THE
DAUGHTER
IN LAW

BOOKS BY SHALINI BOLAND

THE
DAUGHTER
IN LAW

SHALINI BOLAND

bookouture

Published by Bookouture in 2022

An imprint of Storyfire Ltd.
Carmelite House
50 Victoria Embankment
London EC4Y oDZ
Uniter Kingdom

www.bookouture.com

ISBN: 978-1-83888-154-2
eBook ISBN: 978-1-83888-153-5

For my wonderful editor, Natasha Harding.
Thank you for an incredible five years. I couldn't have done this
without you!

PROLOGUE

The torch throws light and shadows onto my rusted spade as it bites into the ground. As it squelches into earth that's thick and sodden with weeks of rain. Rain that's still falling, sliding down my face and oozing through my clothes, trickling around my neck and along my spine, clinging to my lashes and soaking my hair, mingling with the damp, hot sweat of my labour.

A half-moon briefly lights up the night as heavy clouds scud past. The forest thrums with a tattoo of rain and wind, spattering onto leaves and howling through the branches. At least all this water means the ground is soft, which makes things easier. I lift the spade and dump more saturated earth onto the growing mound by my side. The hole is almost halfway dug now. Or maybe I should call it what it is – a grave.

She's lying face down in the mud. I turned her over so I didn't have to look at her any longer. At those blank features hiding all that hurt and accusation. But what did she expect? After everything she said, did she really believe I would let her ruin it all?

Did she really believe I could let her live?

ONE

CAROLINE

The taxi slows to a stop outside a stunning Christmas-card thatched pub set back from the road. It's dusted with snow and twinkling with Christmas lights. A warm glow emanates from the windows where I make out the shapes of people sitting, eating and drinking. It's picture-perfect, making me catch my breath in awe. Seb takes my hand and gives it a squeeze. My heart is thumping so loudly I'm sure the taxi driver can hear it.

'Here we are,' Seb says proudly, his grey eyes lingering on my face. 'Home.'

'It's gorgeous,' I reply, returning my gaze to the weathered limestone building that has somehow already captured my heart. Seb wasn't kidding when he said Stalbridge was a beautiful place. Set in the Blackmore Vale just across the border from Somerset, it's the smallest town in Dorset. It runs from the church near the top of the hill, past the fifteenth-century market cross, to the narrow high street beyond. Just past the cross sits my new husband's home and family business – the Royal Oak pub.

It's a far cry from my own home. Or should I say my *old* home. This quaint pub in an English village couldn't be any more different to my apartment in the coastal town of Byron Bay, Australia. *No.* This place is straight out of a Brothers Grimm fairy tale. The main word that springs to mind is *magical.*

'Wait till you see inside.' Seb opens his door and steps out of the cab. 'There's always such a great atmosphere.'

A blast of icy air rushes into the taxi. For a moment, I'm almost paralysed by nerves. Here I am, about to embark on a new unfamiliar life. To meet my husband's parents for the first time, maybe even some of his friends and work colleagues. All while still jet-lagged. Seb and I had to take separate flights as I couldn't get a seat on his, but I managed to get one the day after. Perhaps we should have checked into a B & B for a couple of days to acclimatise first. Too late now. We came straight from the airport. To the place where my husband lives and works with his family.

In a daze, I exit the taxi and shrug on my new parka – a gift from Seb – drawing it tightly around me and pulling the hood up over my wavy blonde hair. It's bloody freezing out here, colder than when I first landed at Heathrow this afternoon. I think wistfully of Byron Bay, of my shared apartment with its sprawling balcony. Of warm summer evenings and familiar faces. But then I see my husband grinning at me as he walks to the rear of the cab, and I remember why I'm here. I return his grin with a nervous smile of my own.

'Don't look so worried, Caroline,' he says, heaving one of my cases out. 'They're going to love you.'

Seb's mum and dad are the landlady and landlord of the Royal Oak, but since graduating from catering college nine years ago, Seb says he's gradually taken over most of the running of the place. All the same, I wonder what his parents are going to think of me, his new wife coming here and inserting myself into their life. I wanted Seb to give them a heads-up before we landed, but he insisted that it would be better as a surprise. So here we are, about to break the happy news.

Seb pays the cab driver and lifts the two heaviest cases – mine. I take the smallest case – his – and follow him through the wrought-iron gate and down the short, well-tended path towards the pub entrance. My breath floats out in white misty clouds and my boots crunch and squeak over the snow. Victorian style lamps light our way, and I feel like I've entered Narnia.

'There's a private door round the side,' Seb calls back to me, pointing to our left. 'But I want you to get the full pub experience this evening.'

I swallow and give myself an internal pep talk as we head towards the main entrance. I'm tired and nervous after the flight, that's all. It'll be fine. Seb loves me. I'll get used to living here. This is what I wanted. His family are now my family. I'm sure they'll be perfectly nice and we'll all get on really well.

Seb pauses outside a traditional wooden door studded with impressive metal rivets. 'Ready?' he asks.

'Yes.' I give a decisive nod and follow him into the pub.

The noise and warmth hit me straight away. Laughter, chatter, the clink of glasses and cutlery. The smell of wood, polish, garlicky food and the tang of beer overlaying everything. I pull down my hood and let my gaze sweep the room, taking in the oak beams and flagstone floor and the inglenook fireplace at the far end with a log fire blazing in the hearth. The long oak-panelled bar is hung with Christmas garlands and fairy lights. There's a good-looking guy in his twenties behind the bar pulling a pint.

The inside is far bigger than I thought and the décor is like something out of a swanky interiors magazine. The whole place has far exceeded my expectations. Every table in the place is taken – family groups, couples, friends, all quite expensive-looking people in designer clothes and shiny hair. More than a few customers give Seb a nod or a wave. They also give me the once-over – not very discreetly – but no one catches my eye with a nod or a smile. I'm a stranger here. Hopefully that will all change soon.

'What do you think?' Seb turns to me with pride in his eyes.

'It's incredible. Beautiful. I love it.'

'Knew you would.'

'It's a proper English pub. I mean, we have pubs in Australia, but this feels different.'

'Yeah, I know what you mean. It's sixteenth century so you can feel the history.'

He scans the room. 'Mum and Dad aren't here. Let's go through to the back.'

'Hey, Seb, nice tan.' A young woman in black jeans and a T-shirt emblazoned with 'The Royal Oak' walks past carrying a stack of empty glasses, dark-brown curly ponytail swinging, black eyeliner flicks, silver rings and a silver chain around her neck. She glances at me briefly and then turns back to my husband. 'How was Oz?'

'Amazing,' Seb replies, setting down my cases. 'I brought back a souvenir.' He gives me a playful nudge. 'This is Caroline. Caroline, this is Mariah; she works mainly in the restaurant, but sometimes helps out behind the bar.'

'Hi,' I offer with a smile.

Mariah gives me a nod but no smile. Not exactly a warm welcome, but that's okay, she looks busy.

'Is Mum in the restaurant?' Seb asks.

'No, she's just gone upstairs for a quick bite. Think your dad's up there too.'

'Okay, cheers. See you later.' Seb picks up the cases and leads me past the bar. He tries to catch the barman's eye, but he's busy serving a customer and doesn't notice. Seb gives me an awkward shrug and beckons me through a door marked 'Private'.

At the other end of a corridor a twenty-something blonde guy carrying two plates barges his way through a wide swing-door with a circular glazed panel.

'Seb, you're back!' he says.

'Hugo, how's it going?'

'Busy.' He grins.

'I'll let you go. This is Caroline, by the way.'

'Hi.' I wave.

'Nice to meet you.' He gives me a friendly smile as he walks past us out into the bar.

Seb leans over and kisses my lips. 'I'll introduce you to everyone properly once we've spoken to my mum and dad.'

'Sure, no problem.' Of course he'd want his parents to be the first to know that I'm his wife.

Seb heads towards a set of stairs on our left. 'Hugo's been with us a year now. He started in wash-up but now he's part of the wait staff as well. You'll get to know everyone soon enough. We're all like family here.'

I take a breath and tell myself that it's natural to feel a little overwhelmed by my new situation. I've been used to a life in Australia, this is bound to take a little adjustment. I switch the case to my other hand and follow him up the wooden staircase.

'Up here's the private area where we live,' Seb explains. 'It's a three-bedroom apartment.'

'An apartment?' I query. 'I thought it would just be a couple of rooms above the pub.'

'I thought I'd told you about it?' Seb smiles. 'I promise you'll love it.'

My heart is thumping and my mouth is dry. I'm about to meet my in-laws. From what Seb's said, they're great people, but I also get the sense that his mum can be quite stern. She's the landlady of the pub, so she doesn't take any nonsense. That's fine. I'm a straight-talker too. Hopefully, that means we'll get on okay.

Seb pushes open the door at the top of the stairs which leads into a wide hallway with a dark wood floor and thick Berber-style rugs. He dumps my suitcases next to a white marble console table on which sits a vase of fresh flowers, a bowl of keys and some unopened mail. I set Seb's case next to mine and wipe my palms down the side of my coat. I realise I'm sweating now. The apartment is warmer than I'm used to. We have air con back home rather than central heating. Once I take off my coat, I'm sure I'll be fine.

'You okay?' Seb asks, taking my hand and kissing my knuckles.

I nod, but the truth is I'm weary, disoriented and longing for food and bed. The last thing I feel like doing is meeting my in-laws for the first time.

Seb keeps hold of my hand as we walk along the hall towards the sound of voices. The walls are adorned with bright abstract artwork that I can tell has been inspired by the local area with sweeps of green and blue to represent hills and sky.

I guess his parents must be in that room at the end. The door is slightly ajar. Seb lets go of my hand and pulls the door open. I hang back in the hallway.

Things go quiet for a beat. And then a woman speaks. 'Seb! You're home!'

'Hi, Mum. Hi, Dad.'

I can't quite see my in-laws as Seb is blocking the door. As he moves further into the room, I see his parents sitting at a white circular dining table, the remains of dinner on their plates – a few potatoes, some broccoli and what smells like roast chicken. His mum is good-looking with glossy brown hair held back in a chignon, and immaculate make-up. His dad is a silver fox with broad shoulders and a kind face – an older version of Seb.

The room is gorgeous – a perfect mix of old charm and modern comfort. But I barely take it in as most of my attention is drawn by Seb's parents who both stand as he leans in to kiss his mum's cheek. She's smiling broadly and then startles as she catches my eye. She looks to her son for an explanation as I follow my husband into the room.

'Hello?' Seb's dad says tentatively to me, checking his shirt is tucked in. He gives Seb a hug.

My eyes scan the kitchen, taking in the sleek charcoal-grey units sitting confidently alongside oak beams, picture rails and dark polished floorboards.

'Mum, Dad, this is Caroline. Caroline, these are my parents, Lilian and Brian.'

'Oh.' Lilian frowns and gives me a confused and slightly frosty smile. She turns back to Seb. 'I didn't know you were coming home today, Sebastian. Who's your friend?'

'How was Australia?' Brian asks. 'Good holiday?'

'The best.' Seb puts his arm around me and draws me to his side. He clears his throat. 'I've got some news. *We've* got some news.' Seb's chest puffs out and he pushes his hair back with one hand.

Brian looks curious, but Lilian's face is darkening, her brown eyes narrowing to slits.

'This is Caroline... she's my wife,' Seb declares. 'We got married in Australia.'

'It's so lovely to meet you both,' I say, wondering if I should move in for a hug, but I realise a hush has fallen over the room. It's totally silent. You can't even hear any noise from the pub below. I feel like I should say something else to break the tension, but every word I know has fallen out of my head. Lilian hasn't moved and Brian is nodding like one of those toy dogs you sometimes see in cars.

'Well?' Seb asks them, crushing me against him a little too tightly. 'Aren't you going to congratulate us?'

'Seb, can we talk to you in the living room for a moment?' Finally, Lilian moves, tucking her chair under the table.

'Uh, yes, okay.' Seb sounds strangely unsure of himself. 'Let's all go and have a sit down and a drink.'

'Just the three of us,' Lilian says to him without catching my eye at all.

'The three of us?' Seb echoes.

I step out of the way to let Lilian and Brian file past, out of the kitchen. Seb turns and mouths at me to give him a minute. He follows them out of the room, leaving me standing alone in the beautiful kitchen feeling slightly sick and wondering what the hell I'm supposed to do now.

TWO

LILIAN

I can't believe what Sebastian has just told me. It's a joke. It has to be. *Married?*

Brian rests a hand on my upper arm, trying to quell the hurricane that he can sense building in my chest. I shrug him off with an angry jerk.

The girl is stunning in a hippyish kind of way. Blonde wavy hair, ripped jeans, a flowing top, nose ring – and I think I saw a tattoo on her wrist. I'm also fairly sure she has an Australian accent. But who on earth is she? *Oh, Seb, what have you done?*

The three of us congregate in the living room. Brian and I sit on the small sofa, but Sebastian remains standing, a stubborn, hurt look in his eye. The same look he used to get when he was a little boy and I told him he couldn't have seconds of pudding.

'What's this about marriage?' I ask, getting straight to the point. 'Surely you're not serious.'

Sebastian shushes me and closes the living room door. 'I am serious. We love each other.'

'You've only been away for three weeks. How can you possibly know you're right for one another after such a short amount of time?'

'We've been talking online for months.'

'*What?*' This is news to me. When Sebastian said he wanted a holiday, I thought it was a good idea. He'd been working flat out for months and said he needed to get away to clear his head. But now I realise he wasn't being entirely truthful. It wasn't so much a holiday to recharge as a visit to see his online *girlfriend*. 'What do you actually know about this girl?' I ask, unable to temper my snappish tone. 'She might have known about the pub and be looking for a free ride. She could be scamming you. You read about it all the time. People reeling you in online. Catfishing, I think it's called.'

'Don't be ridiculous.' Sebastian curls his lip. 'I'm not an idiot, Mum.'

He's never spoken to me in this tone before. Never pulled that face at me. I'll have to tread carefully if I'm to avoid angering him further.

'Don't talk to your mother like that,' Brian says. 'She's only concerned for you, lad. So am I.'

Our son flushes. 'Sorry. You're right. It's just... I want you to be happy for me. For us. If you just take the time to get to know her, you'll love her, I know you will. I wanted to tell you guys about Caroline when we first started talking, but I thought it would be better to fly out and meet her in person before I told anyone. And then, when I got there and saw her... it just hit me that I love this girl. I mean, really love her. She gets me.'

'I'm sure she's lovely,' I say, not actually believing it. 'But couldn't you have carried on seeing one another without actually tying the knot? You can't know her properly. Not really. Chatting online is very different to seeing someone day in, day out. Maybe you could get an annulment? Carry on as girlfriend and boyfriend, or even be engaged. Set the wedding date a year from now. That will give you both time to work out if it's real or not.' As I bluster out my words, I know it's useless. Sebastian's mind is made up. My suggestions are only irritating him.

His expression is one of frustration and disdain. He folds his arms across his chest and clenches his jaw. 'That makes no sense, Mum. Why would we annul our marriage if we were going to do it again next year anyway?'

I want to yell at my pig-headed son. *It's too soon! Who is she? Why did she want to marry you?* Through sheer effort, I restrain myself. Instead I take a breath, swallow and get to my feet, massaging my breastbone. My dinner feels like it's lodged in my gullet.

'You okay, Lil?' Brian asks.

'Fine, just a bit of indigestion.'

Brian harumphs. 'I think those roasties were a bit undercooked.'

'My indigestion has nothing to do with roast potatoes,' I mutter under my breath.

My husband continues. 'I can't wait for Felix to get back in the kitchen; his roasties are top notch. That boy's been away too long. Well, at least one of our sons is home.' He stands and claps Sebastian on the shoulder.

Seb gives him a grateful smile.

Once again, I'm turning out to be the bad guy. I wish Brian could see that this whole situation is madness. If I'm not careful, I'll end up alienating my son, and I can't have that. I pride myself on having a great relationship with Sebastian and Felix. I'm not a soft touch, but they always know I have their backs. It's not every family that could live and work together as smoothly as we do. I don't want this girl getting in between us and upsetting our family dynamic.

'I'm going to see how Caroline is,' Sebastian grumbles. 'If you can't be nice to her and give us your blessing then... I dunno, we'll check into a bed and breakfast or something.'

'Don't be silly. Of course I'll be nice to her. It's a shock, that's all.' I muster up a smile. 'It's not every day that your son walks in and tells you he's married to someone you've never met.'

Sebastian's shoulders sag. 'I know, Mum. I'm sorry. We got swept away in the moment. But it feels right. When you know, you know.'

The three of us stand in the living room facing one another. I realise I have to swallow my worry and be the bigger person here. 'Come on, then. Let's not leave the poor girl waiting on her own any longer. Brian, nip downstairs and snag a bottle of bubbly.'

'Cava? Or champagne?' he asks.

I hesitate, feeling our son's gaze on me. 'Champagne, of course.'

'Great.' Brian gives me a nod. 'I'll tell Mariah and the others to hold the fort for an hour or so.'

Sebastian's eyes blaze with happiness. 'Thanks, Mum, Dad. You're the best. You'll love her, I promise.'

I wish I could share Sebastian's optimism, but he's not exactly had the best judgement these past couple of years.

Far from it.

THREE

CAROLINE

Well, this isn't awkward at all.

Standing alone, I drag my gaze around the Fletchers'
immaculate kitchen, noting the expensive-looking appliances
and Farrow & Ball paint on the walls, trying not to think about
what's going on in the room next door. Seb's parents are obviously unhappy about my arrival. I knew it might be a surprise,
but I didn't expect them to react quite so badly. I was stupid to
let myself be drawn into Seb's optimism. He told me they'd be
pleased, excited, that they'd love me. And I foolishly believed
him. I should have prepared myself better. Never mind. I'll
make it work with or without his parents' blessing. But it would
be so much easier *with*.

The room is stiflingly warm, the strong smell of food almost
unbearable. My armpits are prickling with sweat. It's no good,
I'm going to have to take off my parka, even if it looks like I
might not be welcome. I'm in the process of removing it as Seb
returns to the kitchen.

'Caroline,' he says, his eyes full of apology. 'I'm so sorry we
abandoned you like that. Come into the lounge. Here...' He
takes my coat and drapes it over the back of one of the chairs.

'Your parents—' I begin.

'Don't worry. They're fine. Just a bit shocked, that's all. Dad's gone to get some champagne so we can celebrate properly.'

'Really? What about your mum?' I ask, only slightly reassured by his words, although a glass of champagne would be very welcome about now.

'Mum's fine. Honestly, she just wanted to find out what's happened.'

'Are you sure she's fine with it?' I search Seb's features for any hint that he's simply trying to smooth things over.

He takes my hand. 'Come on. Come and meet her properly.'

With sweaty palms and a thumping heart, I walk with my husband into a large but cosy living room with a stone fireplace, yet more wooden beams across the ceiling, squashy cream sofas and a vibrant Persian rug. I'm surprised at how spacious the apartment is considering this is a sixteenth-century thatched building. I was expecting dark, poky, little rooms and ultra-low ceilings. Seb's mum stands by the mantelpiece, a fixed smile on her face.

'Caroline,' she says. 'Welcome to the family. I'm sorry about earlier. It was a bit of a shock, that's all.'

I attempt a smile. 'No worries, I totally understand. I told Seb he should have given you both a heads-up, but he wanted it to be a surprise.'

Lilian and I share an eye-roll moment at Seb's expense, and the three of us laugh. The tension eases and I suddenly feel a lot better.

'Here we are!' Seb's dad proclaims, returning to the living room brandishing a bottle of Taittinger and four crystal champagne glasses held upside down by their stems.

Minutes later, the four of us are seated with full glasses in our hands, Seb and I next to each other opposite his parents.

'Cheers!' Brian holds out his glass and we all lean forward to clink.

'You have a beautiful home and pub,' I say.

Lilian smiles and nods. 'So, you met on the internet?' she says, glancing from me to Seb.

'Instagram,' Seb replies. 'We both like the same band and got chatting about them. Then we realised everything else we had in common, and found out we're both in hospitality.'

'Really?' Lilian says, taking a sip of her champagne then placing her glass on the wooden side table. She transfers her gaze to me. 'What do you do?'

'I was managing a great little bar by the beach.' I think of my job back home. It was a bit of a love-hate relationship. I enjoyed the responsibility and the creative control, plus I got on really well with the owner who pretty much let me have free rein. It was a fun job. But the hours were so antisocial that I barely had a life outside of work.

'A bar?' Brian says, looking impressed. 'How long have you been doing that?'

'Just over two years,' I reply. 'But I've been working in bars and restaurants since I was eighteen.'

'How old are you now?' Lilian asks.

'Thirty.'

Lilian's frowning. 'You said you "were" managing a bar. So you don't do that any more?'

'Well, I had to quit because...' I give an awkward shrug. 'Because of coming here, to the UK.'

'Aah.' Lilian steeples her fingers. 'So, do you have any plans for work while you're here?'

'It was all so last-minute...' I tail off, trying to catch my breath between responses. Lilian is firing questions at me so fast that I can barely think straight.

'Because there aren't an awful lot of opportunities around

here,' Lilian continues. 'It's not a big town. Not like the places you'll be used to. I hope you don't find it too quiet.'

'I'm sure it'll be fine.' I give a nervous laugh. 'My partying days are behind me. I'm looking forward to settling down, being part of an old married couple.'

Seb laughs too. 'Same here.'

'Marriage is quite a big step, you know,' Brian interrupts with a jokey smile. 'But if you're both happy, then I wish you all the luck and happiness.'

'Thanks, Dad.' Seb stands and goes over to give him a hug. Lilian holds out her arms next, and Seb leans down to reciprocate, but she still looks pretty shell-shocked to me.

While Seb and Lilian are hugging, Brian beckons me to my feet and gives me a warm squeeze. 'Welcome to the family, love.'

'Thanks, Brian. That means a lot.'

'Love the Aussie accent too. G'day, mate. Bonza.'

'Da-ad!' Seb shakes his head at his father. 'You're so embarrassing.'

'What? Just trying to make the girl feel welcome!' He grins and gives me a wink.

I think his jokey manner is endearing. I notice that Lilian doesn't make any attempt to hug me and I'm not quite brave enough to make the first move. Maybe she simply needs time to get her head around the situation. I should cut her some slack, but it's hard not to start feeling paranoid.

'Meeting online seems to be the norm now,' Brian says. 'Not like in my day where you actually asked people out face to face.'

We sit back down and Seb replies. 'Well, it started out as a chat thing, but the more we talked, the more we realised our feelings went deeper. So I decided to take the plunge and go out to Australia to meet. See if what we had was as real as it felt online.'

'It was so nerve-wracking,' I admit, taking another welcome

sip of champagne, the bubbles fizzing down my throat. 'Before Seb arrived in Byron, I thought I was going to throw up.'

'Same here!' Seb admits. 'But as soon as we saw one another we knew.' He squeezes my hand. 'We both felt sparks. It was like we'd·known one another our whole lives.'

'Do you have family back home?' Lilian asks, not succumbing to the romance of our first meeting.

I pause and swallow. 'No. I, uh, I grew up in care, in Brisbane.'

'Oh.' She pauses. 'Sorry, that must have been difficult.' She shifts in her seat. 'Do you keep in touch with anyone from your childhood?'

'No,' I reply tersely before softening my tone. 'There was a care home and a few different families. I didn't really form any strong attachments.'

'We're her family now,' Seb says. He strokes my cheek and I feel tears pricking behind my eyes. I take a deep breath and manage to stop them before they fall.

'Seb's older brother, Felix, is working on a yacht at the moment,' Brian says, coming to my rescue and changing the subject, 'but he'll be back next week. He's usually our chef, but this incredible opportunity came up to work for a movie producer and earn a lot of money for a couple of months, so he took it.'

'Seb told me,' I reply. 'It sounds exciting. Felix has a wife and baby, right?'

'Yes. Nicki, and baby Teddy.' Brian's expression softens. 'I'm sure Nicki will love having you here. They all live in a little cottage in the grounds of the pub. You'll meet them soon enough.'

Seb clears his throat. 'Actually, Mum, Dad, I thought it would be great for Caroline to help out in the pub while she sorts out her visa,' Seb says. 'She's got great experience and, well, it *is* a family business.'

'We can certainly talk about that,' Lilian says, glancing across at her husband who's beaming at us both, seemingly unaware of Lilian's reservations.

'We can always do with help behind the bar,' Brian adds.

'Hmm,' Lilian says, 'the bar is quite well staffed at the moment. We're short on wait staff though.' She turns to Seb. 'Fliss handed in her notice while you were away.'

Seb frowns. 'That's annoying, we only just trained her up.'

'I don't mind helping out as a waitress,' I say, pleased that I might be of some use.

'That's settled, then,' Brian replies.

'Perfect,' Seb adds.

Lilian gives a brief nod, but her lips are pursed and she doesn't quite catch my eye.

I clap my hand over my mouth as a huge yawn escapes.

'Oh, someone's tired,' Brian says.

'Isn't it supposed to be your morning now?' Lilian says.

'She didn't get any sleep on the plane,' Seb replies.

I think back to my nightmarish journey sandwiched between a drunk man who kept belching, and a woman whose headphones were so loud that I could hear every word of the film she was watching.

'Do you want to get some rest?' Seb asks.

'Would you mind?'

'Course not. I'll show you our room.'

'We're going back downstairs now, Seb, okay?' Lilian rises to her feet. 'Hopefully Hugo hasn't set the place on fire like last week.'

'*What?*' Seb's eyes widen.

'Daft idiot was smoking next to the recycling bin.' She rolls her eyes.

'I had to sling a bucket of water over it and him,' Brian says with a chuckle.

'It's not funny, Brian.'

Their words are all merging now. After the anticipation and stress of meeting my new in-laws, I'm now desperate to lay my head on a soft pillow and fall asleep. Seb's parents finally head downstairs, leaving the two of us alone.

'Welcome home, Mrs Fletcher,' Seb says, sliding his arms around me and pressing his body close. His lips brush mine and it's clear he wants more than just a kiss.

I pull back. 'Do you think they like me?'

He frowns. 'What? Course they do. Who wouldn't?'

'Seriously, though. I think your mum seemed worried about how quick it's all been.'

'She'll be fine. Come on.' Seb takes my hand and leads me out of the living room and back along the hall where he pushes open one of the doors. 'This is us,' he says a little shyly. 'I hope it's okay. Obviously, we'll look for our own place further down the line, but for now...'

In a haze of exhaustion, I gaze around the squarish room. It has low wooden beams and a deep-set window opposite the door. The walls are white and the carpet is beige, but a red patterned Afghan rug makes the place feel warm. A couple of modern framed prints hang on the wall next to a double bed which butts up against a large chimney breast. Facing the bed a mahogany wardrobe stands next to a door which leads through to what looks like an en suite shower room. I'm pleasantly surprised by the choice of decor and feeling of homeliness.

'What do you think?' Seb asks, chewing his lower lip. 'Is the room okay?'

'It's great,' I reply. '*Way* nicer than I thought it would be. You made it out to be an old-fashioned hovel! Not this stunning apartment that looks like it should be on the front cover of *Homes and Gardens* magazine, or whatever it's called.'

'Ah, see, I lowered your expectations so you wouldn't be disappointed.'

'Sneaky.' I elbow him lightly. 'Is the water hot? Can I have a shower.'

'Yeah, sure. You don't have to ask. This is your place too. I'll grab our cases.'

As Seb leaves the room, I sit on the bed and rub my tired scratchy eyes. I can't believe I'm actually here in the UK with my new husband. It's all been such a whirlwind and right now everything still feels surreal. I gaze around me again, trying to take it all in. Trying to realise that this is my home now, for the foreseeable future. At least the initial meeting of the parents is over with. His dad's a sweetie, but his mum...

I think it's going to take more than a few days to win her round.

FOUR

LILIAN

I bolt the entrance door behind the last drunken straggler and take a moment to catch my breath. It's been a busy night what with one thing and another.

'I'm off now, Mrs F,' Mariah calls from behind the bar, interrupting my thoughts.

'Is everything shipshape back there?' I ask, walking back towards her. 'All stocked up for tomorrow?'

'Yep. We're low on lemons, but I've added them to the list.'

'Great, thanks for holding the fort earlier.'

'No worries. You must be pleased to have Seb back.'

'Hmm? Yes,' I reply. 'Yes, it's lovely.' I give an inward sigh. Of course I'm happy to have my youngest son home again. I just wish he hadn't been so impetuous. I mean, *marriage*? What was he thinking? I suppose he wasn't. That's the point.

'Was that his girlfriend he brought with him, or just a friend?' Mariah asks, trying to be casual, her whole body rigid, waiting for my reply. The girl's had a crush on Sebastian since she started working here, but I'm not explaining his situation to her right now. I can barely wrap my head around it myself.

'Sorry, Mariah, let's chat tomorrow. I'm off to bed now.'

Her shoulders droop. 'Course, yeah, see you tomorrow.' She shakes out her ponytail, letting her curls loose, gives me a wave and disappears through the back door.

The bar is silent. I usually like this time of night, once everyone has gone home and the place is clean and tidy, ready for tomorrow. The distant echo of talk and laughter. The residual warmth of the fire. The air settling. But tonight, all I feel is a deep sense of foreboding, a dull thud of dread knocking against my ribcage. Why does nobody tell you that having young children is the easy part? It's once they get older that things really start to get tricky. A grazed knee is fixable. A grazed heart isn't quite as simple.

I make my way around the bar, my low heels clicking against the flagstones. Why did Sebastian really marry this girl? Surely he can't be in love with her, not in such a short space of time. Was it a reaction against everything that's gone on before? A plaster to stick over his problems?

'You coming up, love?' Brian pokes his head through the door to the bar.

I give him a tired smile. 'Yes, I'm coming.' I switch off the bar lights and follow my husband out into the corridor.

'What about Seb, eh?'

'Oh, Brian. What are we going to do?' I wait at the foot of the stairs while he switches off all the pub lights.

'Do?' he asks. 'I think it's already been done, hasn't it?'

'You know what I mean.' I follow him up the stairs. 'Who is this girl? We know absolutely nothing about her.'

'Keep your voice down, Lil.'

'See? We can't even talk freely in our own home.'

Brian lets out a loud yawn. 'Let's go to bed. Things always look better after a good night's sleep.'

'How's this going to be better?' I hiss. 'He's jumped out of the frying pan and into a raging hot inferno.'

'It's not that bad,' Brian says with infuriating calm. 'She

seems quite sweet. Let's give her a chance.' He heads to the kitchen. 'Want a glass of water?'

'Yes please.' I stare at Sebastian's bedroom door, wondering if they're still awake before giving myself a shake and almost bolting into our bedroom. I sit on the edge of the bed, slightly breathless, and kick off my shoes, rubbing my aching toes.

I know my husband's right about giving her a chance, but I can't stop this well of fear bubbling up in my chest. This Caroline girl is a total stranger who's suddenly now supposed to be part of our family. I really do hope and pray that Brian's right and she's as sweet as he thinks she is, but I have a mother's intuition that there's something not quite right there. That something is... off.

As Brian comes into the room with two glasses of water, I resolve to try to put these dark thoughts away and make the best of things. 'I think Mariah's disappointed,' I say.

'Disappointed?' Brian raises an eyebrow.

'About Seb and Caroline,' I clarify.

'You told her he's married, then?'

'No, but I think she realised they're more than just friends.'

'Poor girl. I remember what that's like.' Brian gives me a look. 'Unrequited love.'

'*What?*'

'Don't pretend you didn't keep me on a hook for months before you agreed to go out with me.'

'I did no such thing!' I smile at my husband's teasing. He loves to remind me that I didn't pay him any attention in the early days, when he was besotted with me. Back then, I could have had my pick of the boys – much to the annoyance of my sister who was more than a little jealous of me. But for all my pretence that I couldn't care less about him, Brian Fletcher was the one I had my sights on. I knew I would get him eventually, but I also understood that I couldn't appear too keen. That I had to play the long game in order to make it last. To make him want me so badly that he'd never want to let me go.

That's why I'm so worried about Caroline.

What did she do to make my son want her so badly?

FIVE

CAROLINE

We stand under the dripping porch waiting for Seb's sister-in-law, Nicki, to open the door to her and Felix's place, a cute little cottage at the rear of the pub, partially screened by a neatly clipped laurel hedge. Yesterday's snow has turned to slush and a steady drizzle blows across the pub car park, swathing the trees and houses beyond in a blur of grey mist.

'You'll love Nicki,' Seb says confidently. 'She's feisty and fun. A bit like you, actually. She's going to love you too.'

I hope he's right, but after yesterday's lukewarm reception from his mum, I'm not taking anything for granted.

Seb and I both slept late this morning and by the time we got up for breakfast – which was actually more of a brunch – his parents were already downstairs preparing for the lunchtime trade. Seb's mum wants to have a meeting with him this afternoon to get him up to speed with the pub while he's been away, so Seb suggested I hang out with Nicki for an hour or so. He called to tell her about us this morning. Apparently, she's really excited to meet me.

Seb rings the doorbell again.

'How old's her baby?' I ask.

Seb frowns. 'Almost one, I think. Yeah, he was born in the new year.'

The door is jerked open by a very harassed looking woman in sweatpants and a ratty jumper, her short black hair pinned back off her face with a couple of hair grips. 'Didn't you read the sign?' she snaps, her dark eyes flashing.

'Uh, *sign?*' Seb takes a step back and looks at the door frame.

'Stuck to the door,' she says, turning to look at the open door. 'Oh.' She glances around and then points to a scrap of cardboard on the ground behind us. 'There. It must have come off. It says don't ring the bell because I just put Teddy down for his nap.'

Sure enough I can hear the sound of a baby's distressed cries.

'Shit, sorry,' Seb replies, bending to pick up the soggy card and handing it to her.

'It's a bit late for that,' she says huffily. 'Come in.'

'We can come back another time, if that's easier?' I offer.

'You're here now,' she says, striding off into the gloomy hallway.

Seb and I pause outside for a moment. He gives me an *oh dear, I'm sorry* glance, and then I follow him inside.

When Seb told me I was meeting Nicki today, I wanted to make a good impression, so I curled my blonde hair and took extra care with my make-up and clothes. But now that I see how casual everything is, I can't help feeling overdone. Like I'm trying too hard. I take a tissue from my bag and surreptitiously wipe off my lipstick. I then rummage around for a hair tie and pull my hair up into a messy bun.

'What are you doing?' Seb asks.

I shake my head and mouth, *Nothing.*

He gives me a bemused smile.

'Go through to the lounge!' Nicki calls. 'I'm just going to settle Teddy.'

While the outside of the cottage is chocolate-box perfect, the inside appears to be the polar opposite. Seb and I step into a dingy room that smells of damp laundry. A saggy beige sofa faces a small pine TV unit, and there's a small dining table by the window. Three dining chairs and the radiator are strewn with washing, the rest of which is piled high in a blue plastic laundry basket that sits on the table. I wonder at the difference between the interior of this cottage compared to the glamorous charm of the pub and apartment. *Thank goodness I'm not staying here.*

'I should have brought some flowers or something,' I mutter.

'No, it's fine,' Seb says, gesturing to me to sit down on the sofa. 'Nicki's laid-back; she doesn't like fuss.'

'Shouldn't we wait to sit down?' I ask.

Seb shakes his head and pulls me down onto the sofa next to him, but as Nicki comes into the room with a red-cheeked baby in her arms, I shoot back up again, uncomfortable at making myself at home.

'No, it's fine, sit down,' she says. 'I need to walk around and jiggle him to sleep otherwise he's going to scream his head off.'

'He's so cute!' I gush, sinking back down. 'Look at those dark curls. Gorgeous.' I'm suddenly determined to crack her frosty exterior.

'Yeah, well, I guess he is quite a stunner. Then again, I am biased.' She shrugs.

Teddy stops grizzling for a moment to stare at me. Then his face contorts into a cry of tired rage.

'Come on, Ted,' Nicki croons to her son, and sticks her little finger in his mouth. 'Close your eyes now. You're overtired, little man. Seb, can you put the kettle on? I've got my hands full here.'

'Sure. Tea?' He gets to his feet.

'Please,' she replies. 'I think there's some biscuits in the tin.'

'Tea's great,' I add, watching my husband leave the room.

Nicki's pacing the small room. Teddy's quieter now, but his face is flushed and tear-streaked.

'So...' Nicki and I say at the same time.

I give a small laugh, but she just nods at me to go first.

'So, I guess we're sisters-in-law,' I say with a smile.

'Yeah. Congrats on the wedding,' she replies with minimal enthusiasm.

'Thanks.' I feel awkward sitting on the sofa while she's walking around the small living room, exuding irritation. Teddy's eyes are drooping now, his head sinking onto his mum's shoulder.

'Seb's a great guy,' she says. And it feels like a warning. Like she thinks I'm going to hurt him, or that I'm not good enough or something.

'The best,' I add.

There's a long, uncomfortable pause where I rack my brain to think of something, *anything*, to say. It's not like me to be lost for words, but my mind has gone completely blank.

'You met online,' she says, a statement rather than a question.

'We did!' I wince at how overenthusiastic I sound. 'We just clicked. I felt like I'd known him my whole life. Then, when he made the trip to Australia and we met up in person, it just confirmed that... he was the one.'

'Is he, though?' She stops walking and tilts her head, looking at me.

I swallow, shocked by the baldness of her statement. The rudeness.

'Two teas!' Seb walks into the room carrying two mugs and a plate of chocolate biscuits on a red tin tray.

'You not having one?' Nicki asks him.

'Sadly not. I hate to love you and leave you, but Mum's expecting me for a quick staff meeting before the evening crowd descends.'

My heart plummets at the thought of having to make conversation with this prickly woman on my own. Either she's fiercely loyal and territorial of her family, or she's resentful of the fact I woke her baby and probably interrupted her quiet time too. Either way, I'm definitely not her favourite person in the world right now. Even if she is technically my family too. *My sister-in-law.* I steal another glance at her, but she's looking at me too, so I hastily avert my gaze.

Seb leans down to give me a lingering kiss, but I pull away, embarrassed by such a public display of affection after Nicki's made it clear she doesn't approve of us. 'Have fun,' he says to both of us before leaving the room.

The front door slams, and now it's just me, Nicki and Teddy.

'I need to put him in his cot,' Nicki says. 'Back in a minute.'

I wonder whether, when she returns, I should just make my excuses and leave. I'm still jet-lagged and don't feel remotely on my game. I really wanted to come to the UK with Seb, but now that I'm here, I'm nervous and unsure. This isn't how I thought it would be. I'm an outgoing, confident person, popular and sociable. I usually get on with people straight away. This hostility isn't something I've experienced since I was back at school, when I had to deal with the mean kids. I'm hoping that it's just because the Fletchers are protective of Seb. That once they get to know me, they'll start opening up and welcoming me in.

Nicki comes back into the room, making me jump.

'He's usually pretty good at getting off to sleep, but he's teething at the moment.'

'Poor thing,' I reply.

'Yeah, it's a bit miserable for him.' She walks past me to the dining table and shifts some laundry from one of the chairs to the overflowing basket before sitting down. 'I think he's finally asleep, thank goodness.'

'So sorry we disturbed him.'

She gives a slight eye-roll. 'To be honest, he would have taken ages to go down anyway. Bet you think I'm a right grumpy cow, and you'd be right. Sorry.'

I suddenly feel lighter, reassured that maybe we can be friends after all. 'No worries. It must be hard when they're unhappy. I'm sure the teething stage will pass soon.'

'Here's hoping.' She picks up her mug of tea and raises it to me. I cheers her back. 'Biscuit?' She points to the plate.

'Go on then.' I'm not hungry, but I feel it would be rude to refuse. It's strange how she's switched from being downright rude to friendly. It's a bit unsettling, but I'm not complaining. I want to win her over. Get her to like me. 'So, you're married to Seb's brother, Felix, right?'

'I am. Although you wouldn't know it at the moment. I feel like a single mum.'

'Oh, sorry, yeah. Brian said Felix is working away at the moment?'

'Yeah. Some friend of a friend got him a chef gig on this superyacht. The money was too good to pass up, but it's been hard, him being away. I'm pretty much stuck at home as I don't drive, and his parents are so busy I barely see them.'

'He's coming back soon though, isn't he?'

'Next week. Hallelujah. I can't wait.' She breaks off a bit of biscuit and dunks it in her tea. 'Seb's been amazing, helping me with Teddy and keeping me company. No offence, but I've missed him while he's been away.'

'Sorry about that,' I reply with a grin.

She doesn't quite grin back, but at least there's the fleeting hint of a smile.

'What about your own family?' I ask. 'Are they close by? Do they help out at all?'

Her face closes down again.

'Tell me to mind my own business,' I add hastily.

'No, no, it's fine. I... well, it's just that I'm not in touch with my family any more. We don't really get on.' She rolls her eyes and takes a breath.

'Sorry,' I reply.

'Not your fault.'

There's an awkward silence. I nibble on my stale chocolate biscuit, wracking my brains to think of something neutral we can talk about.

'I can't believe Seb kept you a secret from all of us.' Nicki shakes her head, her dark eyes boring into mine.

'I think he wanted to wait and see how we got on in real life before going public.' I sip my tea and grimace. It's lukewarm and Seb's put too much milk in it.

'It's hardly "going public" to tell his family.' Nicki's tone is veering towards antagonistic again.

I don't want to start justifying myself to her. Why can't she just be happy for us? I curb my instinct to defend our relationship, instead changing the subject. 'How long have you been with Felix?'

'Oh, years,' she says airily. 'I actually knew him from school but we didn't hook up until he came back home after catering college.'

'Do you help out in the pub too?' I ask, wondering if I'm going to have to work with her.

'God, no.' Her eyes widen in horror. 'I can't imagine us working and living together. We'd end up killing each other. I've got an admin job at the local builder's merchants, but I'm on maternity leave and have to decide whether I'm going back or not after Christmas.'

'What do you think you'll do?' I ask.

'Not sure yet, but I'll probably have to go back because of finances.'

'What will you do with Teddy if you go back to work?' I ask.

'Not sure. Childcare costs an arm and a leg, so it might not be worth me even going back. I'm hoping they might let me work from home.'

'That would be good.'

She shrugs and curls her lip unenthusiastically. 'It's not exactly my dream job. What about you? Are you going to work over here?'

I nod. 'The plan is for me to help out in the pub while I sort out my visa.'

'Good luck with that,' she says, her voice laced with scepticism.

'You don't sound very optimistic,' I reply.

'Let's just say that Lilian likes things done just so. As long as you toe the line, you'll be fine.'

I swallow. Having managed a bar, I'm not used to taking orders from other people. I'll just have to hope her management style doesn't rub me up the wrong way. 'That's fine,' I say. 'It's their pub, not mine. I'll just do what I'm told.'

Nicki raises her eyebrows, but doesn't comment. There's a brief silence while she sips her tea and I pretend to sip mine.

'So, tell me about you,' she says. 'Whereabouts in Australia are you from? Seb said you live by the sea.'

'That's right. A place called Byron Bay on the east coast. It's small but lively.' I get a sharp pang of homesickness as I think about the surfing beaches, bars, boutiques, cafes and the lush hinterland. It's pretty here in Dorset, but it doesn't feel like home. Not at all.

'Must be quite different from here. Have you been to the UK before?'

I shake my head. 'Never.'

Nicki sucks in a breath. 'Brave move, getting married and moving to a country you've never seen before.'

I shrug. 'It was worth the risk. For Seb.'

'You're not wrong. He's a good guy.'

I nod. But I'm 99 per cent sure that she's left off the end of her sentence. That what she really wants to say is Seb's too good for someone like *me*.

SIX

AMY

'I'm home!' Amy Nelson closes the front door behind her and dumps her bag in the hall, a thick, heavy exhaustion swamping her.

'Amy? Is that you?' Amy's mum pokes her head out of the living room, her face breaking out into a huge smile that warms Amy's heart. She's missed her mum so much.

'Hi, Mum. I'm only here till tomorrow, and I have to study. But I needed a night at home, hope that's okay?'

'Of course it is.' Her mum wraps her up in a warm hug that almost makes her cry. 'Ooh, I've missed you, Amy. We're so proud.'

Amy is now in her first year studying medicine. But it's been more gruelling than anticipated. She's doing okay, but the pace has been relentless and she's worried about falling behind. She thought a night at home might help recharge her batteries. Right now, all she wants to do is go up to her room and sleep.

'Dave! Michelle! Look who's back from uni!' Amy's mum yells up the stairs, before turning back to her daughter with a concerned look on her face. She smoothes Amy's chestnut hair off her brow. 'You look tired, darling. Have you been eating properly? Let me get you something.'

'Hey, Amy,' Amy's younger sister, Michelle, comes bounding down the stairs. 'How's it going? It's been really weird here without you.'

'Hi. Michelle. Uni's intense.' Amy smiles at her sister. Back when she lived at home full time, they fought like cat and dog. Michelle was always stealing her clothes and wrecking her make-up, going through her stuff and generally invading her privacy. But now, after time away, she can't believe she's actually happy to see her kid sister. She misses the easiness of being able to speak your mind to another person. Being totally relaxed. Even if she can be a giant pain in the arse.

'Amy!' Her dad is coming down the stairs now, a giant grin on his face. 'How's my daughter, the doctor?'

'I haven't even done half a term, Dad. Not quite a doctor yet.'

'No, but I bet you're already top of the class, aren't you?'

Amy forgot how full-on her parents are. She'll be lucky if she gets a moment's peace to study. She picks at the skin around her fingernails and follows them into the kitchen.

They all sit at the pine table while her mum makes tea and rummages about in the cupboards for some cake and biscuits. It feels like she's snapped straight back to the old days, but also like she's looking in on a memory from far away.

'So, tell us all about it, Amy,' her dad asks, scratching his salt-and-pepper beard.

Amy takes a breath and starts to fill her family in on university life. She tries not to think about the textbooks in her bag that are calling to her, figuring that the sooner she satisfies her parents' curiosity, the sooner she can disappear upstairs.

Eventually, after two cups of tea and a large slice of Victoria sponge, her parents' questions start to tail off. Amy knows how much she owes them. They've been so supportive, supplementing her student loan with their own money to pay for her food and accommodation. There's no way she'd have been able to do this without them.

Amy notices that Michelle's put on quite a bit of weight since the summer. Her normally glossy brown hair hangs in lank strands down her back and there are breakouts on her chin and forehead. 'How are the A-levels going?' she asks her sister.

Michelle tips her hand back and forth. 'Yeah, okay. I'm predicted an A in art.' Her features perk up a little at this.

'That's amazing, well done, sis.' Amy gives her a smile.

'Have you thought any more about what you're going to study at uni, Michelle?' their mum asks. 'You need to fill in your UCAS form soon.'

Michelle doesn't reply, instead she stares down at her lap.

Amy feels for her. She knows what their parents can be like. Thankfully, Amy always wanted to study medicine, so she never had her parents on her back.

'Maybe you could take a year out?' Amy suggests. 'Have some time to think about what you want to do.'

Their mum gives her an annoyed glare. 'That's not helpful, Amy. Michelle needs to focus now, not swan around for months on end. Michelle needs something definite to go to afterwards, otherwise she'll just end up drifting.'

Michelle sits up straighter in her chair and clears her throat. 'Actually, I am focused, and I do know what I want to do with my life.'

Amy notices her parents exchange a worried glance.

'I want to go to art college,' Michelle announces.

'Art's a hobby, not a career,' their dad says, predictably. 'We'll talk about this once Amy's back at uni. We can all sit down and look at career options together.'

'I don't need to look at career options. I want to be an artist. You already know how good I am at art, but you never say anything about it. Why can't you be proud of me too? Miss

McCormack says I'm exceptionally talented. Why aren't you pleased about that?'

'Michelle...' Their mum's eyes are hard as she gets to her feet and starts clearing the table. 'Why have you got to make a scene just as Amy's arrived? Your dad's just said we'll talk about it next week, but no, you have to make yourself the centre of attention. You need to grow up and realise that the world doesn't revolve around you.'

Michelle scrapes her chair back and stands up, her whole body trembling with anger and frustration. 'You were the one who asked me what I wanted to do, so I told you! Just because I don't want to be a doctor or a lawyer or some other traditional job, I'm not good enough. You act like I'm going to start up a meth lab or something!'

'That's enough, Michelle!' Their dad's voice rumbles through the kitchen. 'We don't want to see you waste your brains, that's all.'

Michelle swipes at her eyes with the back of her hand. Amy tries to think of something to offer comfort, but she doesn't want to add to the argument, so she stays quiet. She'll speak to her in private a little later. Her sister always manages to rub them up the wrong way. She needs to be clever about it rather than charging in without thinking. Michelle glares at everyone before slamming out of the room, her feet clomping up the stairs.

'Sorry about that, Amy love,' their mum says. 'She's such a drama queen, that one. Do you want another cuppa?'

Amy shakes her head. She feels sorry for her sister. She's tried to get her parents to go easier on her, but they're stuck in this stubborn circle of miscommunication where neither side is prepared to listen to the other. Amy just doesn't have the headspace to deal with it right now...

SEVEN

LILIAN

'That's thirty-two pounds and forty-five pence.' I hold out the card machine to Fiona Davies, who taps her debit card and thanks me.

'Did you get my deposit for our Christmas do?' she asks. 'I transferred it last week.'

'I did, thanks, Fiona. You're all booked for the twentieth.'

'Great. The staff and I are all looking forward to it.' Fiona owns a local beauty salon that's been featured in several lifestyle blogs and Sunday supplements. I try to book myself in for a treatment every couple of months or so. The hot stone massage is to die for.

Fiona has lived in Stalbridge all her life too. Same as most of our clientele. It's nice having that shared history. Our kids going to the same school, growing up together, celebrating each other's milestones. Of course, there are a few who've left to start afresh in other towns and cities, maybe even abroad. But most of us are born-and-bred locals. We're part of each other's lives and know one another's characters, the good, the bad and the ugly. It's reassuring. Safe.

I glance across the bar, through to the dining room beyond,

to see Caroline standing at a table with a notepad in hand taking a Sunday lunch order from the Sticklands. John Stickland is the headmaster of the local primary, and his wife, Susie, runs a local arts charity. I've known their three teens since they were born. My son's new wife is chatting easily to them, making them laugh. I suppose that's something. The fact that she's making a good impression with the customers. With our friends.

Both the bar and restaurant are packed today, the rumble of voices vibrating through the beams. We're always booked up over the weekend, mainly thanks to Felix's talent as a chef. Our stand-in is okay, but nowhere near as good as my son. We've already had a few minor complaints – I hope they're not bad enough to lose valuable custom. But we pride ourselves on our excellent service. If there's any legitimate issue with the food, I'll always go big on the complimentary alcohol or waive the bill altogether. That's why I'm fanatical about everything being perfect in the first place. I don't want to give away our profits.

There's a lull at the bar, so I leave Tarik to it while I do the rounds. Brian and I like to greet all our customers personally whenever we can, asking them if everything's to their liking, checking that it's all as it should be. I don't hover or intrude, but simply glide through the pub, nodding and saying hello every couple of hours or so. Most people like to feel special. It's our job to make them feel that way.

I head through to the restaurant, where Sebastian is talking to Caroline by the till point. I notice the way he gazes at her. The way he takes every opportunity to touch her – a stroke of the arm, a guiding hand at her back, a brief kiss on the lips. He's only been home two days, but I can see the different in him since he left.

Before his trip to Australia, he was anxiety-ridden, surly and unresponsive. He would go AWOL for hours without telling anyone. He would snap whenever I asked him how he was doing. Now, he's bright and enthusiastic, driven again. He's back to how he used to be before...

I shake away the memories of what happened. I shouldn't dwell on the past. I shouldn't compare then and now. I should just be grateful that I have my sunny Sebastian back. I should be grateful to Caroline for restoring my boy.

So how come I'm not?

The thing is, I've noticed that he seems far more infatuated with Caroline than she is with him. He gazes adoringly at her while she accepts his love as her due. Perhaps she's simply a more guarded person. Maybe it's just a case of her taking time to settle in and open up properly, but I'm not convinced. Also, I may be mistaken, but Sebastian's new happiness seems tinged with a hint of fear. Like he's caught this perfect butterfly in his hands, but isn't sure how to keep it.

When Seb was explaining how they met, all I could think was, *How could he be so naive?* It's all very well having a spark when you first meet someone, but those sparks don't always last. You have to back them up with something real. With a solid foundation. You have to get to know someone properly before you commit to spending the rest of your lives together. Does Caroline have what it takes to put the work in? I suppose only time will tell.

The bowls club lunch are leaving now. I go over and shake Bob Whittaker's hand. They're all very complimentary about the food and the service, so that's nice to hear. From the corner of my eye, I notice a rowdy table of lads in the corner. Pat and Joanne Chancellor's eldest boy and a few of his mates from the rugby club. They're all plastered. I'll need to monitor the situation. I can't have them disrupting the other diners. They all come from good families but tend to get a bit carried away when they've had too much to drink. They really should know better.

'Mariah.' I pull her over to one side. 'Take a couple of

baskets of bread over to table four. And if they order any more to drink, take your time giving it to them.'

She nods. 'They're a nightmare.'

'Maybe tell chef to make their food a priority. They need something substantial to soak up the alcohol.

'Good idea.'

'Want me to get Brian to deal with them?' I ask.

'No, it's fine. Take more than Tom Chancellor and Benny Mitchell to faze me. Tom was a right little crybaby at school. Always wanting his mum, that one.'

'Fine. Thanks, Mariah. I'll leave them in your capable hands.' I head back to the bar with worries about Caroline and Sebastian still dominating my thoughts.

I'm concerned about Caroline's background. She's a stranger with no family to speak of. I understand that isn't her fault, so I do have some sympathy. Of course I do. Haven't I already welcomed Nicki into our family after her own family turfed her out? No surprise there; she's a prickly one.

At least Caroline's situation wasn't of her own doing. Growing up in foster care must have been hard. I can't imagine what that was like for her. Most people would be at least a little scarred by the lack of a stable childhood home. What is it with *both* my boys having partners with unstable backgrounds?

My main worry is, can Caroline really be the bright bubbly person she's presenting to the world? She seems too confident, too perfect. Another more sinister thought pops into my head. What if she married him to get British citizenship? I don't like to be suspicious and sceptical, but Sebastian is my son, and right now he's completely blinded by love. Or, more likely by *lust*. Is this brash Australian girl taking advantage of Seb's sweet nature?

EIGHT

CAROLINE

'I think you're impressing Mum with your waitressing skills,' Seb says, running a finger down my cheek. He's been working in the back office all morning, catching up on the books, and he's thoughtfully nipped into the restaurant to see how I'm getting on during my first shift.

'Well, I haven't managed to drop any plates yet.'

It's a busy Sunday lunchtime at the pub – a baptism of fire – but it's nothing I can't handle. This is me in my element. I'm always good with customers. I've had years of practice. I wonder what Lilian really thinks about how I'm doing. I hope Seb's right and I really am impressing her. Surely, she can't have found anything to criticise. I've noticed her gaze following me around the restaurant. She thinks she's being subtle, but she's absolutely not. Not that I mind. If she's pleased with my waitressing skills then hopefully that will be a point in my favour. I'll gradually win her round if it's the last thing I do.

'Are you going to be okay if I go out for a couple of hours?' Seb asks. 'Nicki asked if I'd take her into Blandford to do some Christmas shopping. It's been hard for her to get out while Felix is away. She doesn't drive and the buses are crap on Sundays.'

'Yeah, sure, no problem,' I reply, realising how thoughtful Seb is. I smile up at him. 'I know she doesn't get on with her family so it's sweet of you to do that.'

He shrugs. 'She's part of our family now.'

'Okay, well, I better deliver this order to the kitchen. I want to stay in your mum's good books.' I'm clutching my order pad, surprised by how nervous I am. At how much I want to impress Lilian.

'Don't worry. You're doing a great job.' Seb plants a kiss on my nose. 'But you know you didn't have to start working straight away. I meant what I said about you taking some time to acclimatise to the UK, get your bearings. I was thinking... we could book into a hotel for a couple of nights. Have a proper honeymoon. I have the money for it...'

'I don't think your parents would be too happy with me if we did that! You've been out of the country for weeks. The last thing I want to tell your mum is that we're now off on a mini-break.'

His face falls. 'I guess you're right. But that doesn't mean *you* can't have a few days off to settle in.'

'I'm not going to laze around while you're all working,' I reply. 'I'm happy to pitch in. Anyway, I'll acclimatise quicker by throwing myself into things.'

'You're amazing, Cal. Okay, see you later. Speak to Mum or Dad if you need anything.'

'Say hi to Nicki from me,' I say, although I still feel a little confused by my sister-in-law. I can't work out whether we clicked or not. Maybe she's just one of those people who take a little time to open up. I'll have to visit her again, maybe offer to look after Teddy so she can have some time to herself.

'Will do,' Seb replies, giving me another kiss before disappearing through the restaurant.

I take my order out to the kitchen where Mariah hands me two baskets of bread rolls.

'These are for table four,' she says.

'Okay,' I reply, even though that's one of *her* tables. 'Is that the one by the bay window?'

'No, it's in the far left corner.'

'Ah, the one with the four drunk guys,' I reply, realising why she's given me the bread. Maybe she doesn't want to deal with them, or maybe she wants to see how I handle them. I take the baskets and head back into the restaurant.

'Oy, oy!' one of them shouts as I approach.

The restaurant is noisy enough for it not to be disruptive, but a few of the other customers shake their heads in irritation.

'Some bread rolls for you gentlemen.' I place the baskets on the table.

'Forget the bread, I'll just have a roll,' one of them slurs.

The other three laugh at his lame joke.

'You an Aussie?' the same guy asks. He's dark haired with gym muscles, a baby face and receding hairline.

'I am.'

'Wanna go out for a drink sometime?'

'Thanks for asking, but I'm a married woman. Let me take some of these dead glasses for you.' I lean across the table to collect the empties and feel one of the other lad's hands on my denim-clad arse. Lightning quick, I take hold of his arm and twist it upwards, making him cry out in pain.

'Keep your hands to yourself, mate,' I say lightly, without animosity. What I really want to do is knee him in the balls, but I'm aware that I'm on trial here, that Lilian or Mariah might be watching. I don't mind a bit of near-the-knuckle banter, but I draw the line at molestation.

'What d'you do that for?' the culprit roars. He's also in his twenties, thickset with a bull-like neck and small blue eyes. He's rubbing his forearm and glaring at me. 'I think you've done some real damage to my wrist, you psycho.'

My heart sinks as his friends start jeering. Calling him a

wuss and a pussy. Telling him he's been beaten up by a girl. Banging on the table with their cutlery and laughing. Their behaviour isn't going to do his bruised ego any good.

'That's assault, that is,' he cries, getting to his feet and staring around the room. 'Did you see that?' He's trying to engage the other diners. Trying to imply that I've done something wrong. To get them to take his side.

I need to shut this down. I've seen plenty of this kind of drunken macho behaviour before, of course I have. But why did it have to happen today of all days? On my first shift when Lilian's watching my every move. Hopefully she'll realise that it's simply a group of lads who've had too much alcohol on an empty stomach. I notice Mariah over near the till. She raises her eyebrows and gives me a bitchy smile that lets me know she has no intention of coming to my rescue. That she almost knew something like this would happen. Fine. I'll sort this out myself. I smooth my T-shirt and manage to give the arsehole a smile. 'Let me get you a drink and we'll call it even, hey?'

'You can't buy me off with a drink,' he grumbles.

'She needs to buy us *all* a drink,' one of his friends says, pointing at me.

'What's going on over here?' It's Lilian. She's speaking quietly but firmly, and her question is directed at *me*.

'She assaulted me!' the man interrupts.

'He put his hand on my backside,' I tell Lilian quietly. 'So I removed it.'

She acts as though she didn't hear me. 'Is everything all right now, gentlemen? Chef said your lunch will be just a couple more minutes. Today's meal will be on the house.'

'I should bloody well think so too,' the sleazebag mutters. 'If she's done any permanent damage to my arm, I'm gonna sue. I'm a professional rugby player, you know? She better not have wrecked my season. Just 'cause she's got big tits and a pretty face she thinks she can do what she wants.'

'Caroline, you can go back upstairs for now,' Lilian says.

'It's no problem, I'm fine,' I reply.

'Now, please,' she insists.

I realise she isn't asking me out of concern. She's dismissing me as if I've done something wrong.

'You should give her the sack, Mrs F,' gym muscles says, throwing me a smirk, like he thinks this whole thing is hilarious. 'She's a danger to your customers. Haven't you heard of customer service, love? Don't they have that in your country?'

'Caroline, please,' Lilian says, giving me a firm stare.

I nod, my cheeks hot as I leave the restaurant, weaving through the tables and chairs, feeling everyone's eyes on me. I can't believe Seb's mum didn't have my back. That she didn't stick up for me in front of them. Actually, I'd rather she hadn't come over at all. I would have calmed them down if she'd only let me get on with it.

Out in the hallway, I decide not to skulk away upstairs. Instead, I wait outside the kitchen for Lilian, my heart thumping with embarrassment and a growing anger that I'm trying to dampen down. I wish Seb hadn't gone off with Nicki. I could really do with his opinion on this. Did I overreact? I don't think so. No. Definitely not.

Mariah comes through with arm armful of dirty plates.

'What did you do to Tom?' she asks, stopping outside the kitchen door.

'Is that the guy who groped me?'

'He groped you?' She raises a disbelieving eyebrow.

'Yeah, I gave him a lesson in how not to treat women,' I reply.

'Hmm, Mrs F isn't going to like you assaulting the customers. I'd say you're about to get a bollocking. You should lie low upstairs till she's calmed down.'

'It was hardly assault,' I reply, crossing my arms. 'It was self-defence. He's lucky I didn't do worse.'

'Your funeral,' Mariah replies, shoving open the kitchen door with her shoulder and disappearing inside.

NINE

LILIAN

Well, this is all I need – my son's bolshy new wife upsetting the clientele. Granted, those boys are a little inebriated, but if Caroline had half as much experience as she says she does, then things would never have escalated like that. What was she thinking?!

I told Mariah to comp their meal and any drinks they've had so far. That seemed to calm them down. At least they're behaving themselves a bit better now. But what's really worrying – aside from the appalling customer service – is that this whole episode doesn't bode well for Sebastian and Caroline as a couple. I hope she's not going to be as quick to fly off the handle with my son. He's a gentle, trusting soul. Too trusting for his own good sometimes.

Memories of Sebastian's disastrous love life flash through my mind. I thought I'd taught him better than this, but he's inherited his dad's romantic nature. The belief that everything is meant to be. That destiny and soulmates and love at first sight are a thing. I give an inward snort. What a load of sentimental nonsense. Relationships are about character, compromise and hard work. No doubt his premature marriage came about due to an overload of hormones and sunshine.

I take a breath and resolve to put it all out of my head for the next hour or so while I take over Caroline's shift. I'd been hoping she might replace Fliss, who left last week after she was offered a singing gig on a cruise ship. I bet when that's over, she'll want her old job back. But it'll be too late then, missy. You can't swan in and out of jobs just like that. I take a breath. Oh, I really am out of sorts. I need to calm down and give Mariah a hand. This whole Caroline business has got me all riled up.

The next hour rushes by with no time to think of anything but serving food, clearing tables, singing 'Happy Birthday' to eighty-year-old Margery Hawkins, taking drinks orders and making sure the chef isn't knocking back too much red wine. Thankfully, the rugby lads left soon after the incident, with unhappy murmurings about how we're lucky they aren't going to sue, and how they hope that Australian psycho has lost her job. It's all bluster, of course. I'm not too worried about them following it up with anything official.

As the restaurant slowly empties out, I think about going upstairs to have a word with my new daughter-in-law. See how she's taken her dressing down. I'm betting she's going to be annoyed and defensive, but perhaps she'll surprise me and apologise. It was probably a bad move, throwing her in at the deep end like that. The Sunday-lunch crowd is demanding and rowdy. Maybe she was trying to impress us, exaggerating how much experience she actually has.

'Will you be all right on your own for fifteen minutes or so?' I ask a sweaty-looking Mariah, her cheeks pink from rushing between the cosy restaurant to the oven-hot kitchen.

'Yes, sure.' She tightens her ponytail and grabs two portions of the salted-caramel cheesecake. 'It's all puddings, coffees and liqueurs now.'

'Great. I'm upstairs if you need me. Or get Brian from the bar.'

She nods and leaves the kitchen, cheesecakes in hand.

I can't put it off any longer. I leave the kitchen, ignoring our glassy-eyed chef; it's a miracle he's still standing. Thank goodness Felix is coming back this week to save the day.

I head upstairs, trying to work out what I'm going to say to the girl. I'll have to choose my words carefully so I don't upset Sebastian. If anybody else had assaulted a customer they would have been out on their ear. The flat feels empty. I walk along the hall and peer into the kitchen and then the living room. I suppose she must be in her room. It's not ideal having her living here with us. I'm not going to be able to relax properly with a stranger in our home.

I retrace my steps along the hall and come to a stop outside Sebastian's room. I pause and give a double rap with my knuckles. 'Caroline? Can I have a word?'

There's a brief silence before I hear footsteps. The door opens and I get a waft of her vanilla perfume. It masks the usual scent of Sebastian's room – soap and his citrus aftershave.

'Hi,' she says with no expression in her voice. She's changed out of her black uniform into grey joggers and a thick navy sweatshirt. Her blonde hair is piled up in a messy bun, her face scrubbed of make-up.

'I wonder if we could have a chat?' I ask.

'Uh, sure. Do you want to come in?' She gestures into the room as though it's hers.

'Why don't we go into the living room?' I suggest. 'Would you like a drink?'

'No thanks.'

There's an awkward shuffle as she walks through the door and we're not sure who's going first. I gesture to her to go ahead, and follow behind. I'm actually glad Sebastian isn't here, getting all defensive. I'm going to treat this professionally and then we can put it behind us.

I sit in my usual spot on the large sofa, while Caroline perches on the edge of the smaller sofa where Felix normally sits when he's here.

'So...' I begin, taking charge of the conversation, 'that was quite a bit of drama downstairs.'

'That guy put his hand on my arse,' she says bluntly.

'Are you sure about that?' I ask, wondering if he may have brushed her accidentally.

'Am I sure his whole hand was squeezing my left buttock? Yes. I am.' She presses her lips together and her fists clench in her lap.

'Okay. Did you ask him to remove it?'

'I removed it myself,' she replies with a defiant glare.

I expel air through my mouth as I realise that my son's new wife is possibly going to be too feisty to put in front of customers. I need to tread carefully. 'Those boys had far too much to drink.' I shake my head in what I hope looks like solidarity. 'But I've known them since they were little. They're harmless enough. Just a bit excitable, that's all.' I cringe somewhat as I'm saying this. If Tom did grab her behind then that's unacceptable, but I need to diffuse the situation, and Caroline's bolshiness isn't inspiring me with confidence. I honestly don't think she's the right person to work front of house.

'"Excitable" isn't the word I'd use,' she replies.

'No, it was obviously quite ambiguous. And if he were to press charges, then it would be a "he said, she said" situation.'

'There were witnesses,' she drawls. 'But I did actually have everything under control. If you hadn't come over, I would have smoothed the situation.' She shifts in her seat and takes a breath. 'To be quite honest, if that had happened in my bar back home, I would have asked him and his mates to leave.'

'Hmm. You see, that's the difference. Our pub prides itself

on being friendly and welcoming. We know most of the customers personally, and they know they can come here and get a home-from-home experience.'

'I'm glad I don't live in that guy's home, then,' she mutters under her breath.

'Look, I understand it was upsetting. Why don't you take a break from working in the pub. Settle into the area first. Get to know Stalbridge a bit better.'

'I'd still like to carry on, if that's okay? Seb was really excited about us working together. And I don't suppose being groped is an everyday occurrence – unless it *is*, here?'

'Of course not!' I snap. 'I'm not condoning what he did. I'm just saying we have different ways of dealing with things.'

Her face clouds over and I can see she's trying not to lose her temper.

'Okay, Caroline, look, if you don't think you can handle the customers politely, then—'

'It's not that I *can't*! It's that I don't agree with letting things like that slide. It's not right.'

'Whatever the rights and wrongs, maybe you'd be better suited to the kitchen doing food prep.'

She raises an eyebrow.

'Just for now,' I add.

'Fine. If that's what you think, then...' She shrugs and holds out her hands.

'Good. I'm glad that's sorted. Sebastian's brother comes home tomorrow so you'll be helping him. Don't look so worried,' I say, getting to my feet. 'Felix gets on with everyone. You'll enjoy it. Right, I must get back downstairs to help Mariah.'

'Do you want me to come back down?' Caroline asks unenthusiastically.

'No, that's fine.' I glance at my watch. It's almost two thirty. 'Sebastian will be back soon. Maybe you two can go out for a walk or something?' I peer out the window at the grey sleeting afternoon. 'Or maybe not. Why don't you get comfy and watch a film. Help yourself to snacks.'

'I think I'll finish unpacking,' she says, standing up.

We stand awkwardly for a second until I clap my hands together. 'Right, see you a bit later then.'

I leave Caroline in the lounge and stride into the kitchen, feeling relieved that conversation is out of the way. As I reach into the cupboard for a glass, I hear her retreat along the hall, returning to Sebastian's room. This all feels so uncomfortable. I do wish she'd slotted in a little better. I get the feeling that Mariah hasn't taken to her either, although that's not surprising given her crush on Sebastian.

I pour myself a tall glass of water and take it downstairs to the back office where I close the door behind me. I should be helping Mariah like I told Caroline, but the truth is I need a few moments to gather my thoughts. Normally, keeping the staff in check doesn't faze me at all. But this is different. This is personal. Should I have been more forgiving? More understanding? Perhaps. Sebastian isn't going to be happy with me. But I can't make one rule for his wife and another for everyone else. Anyway, if the staff see that I'm not playing favourites, they'll warm to her more quickly. I've probably done her a favour.

The thrum of chatter from the other side of the wall pierces my thoughts as I sit heavily at my desk. Well, it's more Sebastian's desk these days. He's taken over most of the running of the place. At first, I resisted it, unwilling to hand over the reins. Unconvinced that he would do as good a job as me. I still think of him as a child making mistakes and needing my help. But he's actually very good. Both my boys are hard workers. I just need them to not be... led astray by certain people.

The door opens. 'Lilian, there you are!' Brian comes into the office with his solid, reliable warmth. 'I just heard what happened. Did Caroline do something to Pat Chancellor's boy?'

'Oh, Brian, the silly girl overreacted. The lads were drunk

and Tom got a bit flirtatious. She only went and twisted his arm back and now he's threatening to sue.'

'What!' His eyebrows shoot up. 'Don't worry, I'll have a word with Pat and get him to smooth things out with Tom. He owes me after that bust-up at the rugby club.'

'Oh, yes, good point, Bri.' Back in the summer, we were invited to Pat's fiftieth-birthday do in the new state-of-the-art two-storey pavilion. Being a professional club, they've managed to get planning approval for all sorts of new facilities. I couldn't make it to the party – they're a lot younger than us, so not really my crowd – but Brian thought he'd better show his face to be sociable. Especially as a few of them are on the council and it pays to stay in with the planning committee when you run a local business, especially a public house.

Well, at the party, Pat's friends dared Pat to streak around the rugby-club pitch, which he did until the police came along and told him to put his clothes back on. Apparently, some dog walkers reported him. There was a bit of argy-bargy, but Brian managed to calm things down and stop Pat being carted off to the police station.

'Those Chancellor boys can't handle their drink.' Brian shakes his head and plonks himself in a chair. 'How's Caroline doing?'

'She's upstairs having a rest.'

'Poor love. Did you check on her? See how she's doing?'

'Yes, that's where I've been. To be quite honest, I don't think she handled the situation very well.'

'Oh dear. I hope you went easy on her, Lil.'

I raise an eyebrow, amused. 'What's that supposed to mean?'

Brian grunts and gives me a pointed stare. 'You know exactly what it means. She's our daughter-in-law. We need to be nice. Does Seb know what happened?'

'Not yet. He's taken Nicki to town to get some shopping.'

'Hmm. He's not going to be happy. I hope he doesn't go tearing over to Tom's place to do something stupid.'

'Of course he won't. But I'll speak to him as soon as he gets back.'

'Be tactful, Lil.'

I give an irritated snort. 'She's only been here a couple of days and she's already causing chaos.'

'It's hardly her fault,' Brian says.

'I suppose not,' I reply, leaning back in my chair. 'I'll tell Sebastian, but I'll phrase it carefully. He's obviously infatuated with the girl.'

'I'd say it's a bit more than infatuation. They're married, Lil.'

'Don't I know it.'

Brian opens his mouth to reprimand me for my attitude, but I cut him off. 'I'm also worried about Nicki.'

'What? Why?'

'She's become more and more withdrawn recently. We need to perk her up somehow. I think she's annoyed with Felix for going off for so long and leaving her alone.'

'She's not alone, is she? She's got us.'

'You know what I mean. I do wish we'd helped out with Teddy a bit more, but the pub takes up so much time. And what with Seb having gone away too, it's been so busy.'

'Stop fretting, Lil. Nicki will be fine.' Brian has a habit of always looking on the bright side. Of seeing the good in everyone and never wanting to rock the boat. I know this sounds like a great trait to have, but sometimes it irritates the hell out of me. 'She's missing Felix, that's all,' my husband continues. 'She'll be fine once he's back.'

'I hope you're right,' I reply, taking a sip of water. 'I think we'll *all* be happy once Felix finally gets home.' Hopefully then things will start to settle down.

TEN

CAROLINE

I pace around our bedroom, trying to stay calm. That woman is a Stone Age dragon! Letting men get away with groping her staff? What is she *like*? I come to a stop at the side of the bed and glare out of the window. After a moment, the tension drops out of my body. I try to let my mind go blank. Try to centre myself and let today's nastiness wash away. I'm married to Lilian's son. I have to make this work. I have to get her to like me. But how do I do that when I don't like *her*? This whole 'marriage' thing isn't going to be as easy as I thought. Maybe I was mad to do it. I probably was, but it's too late now. I'm here in England, in this quiet place that is so far removed from my life back home that I don't even feel like myself any more.

I sink down onto the bed and lean back against the wall, picking up my book from the bedside table. It's not even like I have any degree of separation from his family, we're all living and working right on top of one another. It's one thing to have imagined what that would be like, but it's quite another to actually live it. I open my novel at chapter two – the same chapter I've tried to read three times, but haven't been able to concentrate on. It's a light-hearted romcom I bought at the airport. I'm determined to give it a go again. I need to switch off the anxious thoughts racing around my brain.

I've made it halfway through chapter four when I'm inter-rupted by a light tap on the door. I look up to see Seb coming into the room, his grey eyes filled with concern.

'You heard, then,' I say flatly.

'Mum and Mariah said there was trouble with some of the lads from the rugby club. Are you okay?'

'I'm fine.' I set my book back on the bedside table.

'What happened?' He comes and sits on the bed and takes my hand, kissing my knuckles. 'Mariah said you twisted Tom's arm back?'

'Did she also tell you he grabbed my arse?'

'*What?!*' Seb springs to his feet, his expression thunderous.

'Hmm, didn't think so.'

'She didn't mention any grabbing. Mum said they were being flirty.'

I shake my head. 'I wouldn't have worked in bars for years if a bit of flirting upset me. No, this was full-on groping.'

'I'm going over there. Sort this out.'

I put a hand on his arm. 'No. You'll only make it worse. Just leave it. It's not worth getting upset about.'

'We can't just leave it!'

'Yes, we can. I don't want it to escalate any more than it already has, okay?'

Seb glowers at a spot just past my right ear.

'*Okay?*' I press.

'Fine.' He snaps his gaze back to me. 'But if I see that little shit out and about—'

'If you see him out and about you'll ignore him. It's been a hectic day, Seb. I just want to forget about it now. How was your shopping trip with Nicki and Teddy?'

'Yeah, it was pretty good actually. We had a laugh. I wish you could have come.'

'With hindsight, so do I.'

'Come here.' He sits back down on the bed and wraps his arms around me, holding me close to his body. After a couple of seconds, he pulls back slightly to find my lips, but after a brief kiss, I turn away. 'Sorry, Seb. I'm not really in a romantic mood right now.'

'Oh.' His face falls. 'No, of course you're not. Not after what happened. I'm an insensitive idiot, sorry.' He lets me go with a reluctant sigh.

'No, it's fine,' I reply. 'I'm sorry. It's just... you know.'

'Yeah, no, of course. But...' he begins and then tails off. 'Ah, I totally understand.'

I realise I need to address the elephant in the room. 'Look, I know we haven't been all that intimate yet, but, well, I didn't realise that we'd be sleeping right next door to your parents. It's... I dunno, it's just uncomfortable to think of them right there, I guess.' I glance at the wall.

'They wouldn't care. And anyway, they're not here right now,' he says with a cheeky smile.

'Yes, but they could come upstairs at any moment. It's not exactly an ideal situation. I'd be mortified if they walked in on us.'

'I get your point.' He thinks for a couple of seconds. 'I could get a lock for the door.'

'Yeah, but they'd still be able to hear us.' I prod his chest with my finger. 'This will give us an incentive to save for a deposit for our own apartment.'

'You want us to move out?'

'Not straight away, but eventually. Soon. Don't *you*?'

'To be honest, I hadn't really thought about it. It's just so convenient living here. You know, with work being downstairs. But, I guess it makes sense. And then when we get our own place, we can christen every room.'

'I can't wait!' I grin.

'Same.' He gives a frustrated groan. 'I might ask Mum and Dad for a loan.'

'No, we need to do this ourselves. I don't want to be in debt. It's a pity I'm totally skint though,' I add. 'After my flight, I literally have about eighty dollars in my account. I'm owed my final wages from the bar, but they'll go towards my final share of the rent and bills back in Byron.'

'I'm skint too,' Seb responds gloomily, running a hand through his hair. 'Spent most of my savings on flights.'

'Never mind,' I say with a smile of solidarity. 'We'll get there eventually.'

'It's a shame that Felix and Nicki got the cottage. That would've been great for us. Felix has always been a jammy sod.'

'Is someone taking my name in vain?' The door creaks open and a man who looks like Seb, but is slightly broader and with darker eyes, stands in the doorway.

'Felix!' Seb's face lights up. 'Thought you weren't back till tomorrow.'

'Yeah, managed to get an earlier flight. Good, hey? Dad said something about a *wife*?' Seb's brother gives me a smile filled with kindness and a hint of mischief.

'This is Caroline,' Seb says proudly, getting to his feet.

'Wow, okay, hello, Caroline, welcome to the Fletcher family.' He holds out his arms and I peel myself off the bed feeling crumpled and sweaty.

'Hi, nice to meet you.' He gives me a hug and then lightly punches Seb's arm. 'Congrats, little bro, I can't believe you went and got hitched. What a mad surprise.'

'A good one, I hope?' Seb says.

I realise he really wants his brother's approval.

'Of course! The best.' He turns to me. 'Mum says you're going to be helping me in the kitchen. Poor you.' He gives me another smile. 'No, it'll be great. I've been working solo for the past few weeks, so it'll be a luxury to have some proper help in the kitchen.'

I nod, suddenly feeling much better about things. I realise that I'd been dreading Felix's return. Worrying that he'd have some issue with me, like his mum and Mariah. But, so far, he seems really nice. Just like a more bubbly version of Seb.

'Anyway, I just popped upstairs to say congrats, but I absolutely have to go and see Nicki and Teddy now. I can't wait to see the look on their faces when I walk in the door.'

Seb smiles. 'She can't wait to have you back, Felix. The girl's been miserable without you.'

'Let's have dinner in the pub later tonight. The four of us,' Felix suggests. 'It'll be great. We've got the temp chef for another night, and I want to catch up on how you two met. Get to know my new sister-in-law over a few beers and some food cooked by someone other than me.'

'Good idea,' Seb replies. He turns to me. 'You up for it, Cal?'

'Totally,' I reply, feeling energised again. Maybe being part of the whole Fletcher clan won't be quite so bad after all.

ELEVEN

LILIAN

After today's drama, it's good to have Felix back home. I hadn't realised how much I'd missed his warm presence around the place. He has a way of lighting up a room and making people feel relaxed. If he wasn't such a great chef, I'd have had him front of house. I stop by the till for a moment to watch my two boys sitting at the window table with their wives, chatting and laughing together. It fills my heart with gladness to put all that awfulness behind us. I hope so much that Caroline is a good person. That she's going to treat Seb with love and respect, the way he deserves. At least she isn't sulking about my decision today.

'Mum!' Felix waves me over. I head across to their table. 'Why don't you and Dad join us for a while?'

'Yeah, you should,' Seb adds.

'We're working.' Both bar and restaurant are busy as usual and we can't afford for both Brian and I to duck out.

'Why don't you take it in turns?' Caroline suggests to my surprise. 'You could sit with us for a while, and then Brian can join us after.' She always looks well put together, but tonight she's simply stunning in pale-blue jeans, a natural linen shirt and cream cardigan, a multistrand gold necklace at her throat, her make-up flawless, and her honey-coloured hair falling in waves over her shoulders. Even her nose ring looks tasteful. No wonder my son is besotted.

In comparison, Nicki fades into the background. She's a pretty girl, but motherhood has washed her out recently. I'll have to tell Felix to spoil her. Take her out for some fun. I notice the baby monitor on the table. She keeps glancing at it anxiously.

'That would be nice.' I pat Caroline's shoulder briefly. 'Maybe just for a short while. Let me tell Brian. I'll be back to join you in a minute.' I hope she isn't trying to win me over so I'll change my mind and let her loose on the customers again.

I head through to the cosy bar where my husband is installed in his favourite place – pulling pints and joking around with the regulars – a mixture of his golf buddies, local business owners and professionals. For Brian, it's more like an exclusive social club than work. I fill him in on the suggestion that we take turns socialising with the kids. 'I'll come and get you in half an hour.'

'Great idea!' he booms. 'You take your time, though. Have some food. I'll catch up for a drink with them later.'

'Okay, but you might have to give Mariah a hand if she gets snowed under with food orders.'

'Hugo!' Brian calls out to our newest member of staff, who's just come off shift. He's only twenty-three, but has proved to be a hard worker. We started him off as a washer-upper and now he's progressed to waiting tables. 'Can you stay an extra hour in the restaurant?'

Hugo rubs at his shaggy blonde hair. 'What, *now*?'

'Yes. I think we've got some big tippers in there tonight.'

'Uh, okay, sure.'

'Good lad!'

'No problem,' he replies.

'Problem solved,' Brian says to me with a wink. 'Go and enjoy. I'll be there in a bit.'

'Hugo, can you add a lemon sole and French fries to Sebastian's order?' I ask. 'Table ten, in the window.'

Hugo gives me a small salute and turns around to head back to the kitchen.

'Shall I order for you too?' I ask Brian.

'No, I'll have some of your chips.'

'You will not,' I reply with mock sternness, and head back to the restaurant. They've already set an extra chair and place setting for me at the head of the table, next to Sebastian and Felix. I experience an unexpected surge of emotion at their thoughtfulness. I often feel surplus to requirements as far as my children are concerned. I know it's the natural order of things. Your kids grow up and they don't need you any more – except when there's a problem. So when they genuinely want my company, it's gratifying.

Sebastian pours me a glass of wine, but I stop him at the halfway mark. 'I still have to work after this.' I'm a stickler for my staff not drinking on the job, so I can't very well go against my own rules.

'One glass won't hurt,' Seb says, ignoring my protests and topping it up anyway.

'Hey, Seb,' Felix says. 'We should have a stag do for you. Did you have one in Oz?'

'No, I didn't, and no thank you. Anyway, it's a bit late for that, I'm already married.'

'You're not getting out of it, mate. I'm your big brother, and I'm sorting it.'

Sebastian grins, happy to have his arm twisted.

'And, Nicki, you should get a few of your friends together to sort a hen night for Caroline.'

Caroline holds up her hand. 'Oh no, that's okay. I'm not really—'

'Definitely,' Sebastian adds, cutting her off. 'It'll be fun, Cal. You'll get to meet some more people.'

She glances over at Nicki, who looks equally unenthusiastic.

'I think it's a nice idea,' I say. 'You don't have to go crazy, Nicki. Just a nice meal out somewhere. You can even do it here, if you like.'

'No, we have to go out properly, otherwise what's the point?' Felix says.

'Okay,' Nicki replies. 'I'm sure I can arrange something. As long as we can get someone to look after Teddy.'

'Don't go to too much trouble,' Caroline adds.

'Mum, Felix was telling us about the yacht owner,' Seb says, changing the subject.

'How was it, working on a boat?' I ask. 'Are you too posh for us now?'

'Absolutely,' Felix replies. 'Totally got ideas above my station. I'll be slumming it here.'

'Charming,' Nicki replies, not getting into the spirit of the joke. 'I think I might pop back to check on Teddy.'

'Is he okay?' Caroline asks.

'He's not crying, and looks fine in the monitor, but it's been half an hour so I want to double-check.'

'Want me to go?' Felix asks.

'No, you stay and talk yachts.'

I can't tell if Nicki's annoyed with him or not. He should have checked with her about the hen night, before asking her in front of everyone. I love Felix, but he's not always the most tactful person.

'Don't be long,' Felix says to Nicki. 'The food will be out soon.'

'Yep, I know.' She squeezes past Felix and makes her way out via the bar.

Definite tension between those two. That makes me anxious. Aside from the hen night thing, maybe she's disappointed not to have Felix to herself this evening. After all, he's been away for over a month. I should have foreseen that and suggested that he spend time with just her. Ah well, hopefully they'll sort it out between them.

'So anyway,' Felix says, unfazed by Nicki's coldness, 'the upshot of my yacht-cheffing experience is that I've made a boatload of money. But, it's put me off ever becoming rich.'

'Why?' Seb asks. 'I thought it would have done the opposite.'

Felix shakes his head. 'So, this yacht owner is a billionaire, but he's the unhappiest person I've ever met in my life.' Felix reaches for the wine bottle and tops up Seb, Caroline and Nicki's glasses before pouring the dregs into his own. 'Hugo!' He waves the empty bottle of white and signals for a new one.

'He's unhappy?' I ask.

'Miserable. The whole time I was there, he was never alone. Mainly in meetings with investment experts, how to make his money "work for him", which properties to buy etcetera. He's constantly worried about people ripping him off. He's so paranoid that he has a tonne of security. And even if you took away the security, he and his family are surrounded by people. He has a chef – i.e., me – waiting staff, housekeeping staff, a massage therapist, nutritionist, personal trainer and on and on. His wife has her own staff separate to his. His kids are time-managed to the hilt - piano lessons, tennis lessons, languages, tutors. Every single second of their days is mapped out. It's horrendous.'

'It must be normal for them,' I say. 'They'd probably be horrified by our boring lives.'

'Give me boring over that any day,' Felix says with a shudder.

'Byron has a lot of rich people too,' Caroline says. 'They've ruined the laid-back feel of the place.'

'Stalbridge's wealthy are the people who love our pub the most.' I add. 'They come for the old-world charm, and the character.'

'Don't forget the top-notch cuisine,' Felix adds with a smirk.

'As if I'd forget that.' I give him an indulgent smile.

'So you're from Byron Bay?' Felix asks Caroline.

'Yeah. It's beautiful, but can get really busy.'

'It's amazing,' Sebastian says. 'We should have a family holiday over there some time. You guys would love it.'

'I'm not fond of the heat,' I say.

'It doesn't get too hot there,' Caroline replies. 'Maybe mid- to high twenties during our summer, and mid-teens in the winter.'

'How have you found it here so far?' Felix asks her. 'Settling in okay?'

'It's only been a couple of days,' she replies. 'But it's a really pretty village. Dorset is gorgeous – what I've seen of it. And the snow when we arrived made everything look like something out of a movie.'

'There are loads of great places to visit,' Felix says. 'And the beaches here are lovely too. We can definitely give Australia a run for its money. Show me Bondi Beach and I'll show you Branksome Chine.' Felix winks. I think he's hoping to goad Caroline into a bit of who's-got-the-best-beaches friendly rivalry. But Caroline doesn't bite.

'I've got a ton of day trips planned,' Sebastian says. 'Lyme Regis, Shaftesbury, Sandbanks.'

Hugo returns with a bottle of white. Felix takes it off him and tops up his glass. 'What did you do back in Byron Bay?' he asks Caroline.

'I managed a bar there.'

He raises his eyebrows, impressed. 'Wow. Sounds like you picked the right girl, Sebby. She'll fit right in here.'

Caroline doesn't reply and neither does Seb. They each take a sip of their wine. An air of awkwardness has suddenly descended.

'We don't need any extra bar staff at the moment,' I say stiffly. 'So Caroline has very kindly agreed to help out in the kitchen.'

'So you said.' Felix gives me one of his infuriating smiles. 'That's okay. She'll have more fun with me in the kitchen than with you and Dad behind the bar.'

'I'm a mean chopper and slicer,' Caroline jokes.

'I can tell,' Felix replies.

Sebastian looks thrilled that his wife and brother are getting on so well, but I can't ignore the beat of alarm thudding behind my ribcage. The girl is obviously flirting with him, which is highly inappropriate given he's a married man with a young family. Maybe Caroline has forgotten that she's married too, and that her husband is sitting right there.

Should I say something to Felix later? Warn him to keep his distance? That might be difficult as she's going to be working in close quarters with him. Perhaps I'll have to rethink that decision and get her back in the restaurant. I'll speak to Brian, but I can already guess what he'll say. He'll tell me I'm worrying over nothing. That I shouldn't interfere and should leave them all to sort out their own lives.

But I left them to it before.

And look how that turned out.

Nicki comes back to the table, red-cheeked and rubbing her hands together. 'It's freezing out there.'

'How's our boy?' Felix asks, taking her hands and blowing on them as she sits next to him. 'You're like a little ice block.'

'Think it's going to snow again,' she says. 'Teddy's fine. Sleeping like a baby.' She smiles weakly at her joke.

I'm happy to see she's cheered up a bit. Perhaps she was simply anxious about Teddy. I can remember that panicky feeling in the early days when my babies were young and help-less. I place a hand on my chest to calm my heart. I still get those panicky feelings now, only they're somehow worse because everything is out of my control. Or maybe it just seems that way because I'm feeling it *now*.

TWELVE

AMY

'Amy, can you...?'

'Mum? I can't hear you very well, you keep breaking up.'

'I said, can you call your sister?'

'Hang on, let me go outside, get a better signal.'

Normally, Amy's parents are good about not disturbing her during the day as they know how busy her schedule is. If she thought the first and second terms were hard, her third term of medicine is on a whole other level. Amy stands out in the bleak magnolia corridor of her halls of residence, where the mobile signal is strongest. She was in the middle of making a quick sandwich when her mum rang and she made the mistake of answering it.

'Mum, are you still there? Can you hear me?'

'Your sister's left home.' Her mum's voice is caustic. Clipped and cold.

'What do you mean, left home? Where's she gone?'

'She's seventeen years old. She's supposed to be doing her A-levels next year, but she's just left me and your father a note. It's so overdramatic. She must have gone sometime last night.'

Amy takes a breath. This is not what she needs right now.

She's got enough on her plate without being drawn into family dramas. 'I'm sure she'll be back later. You know what Michelle's like. She gets emotional. She's probably gone to stay with one of her friends.'

'We had a terrible argument, Amy. We all said things in the heat of the moment. But Michelle, she said some really unforgivable things about me and your father. About you too. I think she's jealous of your academic brain and your dedication.'

Amy's stomach clenches. Why does her mother have to bad-mouth Michelle? She realises things aren't great between her sister and her parents, but her mum shouldn't try to get Amy to take sides.

'Why can't she be more like you?' her mum cries.

Amy walks down the corridor towards the window at the far end, gazing out at the horse chestnut trees next to the bike racks. 'She's her own person, Mum. You need to let Michelle breathe and do her own thing.'

'She can breathe and do her own thing when she's living in her own house and spending her own money. You know, this is all about her wanting to go to art school. She wants us to support her financially while she splashes paint around for three years.'

'She's good at art, Mum. Maybe she could make a go of it. Lots of people do.'

'I'm good at singing in the shower, but that's not going to give me a stable career. I told her she's good enough at arguing, why doesn't she use that talent and go to law school?'

'Mum, listen, do me a favour...'

'What?'

'When Michelle comes home, don't shout at her. Don't tell her what to do. Just let her concentrate on her A-levels. You can figure out the rest later.'

'That's what we've been trying to do, but she keeps telling us how unfair it is that we're supporting you at university, but

won't do the same for her. I'm not going to be guilt-tripped into paying out money for a childish whim.'

Amy sighs inwardly. It's like shouting into the void. Neither her mum nor her sister ever listen to reason, or try to see things from the other side. 'Look, just call me when she gets home.'

'Can you ring her, Amy? Find out where she is.'

'Okay.' She sighs.

The line goes dead. Amy peers out of the window at a group of four students smoking on the front steps. She doesn't understand why her parents can't accept that Michelle has different talents. And even if she doesn't make it big in the art world, what's so bad about studying something you love? You'd still get a qualification at the end.

She calls Michelle's mobile but it goes straight to voicemail.

'Michelle, it's Amy. Mum's doing her nut worrying about you. Can you give her a call and let her know you're okay? Call me back too.'

The group of smokers below are laughing at something. Amy can't actually remember when she last laughed that hard. Everything feels so serious these days. Her phone pings. It's Michelle, thank goodness. She's sent a text message:

> I've had enough. I've left home. I'm not going back so don't bother trying to change my mind. You're obviously the chosen child, so good luck with that.

While Amy does feel sorry for her sister at the way her parents favour her, it's annoying that Michelle blames her for it. She always tries to take her sister's side where possible, but her parents never listen, so how is that her fault? She bangs out an irritated reply:

> Michelle, please just go home. Finish your A-levels and then you can move out and do what you like.

Amy waits for a snotty reply, but her phone screen stays stubbornly blank.

Still nothing.

Amy can't face calling her mum back, so she wimps out and messages her instead:

> *I couldn't get through to Michelle, but she texted me that she's fine. I'll keep trying, see if I can talk to her. I'm sure she'll be home soon xxx*

But Amy is wrong.
Michelle will never return home.

THIRTEEN

CAROLINE

I've spent the last hour peeling and chopping great piles of vegetables in the pub kitchen while Felix reaches into the back of the store cupboard, clicking his tongue.

'I've only been gone a few weeks,' he says, throwing a box of something dubious into a black bin liner. 'You wouldn't think the kitchen could have degenerated into such a disaster so quickly. I hope health and safety don't pay an unexpected visit before I've had a chance to put this lot right. It's taken me almost the whole week to get it halfway decent. And stock levels are still too low.'

'Sorry you had to come back to that,' I say, thankful that the kitchen mess was nothing to do with me.

'Ignore me. I'm just having a whinge.' He throws me a smile. 'It's actually my own fault for not hiring a decent chef. But it was such short notice, I didn't have time to interview properly. And then with Seb going away too, it's all just fallen apart. You're doing a good job with those veggies, Caroline.'

'Thanks, but it's just a bit of chopping.'

He holds up a hand. 'Let me just stop you there. It's not just a bit of chopping. You'd be surprised how many kitchen staff make a right pig's ear of it.'

'Oh, well, glad I'm doing something right,' I reply, aiming for chirpy, but sounding more bitter than intended. I can't believe the original plan was for me to work in the bar, only to be transferred to the restaurant, and now I've been demoted to kitchen skivvy. All in the space of a few days.

'Don't worry, you're an excellent kitchen assistant,' he assures me.

'Hey, what about me?' Hugo sweeps into the kitchen, cheeks red, blonde hair damp from the sleet.

'You're late,' Felix replies.

'Sorry, car wouldn't start, so I had to get a lift from my mum and—'

'Can you fetch one of the small potato sacks from the store cupboard?' Felix interrupts Hugo, who gives me an eye-roll behind his back.

Felix and I have been working together for almost a week and the time has sped by. I've hardly had a moment to myself what with the workload and getting to know the staff better. Hugo is a washer-upper, kitchen assistant and waiter. He wants to become a chef, and is always trying to impress Felix, but keeps getting it wrong. So Felix's patience is wearing a bit thin. I've tried to act as mediator between them, but I think it's probably best if I stay out of it. Especially as I think Hugo might have a little crush on me.

I don't see much of Seb during the day as he's either squirreled away in the back office doing accounts, placing orders and taking bookings, or he's making runs to the cash and carry. By the end of the night, we just fall into bed exhausted.

Not tonight though.

'Looking forward to this evening?' Felix asks, standing by the back door sharpening his knives.

'Hmm, sort of,' I reply, dreading the half-hearted hen night that Nicki's planned for me.

'That's not very enthusiastic. I'd have thought you'd love a night out.'

'I do like going out, but it's weird when you don't really know anyone.' I don't add that the main reason I'm apprehensive is because I'm convinced no one likes me. Mariah is openly hostile, and Nicki is totally unenthusiastic. At least Lilian isn't coming – she's needed to stay and look after the pub.

'Well, that's why it's such a good idea,' Felix says, opening the sack of spuds that Hugo has dumped on the floor. 'It's the perfect opportunity to get to know people. I know Nicki can be reserved at first, but she's hilarious once you get to know her.'

The last adjective I'd use to describe Nicki is 'hilarious', but I keep that thought to myself.

'Honestly,' he continues. 'Give my wife a couple of G and Ts and she's the life and soul of the party.'

'I'll look forward to that,' I reply.

Felix picks out a couple of blackened potatoes, shakes his head and throws them into the bin liner outside the door. 'Take that and stick it in the outside bin. Then wash your hands and come back in and start peeling.'

'Yes, chef.'

None of us get the opportunity to chat further as the Friday lunchtime rush takes hold properly and everything is a blur of steam, shouted orders, banging doors and clanging baking trays.

As well as food prep, I've also been tasked with plating up salads and a few of the starters. I'm quite enjoying it, as it's fast-paced and quite meditative in that there's no time to think about anything other than what I'm doing. The only dark spot is Mariah's sullen face every time she catches my eye. I'm absolutely not imagining it as she's perfectly sunny when she speaks to Hugo and Felix. It's just me she seems to have a problem with.

'You going to Caroline's hen do tonight?' Felix calls to her across the kitchen.

'I'm working, but I'll try to make the club afterwards.'

'Club?' I ask, a little horrified. 'I thought we were going for a meal.'

Mariah throws me a smile, but it's not a nice one. She doesn't reply, just picks up a Caesar salad and a bowl of winter vegetable soup and leaves the kitchen.

'You not into clubbing then?' Hugo asks, stacking plates into the dishwasher.

'Not really. I mean, I don't mind a dance, but I prefer things more low-key.'

'Yeah, same.' Hugo straightens up. 'So, what's your ideal night out?'

'Less talking, more working,' Felix snaps at Hugo.

'Yes, chef,' he replies, turning back to the dishwasher, but not before giving me a wink.

Five minutes later, Mariah returns with the Caesar salad. 'The Cartwrights aren't happy. Barbara's salad's got bacon in it and she's a vegetarian. Her husband says she's eaten some of it and now she's throwing up in the toilet.'

'What?' Felix closes the oven door and turns around to glare at Mariah. 'Well, did she specify no bacon?'

'Yeah, I wrote it on the order.' Mariah resolutely doesn't look at me, even though she knows I'm the one who prepared the salad.

'I'm sorry, I don't remember seeing "no bacon" on the order,' I say, cringing that I might be dropping Mariah in it. I know for a fact it simply said '1 x Caesar 1 x veg soup'.

'Where's the slip?' Felix asks.

Mariah produces it and holds it out so we can both see it. It clearly says '1 x Caesar no bacon', with the 'no bacon' double underlined. Although the writing of 'no bacon' looks different to the rest – messier, and like they didn't press as heavily on the

paper. But I obviously can't accuse her of adding that in afterwards to put herself in the clear.

Mariah looks from Felix to me with an anxious shrug that I
can totally tell she's putting on.

'What's the hold-up with table eleven's desserts?' Lilian
bursts into the kitchen. *Of course she does.*

'There's a bit of a problem with Barbara Cartwright's salad,'
Mariah says, going on to fill my mother-in-law in on my
apparent cock-up.

'Easy mistake to make,' Felix calls over, trying to have my
back.

My cheeks are flaming with fury and embarrassment.
Mariah has either made a mistake and is trying to blame me for
it, or she's set up this whole situation on purpose to make me
look bad. Either way, I need to sort this out and find out why
she's being such a total bitch towards to me. Not now, though.
Not in front of everyone while I'm shaking with anger.

'Caroline,' Lilian says while Mariah looks on, 'the thing is,
reputation is everything in the hospitality industry. We can't
afford to make even small mistakes, not with all the websites out
there like Tripadvisor, Facebook, Instagram and the like.'

While Lilian is talking to me like I'm an idiot, I take a deep
breath and try to stay calm. Arguing with her won't help
anyone, least of all me.

'We need to be impeccable, above reproach,' she continues.

'Absolutely,' I reply, biting the inside of my cheek to stop
myself from slagging off Mariah.

'It's probably my fault,' Lilian says, shaking her head
ruefully. 'I should have given you some proper training. But as
you said, you already manage a bar, so...' She lets her sentence
trail off. 'Anyway, I'll comp their bill and offer them another
free meal. Goodness, Caroline, this is the second lot of freebies
this week. Are you certain you're up to working here?'

I can't even respond to that, because if I do I know I'll say something I'll regret.

'Give her a break, Mum,' Felix says. 'We've all made mistakes.'

She tuts and glares at him before letting out a sigh. 'You're right, you're absolutely right. This week has been your settling-in week.'

I take that to mean that I'd better not make any more mistakes, or else.

Thankfully, the rest of lunch service goes by without a hitch, but I'm still unsettled by the bacon incident and Mariah's apparent hatred of me. Consequently, I keep my head down and try to keep my mind on the job.

'Mum's bark is worse than her bite,' Felix says after his several attempts to cheer me up fail and it's just the two of us in the kitchen. 'As a landlady of a busy pub, she has to be tough. Don't take it personally.'

With all my being, I want to protest my innocence and land Mariah in it, but it's her word against mine and I know I'll come off looking bad. 'Problem is, it's been one thing after another! First the sexual-assault thing, and now this. Your family must think I'm an absolute liability.'

'Hey.' Felix puts down his serving spoon and comes around the counter to give me a hug. 'Don't worry. Like I told Mum, everyone makes mistakes. It's your first week here.'

'Yes, but I'm used to working in a busy bar. I hardly ever make mistakes back home. I don't know what's going on.'

'Probably a bit of jet-lag. Plus you've just got married and flown to a country you've never been to before in the middle of freezing winter, and you've also moved in with a bunch of strangers who are suddenly your "family".' He makes air quotes.

I stare at Felix for a moment, and we both start laughing. 'Okay, when you put it like that...'

'Now, come on, sort out table three's ice-cream order for me. The bowls are there. Two scoops and a wafer.'

'Yes, chef,' I reply with renewed enthusiasm, despite the uncomfortable thought that Mariah and I are going to have to have a talk later.

FOURTEEN

CAROLINE

The restaurant is dark, sedate and nondescript with depressing piped elevator music. The place is half empty and the only other customers are all older couples, aside from one table of six mismatched diners who look like they're having their work Christmas dinner, as they're all wearing bright paper party hats but their faces are sullen. I think a morgue would possibly have made a better venue for a hen night.

To Nicki's credit, she's made a real effort to get glammed-up. Her dark hair is gleaming and she's wearing shiny black jeans, a gold top and spiky heels. My wardrobe isn't really suited to an English winter, but I figure we're not going to be outside much so I opted for a short cream dress with a draped gold-chain belt and a black fitted blazer. I'm insanely over-dressed.

Seb said I looked so good that he was gutted we were going out separately. I told him he didn't look so bad himself, all suited up with the rest of the boys. They've gone further afield, into Bournemouth – about an hour away – while us girls are staying more local, having travelled a mere twenty minutes to Yeovil just across the Dorset border into Somerset.

Now that we've reached the venue, I wish we'd gone to Bournemouth too. But it was nice of Nicki to arrange it, so I shouldn't be too disappointed. Maybe the food will be sensational.

'Table for five?' the waitress asks, casting her eyes over our small group. Brian gave Nicki and I a lift while the other three took a taxi. Nicki briefly introduced us all as we walked into the place. Apparently, she had invited a lot more people but as it was a Friday night on such short notice, hardly anyone had been able to make it. Mariah said she's coming later, after her shift at the pub.

'We've got a booking under the name Fletcher,' Nicki says.

'Oh, right, okay. You're the hen do, right? Who's getting married?' the waitress asks breezily as she leads us to a table in the window. I'm not surprised she put us here, on show. We'll make the place look livelier than it is, maybe we'll draw in more custom.

'That would be Caroline,' Nicki says, pointing to me.

'Congratulations, how exciting! When's the big day?' she asks with more enthusiasm than any of Seb's family or friends have shown.

I smile gratefully. 'I'm actually already married, but I didn't have a hen night, so we're doing it now.'

'Quite right too.' She beams at all of us. 'Friends are so important. You need to celebrate with your besties, don't you?'

There's a bit of an awkward silence as, aside from my soul-mate Nicki, I've only just met these other girls about two minutes ago. 'Totally,' I eventually reply, a little embarrassed.

We shuffle into our seats, and I note that Nicki is sitting as far away from me as she can get. I'm right next to the window opposite a tall blonde girl called Sarah. She's next to a brunette called Camille who I think is her partner. To my right is a curly-haired girl whose name I've already forgotten, and next to her sits Nicki.

The waitress takes our drinks orders and leaves us with the large, laminated menus.

'So, are you all from Stalbridge?' I ask, trying to break the ice.

They all nod except for Camille. 'I'm from Normandy in France,' she says. 'I met Sarah when she came over to nanny for a family in my village.'

'How long have you been together?' I ask.

'Four years,' Camille replies. 'We got married eighteen months ago.' She bumps shoulders with her wife, who smiles at her.

'Congratulations,' I say, feeling an unexpected rush of emotion at their obvious love for one another.

'Same to you,' Camille says.

'Thanks.'

Camille asks how Seb and I met, and I tell them about our whirlwind romance. She and Sarah are engaged in my story, but Nicki and the girl next to me are having their own conversation about children. From the snippets I hear, I gather they both have babies the same age.

Our drinks arrive and we order our food. I opt for the green Thai curry which, when it arrives, is perfectly fine. I spend the entire meal talking to Sarah and Camille. They were living in Normandy up until six months ago when they moved back to Sarah's hometown of Stalbridge to set up a pre-school in the town. It's going well so far. The couple have only just moved back to the UK, so they've hardly seen any of the Fletchers, other than to say a quick hello.

Nicki and the curly-haired girl, whose name I've since gleaned is Annabel, haven't spoken directly to me once. Much as Sarah and Camille seem lovely, the whole evening is forced and strange. My appetite is non-existent and I suddenly feel incredibly homesick.

I try not to think about my life back home in Byron Bay.

About the good friends I've left behind. The glorious weather and the lively bars and restaurants. About my job where I was respected and competent. I know things weren't perfect. I had no significant other there. No one to share my life with, but that didn't seem to matter. Not when my life was full in so many other ways. I had never actively been looking for a boyfriend or a husband. Most of my relationships were fun, fleeting affairs with no expectations and no ties. Which is why the Seb situation is such a big deal. I've upended my life for him, to come to this place on the other side of the world. And, right now, I'm wondering if I might have made a massive mistake.

Thankfully, the meal is finally over and I'm counting down the seconds to when we can call a cab and make the awkward journey back home. I had hoped Nicki and I might have had the chance to chat this evening. To find some common ground and bond a little. I'd wanted to ask her about Seb. About his life before he met me. But we've barely looked at one another, let alone spoken. Both Sarah and Annabel are schoolfriends of Nicki's. They knew Seb, but not that well as he and Felix are a few years older.

'Right then,' Annabel suddenly declares as the bill arrives, 'who's ready for some dancing?'

I try to keep my features from twisting into a look of horror as I contemplate several more hours of trying to socialise with these strangers. I mean, Sarah and Camille have been lovely so far, but the conversation is quite stilted. '*Dancing?*' I turn to look at Annabel.

She smiles, her eyes widening. 'Yes, we're going clubbing next, didn't you know?'

'Nicki didn't mention it,' I reply. Mariah *did* mention a club, though, but when Nicki didn't, I assumed Mariah had misunderstood the plan. Although, thinking about it, perhaps some loud music and a bit of dancing might be just the thing to loosen everyone up. To get Nicki to warm to me. I resolve to make more of an effort to get to know her. It's a pity I couldn't have sat next to her this evening, forced her into engaging with me.

'The bill comes to forty-three pounds each including a tip,' Nicki announces.

I swallow, thinking of my dwindling funds.

'Let's split it between four of us,' Camille says. 'Caroline shouldn't have to pay on her hen night.'

'Oh no, that's okay,' I reply, although it would be very helpful, as I didn't realise there'd be club entry to pay for too.

'Oh, right, sure,' Nicki replies.

I catch Annabel scowling. 'I only had a starter,' she says.

'Yes, but you've also polished off almost two bottles of wine,' Sarah replies with a smile that doesn't quite reach her eyes.

In the end, I insist that we split it five ways. I don't want to fall out with any of these people.

Outside, the icy wind slices through my jacket and freezes my face and legs. 'Jeez, I'm not cut out for this weather,' I say. 'My teeth are actually chattering.'

'You need a better coat,' Camille observes.

'No shit,' I reply with a strangled laugh.

'It's not far,' Nicki says. 'I picked this restaurant as it's close to the club. Mariah's just texted to say she's meeting us there.'

We walk up the road and turn down a side street where the queue for the club stretches along the pavement. I realise I'm going to be an actual ice block by the time we get inside. But, to my intense relief, our little party walks right past what looks like group after group of hen and stag dos that are far more raucous than us, and up to the sizeable bouncer on the door.

'We're on the list,' she says. 'Nicki Fletcher plus four.'

He looks up from his phone and nods, opening up the rope to let us into the blissfully warm foyer.

'Felix is friends with the owner,' Sarah says by way of explanation. 'Nicki always gets in free.'

Everyone hands in their coats, but I keep my jacket on for

now, not yet warmed up enough to relinquish it. Nicki confidently leads the way through the packed, sweaty club to a roped-off area at the back which I deduce is some kind of VIP section with curved, plush red sofas and low black tables. The moment we sit, a waitress comes over with a bottle of champagne and five glasses. She and Nicki greet one another like friends and they chat for a while but it's so noisy I can't make out what they're saying.

The music is cheesy dance and pop and most of the clubbers are jumping around on the dance floor singing along. They all look in their late teens and early twenties. I feel old at thirty, but I don't yearn to have those days back. And then, out of the corner of my eye, I notice a group of people gathered at the edge of the bar over to our right. My heart sinks as I realize some of them are the drunk rugby lads from the pub last weekend. I hope they don't recognise me. I don't want any aggro.

But all thoughts of a trouble-free night evaporate as I see Mariah standing with them – at least I think it's her. She looks so different with her hair down – a cascade of dark tumbling curls – and beautifully applied make-up. She's wearing a black minidress embroidered with gold and red flowers, and I'm furious to see that she's talking very cosily to the guy who groped me.

FIFTEEN

CAROLINE

Knocking back my glass of newly poured cheap champagne, I get to my feet.

'You okay?' Sarah asks.

Nicki looks up. 'The loos are back near the entrance,' she says, assuming that's where I'm headed.

'I don't need the loo,' I reply.

'Are we dancing?' Annabel says, brightening up.

'You go ahead,' I reply. 'There's someone I need to talk to first.'

Nicki and Annabel follow my gaze over to where Tom Chancellor and Mariah are talking near the bar. Now that I'm away from the pub and out from under Lilian's watchful eye, I think I'm going to have a word with those two. I take a step in their direction.

'That's not a good idea,' Nicki says, putting a hand on my arm.

'Is Mariah a friend of that dickhead?' I ask.

Nicki shrugs. 'We all know each other. It's a small town. I'd leave well alone if I were you. Tom's with all his mates and, knowing them, they'll be off their heads on something or other.

Anyway, Mariah's here for your hen night. She probably just bumped into them when she arrived.'

'I'll go and see, shall I?' I sidle past the ridiculous VIP rope and along the edge of the dance floor towards the bar. I note that none of my group has come with me. That's the difference between here and home. Back in Byron Bay, none of my friends would have let me walk over to a hostile man on my own. I'm thinking I might need to make my own group of friends here, rather than relying on Seb's extended family to introduce me. But I should also cut myself some slack. I've only been here a week.

As I draw closer, I realise the cosy chat I assumed Mariah and Tom were having looks more like an argument, their voices carrying over the music.

'No I didn't!' she cries.

'Don't lie. You know you did, Mariah. You got what you wanted and now you're backing off.'

Neither of them notice me approaching.

'I've had enough of this,' she shouts. 'Believe what you want.' She turns to leave but he grabs hold of her arm.

'We haven't finished talking.'

'You might not. But I have. Get off.'

Right at that moment, Tom notices me standing behind Mariah. 'Oh, talk of the devil. Here's the psycho herself.'

'I see you haven't learned your lesson, then,' I drawl, looking at his hand on Mariah's arm.

His face turns crimson with outrage, but he lets her go.

Mariah rubs her arm and turns around. 'Oh, it's you. Having a good hen night?' she asks insincerely.

'I was until I saw *him*. What are you two arguing about? Something to do with last Sunday?' I fix her with a glare.

'*What?*' Mariah's trying to look innocent but she's not pulling it off.

'Yeah, Mariah, what were we arguing about?' Tom says with

a grin. His eyes are bloodshot and his skin gleams under a thin film of sweat.

She throws him a disdainful look before turning back to me. 'Come on, Caroline, let's leave these losers to it.' Surprisingly, she links her arm through mine as if we're suddenly best of friends.

'Oh, right. Fine by me,' I reply. I'd like to stay and find out from Tom what they were talking about, but his friends have started to notice me and I'm suddenly nervous about this conversation becoming more trouble than it's worth. 'I love your dress, by the way.'

'Thanks,' Mariah replies. 'I made it myself.'

'*Really?*' I'm quite impressed. Maybe there's more to this moody girl than I first thought.

Mariah is almost dragging me across the dance floor back towards the VIP area where Nicki and Annabel are watching our progress.

'Are you going to tell me what all that was about?' I ask her, wondering why she was so keen to get me away from Tom Chancellor.

'No,' she replies. 'Let's get drunk instead.'

I inhale, wondering whether or not to push for an answer. But then I decide that her idea is probably the better one. Having a few more drinks with Mariah could be a good opportunity to get her on side. And, also, a night of not having to think about anything heavy is sounding pretty perfect about now.

SIXTEEN

LILIAN

It feels very peculiar walking around the flat knowing that Sebastian is in bed with Caroline just on the other side of that door. She got back at around one a.m., but Sebastian and Felix didn't arrive home until after four. Being a light sleeper, I woke up both times. No wonder they're both still out for the count at – I glance at my slim gold watch, a present from Brian on my sixtieth – nine forty-five.

I wonder if I should bang some crockery around in the kitchen so they don't end up wasting the whole day. But maybe Sebastian wouldn't appreciate that. They both have the day off, so I suppose I should just let them rest. Poor Nicki and Felix won't have the luxury of a lie-in. Not with Teddy still waking at five every morning.

I can't understand why Nicki's parents have never visited their grandson. It's not even as if they live that far away. It's their loss, but it's a shame for Teddy that he won't know them. Nicki's never told me what happened there. Just that she was glad to get away. Her family didn't even come to the wedding, for goodness' sake, and Brian and I have never met them formally. Back when Felix proposed seven years ago, I asked

Nicki if she minded me getting in touch with them, but her reaction was so bristly and defensive, that I decided not to pursue it, even though a part of me is curious as to what caused the rift.

I told Felix I'd cover lunch today, as long as he's done all the prep and can be back in the kitchen for evening service. I've done plenty of cheffing when I've needed to, but I don't like making a habit of it.

Brian is already downstairs setting up the bar with Tarik. I'll need a strong coffee before heading into the kitchen. It's just going to be me and Hugo in there today, but if things get too busy, I might have to ask one of my boys, or possibly even Caroline, to help out.

I'll be glad when these wedding shenanigans are behind us and we can get back to some kind of normality again. It would be different if Sebastian and Caroline had involved the family from the start, but they chose to get married without us there for any of the planning or celebrations, so it all feels a little late to be having hen nights and the like now. I inhale and try not to let myself get riled up. I haven't been myself ever since Sebastian came home with a bride. It's all just been such a shock. Even now, a week later, it keeps hitting me all over again.

I slip on my black court shoes and make my way downstairs to the bar.

'Morning, Tarik,' I call out.

'Morning, Mrs F.'

He's a good lad. Been with us three years now and I've never had a moment's bother with him. With his good looks and that lovely dark hair, he certainly knows how to charm the customers. His dad, Terry, is one of Brian's closest friends, and his mum, Vandana, is a sweetheart. She used to work here when she was younger, until she retrained as a nurse.

'Where's Brian?' I ask.

'In the cellar. He'll be up in a minute. You want me to get him?'

'No, that's fine. Can you make me an americano? With an extra shot.'

'Coming up. Do you want a biscuit on the side too?'

'Go on then. I'm going to need the sugar hit.'

'Oh? Why's that?'

'I'm on chef duty. Actually, can you bring it into the kitchen when you're done?'

'Will do.'

I head into the kitchen and check out the fridges, happy to see that Felix has gone above and beyond what he needed to do. Everything is prepped in labelled Tupperware boxes, ready for me to take out and use as needed. My eldest son may have his flaws, but when it comes to professionalism, he's the best. I nod to myself and wash my hands as Hugo comes in the door bang on ten o'clock.

'Cutting it fine, Hugo.' I glance up at the clock.

'Not late though, am I?' He grins.

'Hmm,' I reply, unimpressed.

'No Caroline today?' he asks nonchalantly.

I give him a sharp look. 'No. She and Sebastian are having the morning off.'

'Right.' He nods and takes the hint to get to work.

Before I know it, it's two o'clock and the lunchtime rush is slowly easing.

'We've run out of order pads!' Jeanie, our newish seventeen-year-old Saturday girl waves an empty stub at me.

'There are more in the office,' I call out.

'Oh, okay. Whereabouts is that?'

'Don't worry, I'll get them.'

Jeanie heads back into the restaurant while I direct Hugo to stop washing up for a minute and take over plating up the puddings. Then I leave the kitchen and head to the back office where we keep all the spare stationery and other bits and bobs.

I open the door and am confronted by a blonde head leaning down, looking into one of the desk drawers. 'Jeanie, I said I'd...'

She looks up and I see it's not Jeanie at all, but a rather red-faced Caroline.

'Oh,' I say. 'I thought you were... never mind. Can I help you? Are you looking for something?'

'Um...' She straightens up and closes the drawer. 'Yes, I was just looking for some painkillers, actually.'

'In the office?' I raise an eyebrow.

Her eyes narrow and she pushes her hair back from her face. 'I couldn't find any upstairs, and I didn't want to disturb anyone.'

'Why didn't you ask Sebastian? He'd have got you some.' I'm trying to sound matter-of-fact, but my voice is coming out harsh and a little accusatory.

'He's in the shower. Sorry, I didn't realise I shouldn't be in here. I'm just a bit hungover after last night and...' She throws her hands up in despair and looks as if she might burst into tears.

I can absolutely do without that kind of emotional drama right now. 'No, no, that's fine, Caroline. Nothing wrong with you being in here. Of course not. You just gave me a surprise, that's all. I wasn't expecting to see anyone.'

Caroline wipes away a tear, making me feel like an ogre. I want to like the girl, but there's something about her I just don't trust.

Or is it simply that past experiences are making me wary?

SEVENTEEN

LILIAN

By three p.m. I'm ready for a sit down and a cup of tea. I'm a hard worker, and used to being on my feet all day, but I think this might be the last time I offer to run the kitchen. Next time Felix has a day off, we're getting in a temporary chef. I'm hot, bothered and exhausted. Which isn't like me at all.

'Hi, Mrs F, have we got any more oat milk?' Tarik asks, poking his head around the kitchen door. 'We're running low behind the bar.'

'Check the door of the big fridge,' I say.

He does as I instruct then turns back to me with a shake of his head. 'Only regular and almond.'

Brian is dismissive of all the varieties of milk we offer. If it were up to him, he'd tell everyone that they could have cow's milk or nothing. But I explained how people have allergies nowadays, and how more and more people are going vegan. I impressed upon him the need to keep up with the times, to move into the future or we'd get left behind and branded dinosaurs. What the customer wants, the customer gets. Evolve or die. He held out his hands to calm me down and ward off my tirade. So, if a customer asks for oat milk, that's what they'll get.

'Can you run up to the supermarket and pick up some more?' I ask.

'Sure,' Tarik replies.

'Great. Hang on. I'll just nip to the office, get you some petty cash.'

I hurry to the office and unlock the bottom drawer to the desk where we keep the petty cash. I lift out the mini safe and open it up but all I find is a fifty-pence piece. That's unusual. Brian or I always keep it topped up with at least a couple of hundred pounds. I open up the notebook and scan down the page to the last entry. The total reads £345.50. So where's all that cash? I flip through the cash book in case some notes have been shoved between its pages, but there's nothing there. Then I look in the drawer again in case the money has been shoved in there instead of in the safe. Nothing. And then I remember Caroline's guilty face earlier as she was rooting through the desk drawers, supposedly looking for painkillers.

I straighten up and frown. When I saw her, Caroline was looking in the top drawer, not the bottom. And she would have had to have a key to open it. Surely she wouldn't risk jeopardising her new life with her new family by stealing from us? *Would she?* I replace the contents of the drawer and relock it – not that there's much point now. Perhaps Brian took the cash and forgot to write in the book.

For now, I rush upstairs and into our bedroom, grabbing a fiver from my purse on the dressing table.

'Is that you, Mum?' Seb calls from the living room.

'Yes! Can't talk now, too busy!' I snap.

He says something inaudible and I hear a female voice respond. He must be talking to Caroline.

I stomp back down the stairs, growing increasingly annoyed with every step.

I head to Tarik in the kitchen.

'He's had to go back to the bar,' Hugo says when I get there.

I take a deep breath and try to calm down. I'm more worked up than I should be over something I'm sure will be easily explained. I make my way to the bar, smiling and nodding to customers as I go, then I hand Tarik the five-pound note. 'Bring me change and the receipt,' I say, although he already knows the drill.

'Course,' he replies. 'I'll just finish serving these customers.'

'Brian.' I tap my husband on the shoulder. He's deep in conversation with a couple of pals.

'Ah, Lil, I was just telling Terry and Paul about our Sebby getting hitched.'

I flash them a warm smile. 'Sorry, I can't chat right now, bit busy in the kitchen. Brian, can I have a quick word?' I walk a little way away and he follows me until we're out of earshot of anyone. 'Did you take any petty cash this week?'

'Petty cash? No, not me.'

'You sure?'

'Absolutely. Oh, hang on...'

'Yes?'

'I did send Mariah up to the newsagents to get a pack of cards... last Tuesday I think it was, because Samuel wanted to show us a card trick he learned on that cruise—'

'Fine, fine,' I cut him off. 'But you didn't take three hundred out for anything?'

'*What?* No.'

'Okay, I've got to get back to the kitchen.'

Brian plants a kiss on my lips and someone shouts out, 'Get a room!'

I shake my head and leave them to it.

Back in the kitchen, Sebastian's standing by the sink, waiting for me. 'Mum, is everything okay? You sounded stressed when you were upstairs.'

'Yes, well, Saturday lunch service is stressful.'

'You should have said. Me and Caroline could have helped out.'

'No, it's fine. Almost done now.'

'Sure there's nothing else?'

'Are you all right in here for five more minutes?' I ask Hugo.

'Yeah, fine. It's just a few desserts now. All under control.'

I nod and lead Sebastian back out to the office where I ask him if he's taken any petty cash out since coming back.

He frowns for a moment. 'No, I haven't taken any. Why? Are we short? I checked it a few days ago and it all looked in order. I think Dad bought some playing cards.'

I tell him about finding Caroline going through the desk drawers earlier, and then later discovering the missing petty cash.

'Are you serious?' he asks.

'I know it's a bit shocking,' I reply, 'but—'

'No,' he snaps. 'I mean, are you seriously accusing Caroline of what I think you are?'

My heart starts racing and sweat prickles down my back. I didn't think he'd be so upset with me for telling him what happened. 'I'm not accusing anyone,' I cry.

'That's what it sounds like, Mum. Don't you like her or something?'

'Don't be silly, Sebastian. I'm just telling you that there's almost three hundred and fifty pounds missing from the petty-cash drawer. Would you rather I hadn't told you?'

'Mum, you said you found my wife going through the desk, and in the same breath you mentioned the cash going missing. You're drawing conclusions that are totally off base. Did you ask Dad or Felix if they took it?'

'Your father didn't take it.'

'Okay, so ask Felix?' Sebastian glowers at me and I suddenly feel small and insignificant. Like my own son is a stranger.

I nod at him, blinking in astonishment at our out-of-character argument.

'Mum, Caroline's my wife and I love her, okay? Can you please try to be nice to her?'

'*What?* I've been perfectly nice to her.'

'Seriously?'

'Look, Sebastian, I am nice to her. It's just—'

'Oh, here we go.' His jaw tightens and he shakes his head.

'It's just,' I continue, 'that you hardly know the girl. For goodness' sake, you only met her this month!'

'Knock, knock. Seb, are you in here?'

Oh, perfect timing. It's Caroline, looking for her husband.

She pushes the door open and glances from him to me and back again. 'Everything all right?' she asks anxiously.

'Yeah, fine,' Seb replies, plastering on a smile.

I keep quiet, wondering just how much of our conversation she heard...

EIGHTEEN

CAROLINE

It's clear I've interrupted Seb and his mum in the middle of a heated discussion so I hastily back out of the office. I'm tempted to linger outside the door to hear what they're talking about, in case it's me they're discussing, but it would be mortifying to be discovered, so I reluctantly head back up the stairs. Maybe Lilian's complaining to him about me searching through the desk earlier.

I take a deep breath and try not to get worked up about it. Looking for painkillers isn't a crime, is it? Unless the reason she was funny about it is because she's got something to hide. Maybe there's something in one of those drawers that she doesn't want me to see. Honestly, I shouldn't be thinking about any of this right now – I'm hungover and exhausted and I'm feeling really overemotional at the moment. I think the stress of such a quick marriage and moving countries is catching up with me. At least I've got today off, what's left of it. I should make the most of my free time and try to relax because I'm back in the kitchen tomorrow.

'Caroline!' I turn at the top of the stairs to see Seb coming after me, a look of concern across his features. 'Were you looking for me? Is everything okay?' He strides up the stairs two at a time and stands with me in the hall.

'No, it's fine,' I reply. 'Just wondered where you were, that's all.'

'I went down to see if Mum was okay. She's been a bit stressed in the kitchen.'

'Oh, sorry to hear that.' I pause. 'Are you sure that's all it was?'

'What do you mean?' He frowns, his grey eyes darkening.

'Nothing, just hope she's not upset with anything I've done.' I can't outright ask if she's been bitching about me, but I'm 99 per cent sure that's what was going on.

'Course not.' Seb gives a dismissive laugh. 'It's just the usual pub stuff, you know?'

'Okay, if you're sure. But, Seb, if we're going to make this work, we need to be honest with each other about everything.'

His ears redden. 'Yeah, totally.'

'I mean it,' I say, taking his hand. 'We're married now. It's us against the world. No secrets. Everything out in the open. If there's a problem, just tell me, okay? I can take it.'

'Yes, I know. If there's anything to tell, I'll let you know.'

I drop his hand and he draws me close for a quick hug, kissing my hair. 'Look, you go relax in the living room, I'll go back down to grab some supplies.'

'Supplies? What do you mean?'

'You'll see.' He gives an enigmatic smile, turns and heads back downstairs.

I close the door to the flat and walk to the kitchen where I pour myself a tall glass of water, drinking it down in great gulps as I stare out of the window into the darkening gloom of the late afternoon. I desperately need to rehydrate. After my run-in with Tom Chancellor at the club last night, Mariah and I got pretty drunk. We didn't exactly call a truce; it was more an unspoken agreement to just have a good night. And that involved a lot of alcohol.

Sarah and Camille left the club early so we were left with the unlikely quartet of me, Mariah, Nicki and her friend Annabel. We didn't talk about anything of any consequence. We just danced, drank and talked shit about how all the twenty-year-olds looked about twelve. It was actually quite a good evening after such an unpromising start.

But now the night is behind me and the effects of the alcohol are battering my body. I haven't drunk like that for years.

I'm heading to the lounge when the door to the apartment opens again.

'That was quick,' I say, thinking it's Seb returning. But as I glance down the hallway, I see Felix standing there.

'Hey, just dropping by to see how you're doing today. Nicki said you all had quite a heavy night.'

'Understatement,' I reply. 'But, yeah, it was good. Really nice of Nicki to organise it.'

'Actually,' he says, following me into the living room, 'I'm escaping the cottage. Teddy's being very screechy today and my head's exploding.'

'So you've left Nicki holding the baby,' I chide. 'What about *her* poor head?'

'I let her lie in all morning, so she's happily sent me on my way. I'm due back in the kitchen at four.'

'Fair enough,' I reply with a smile. 'Don't ask me to offer you a drink though. I need to sit quietly and recover.' I lower myself gingerly onto the sofa.

'No worries. I don't want anything.' He stares at me strangely for a moment.

'What is it? Do I have something on my face?' I pat my cheeks and nose.

'Look, don't think I'm stirring things up,' he says, sitting down on one of the armchairs, 'but I just wanted to check in that you're okay after that thing in the kitchen yesterday with the order mix-up.'

'Oh, yeah, I'm fine. Again, I'm so sorry about that. I honestly didn't see the note about the bacon.'

'I know, I don't think it was your fault,' he replies.

'Oh, thanks,' I reply, taken aback.

'It just...' He pauses. 'There's a reason why Mariah's been off with you, so you need to cut her some slack.'

'I need to cut *her* some slack?' I raise an eyebrow.

'Yes. I know it seems like she's been awful.'

'She *has* been awful,' I confirm. 'But we got on okay last night, so at least that's something.'

'Oh, well, that's good. Because the thing is, the reason Mariah's been the way she has is because she's completely in love with my stupid brother. Well, maybe not in love, but she does have a serious crush on him. So, *you* coming here and—'

'Me coming here having married him...' I nod as it all becomes clear. 'That must have been a horrible shock for her.'

'Yeah. I think she's a bit heartbroken, but instead of moping around, it's coming off as...'

'Bitchy?' I offer.

He gives a sad laugh. 'Exactly.'

'That makes total sense, and now I feel terrible for her. Did they have a fling or some kind of relationship in the past?'

'No. It's all totally unrequited. I don't think she's even told Seb how she feels. Although it's blatantly obvious to all of us.'

'Oh no, poor Mariah.'

'Mm-hm.'

The door to the flat opens and closes. 'I'm back!' Seb calls.

'Don't say anything about Mariah,' Felix mouths at me.

'Okay,' I reply with a questioning shrug, wondering why I shouldn't mention it.

'He's embarrassed about it,' Felix adds.

Seb strolls into the living room brandishing a couple of tubs of Pringles and a huge slab of Dairy Milk. 'Look what I've got,' he says, waving the chocolate around like it's a trophy. 'Oh, all right, Felix, what are you doing here?'

'Nice to see you too,' Felix replies with an eye-roll.

'Chocolate?' Seb offers me the bar.

'That's the nicest thought, Seb, but I just can't face it right now. Maybe later?'

His face falls. 'Really? I thought it would be a treat to stick a movie on and gorge ourselves stupid on unhealthy snacks.'

'Sadly, I'm too hungover to even look at that,' I reply, swallowing down a wave of nausea.

'I know the perfect hangover cure,' Felix says.

'Oh no, not your disgusting hangover drink.' Seb screws up his face in disgust and sinks down next to me on the sofa, dumping his rejected snacks onto the coffee table.

'Don't knock it till you've tried it, Sebby,' Felix replies.

'You'll never get me to drink that disgusting concoction.' Seb wrinkles his nose and places a hand on my knee.

'Caroline,' Felix says, getting to his feet, 'come down to the kitchen with me. I'll make you a glass and you can tell me if it doesn't immediately cure your hangover.'

Visions of milky drinks containing raw eggs almost make me gag.

'Don't look so worried.' Felix laughs.

'Does it involve raw eggs?' I ask, hardly able to say the words aloud.

'No, it does not.'

'If you can't face a bar of Dairy Milk, you'll throw up at the sight of Felix's poison cocktail,' Seb warns.

'Right now, I don't think I could feel any worse.' My recent drink of water is currently sloshing around in my stomach like a pool of wet washing in a machine.

'Okay then,' Felix declares, tilting his head in the direction of the door. 'Shall we?'

'It will either cure me, or make me throw up, either of which will be better than how I'm feeling right now.'

'Don't say I didn't warn you,' Seb says with a grin, looking up from the couch and shaking his head. 'Don't be long, Cal. The day's a wasting and I wanted us to watch a film together.'

'It'll take me two minutes to knock up my cure,' Felix replies.

I follow him back down into the pub kitchen, realising too late that I'll probably have to engage with Lilian. A prospect that's bad at the best of times, but unbearable when hungover.

'Felix!' Lilian's eyes light up as we enter the kitchen. 'Are you here to take over?' Her usually immaculate turnout is looking frayed around the edges. Wisps of conker-brown hair have escaped her chignon, and her trademark perfect make-up is looking a bit patchy, unable to hide the dark circles beneath her eyes. Although I doubt *I'm* looking any better right now.

'Hey, Caroline, Felix.' Hugo comes into the kitchen with an armful of empty plates.

'Hi, Hugo,' I reply.

'Give me five minutes, Mum,' Felix says. 'I'm just going to make Caroline my hangover cure.'

Great. Now Lilian knows without a doubt that I overindulged last night. You think she'd be used to the odd hangover what with running a pub, but the look she's giving me is one of pure revulsion. The annoying thing is, back home, I hardly drink at all. Probably why I'm feeling so bad today. Catching me looking at her, Lilian rearranges her features to form an insincere smile.

'Good night, was it?' Hugo asks me.

'You can knock off, Hugo,' Lilian snaps at him. 'Now that Felix is here.'

'Cheers, Mrs F.' Hugo never seems fazed by the way

everyone talks down to him. I feel a little sorry for him actually. He reminds me of an eager-to-please golden retriever.

'Hi-yah!' A young woman in jeans and a red fleece comes bustling into the kitchen from the storeroom entrance.

'Kim, dear, how are you?' Lilian asks, turning to greet her.

'Hey, Kim, how's it going?' Felix asks. 'This is Caroline. Caroline, Kim's our favourite veg supplier.'

'Hi.' I smile at the woman and she beams back.

'It's lovely to have you back,' Lilian says. 'We've missed you. How was maternity leave? And how's your little one doing?'

'You'll have to drop in to see Nicki some time,' Felix says. 'Teddy's almost one now, so they must be quite close in age.'

'Aw, is he? I can't believe it. Almost one! Yes, I'd love to catch up with Nicki. Spencer's ten months next week. The time's just flying. How's Seb getting on, after Amy?'

There's a brief and very awkward silence where Felix visibly pales and Lilian's mouth drops open.

Hugo throws me a warning look and shakes his head.

'Oh, I'm so rude,' Lilian says, giving me a warm smile that has to be fake. 'Kim, this is Caroline, Seb's wife. They just got married this month. Caroline's from Australia so this is all very different for her.'

'Oh.' Kim's eyes widen and then she composes herself. 'Oh. That's lovely. Congratulations.' She smiles. 'Bet the British winters are taking some getting used to.'

'Definitely,' I reply, glancing across at Felix, but he has his head down, fiddling around with a food blender.

After a couple more seconds, Lilian ushers Kim back out into the storeroom, asking loudly and unsubtly about Jerusalem artichokes and Brussels sprouts, presumably to change the subject from personal matters to professional ones.

'Who's Amy?' I ask Felix.

He's still staring down at the blender, acting like he hasn't heard me.

'Felix?' My heart beats uncomfortably as I wait for him to look up and answer my question.

When he does, his expression is serious and a little uncomfortable. 'Um, I think that's probably a question for Seb.'

'Okay, but I'm asking *you*.'

Felix shrugs and shakes his head.

'Hugo?' I demand.

'Uhh...' He swallows.

'You can go now, Hugo,' Felix says in a tone that no one would argue with.

Hugo raises his eyebrows, gives me an apologetic smile and leaves.

I feel strange asking Felix about Amy, but I'm not going to let him sweep this under the rug. Seb has not once mentioned her to me. And now Felix and Lilian are acting pretty shady about her. All of which I'm finding increasingly disconcerting.

I want answers. And I want them now.

NINETEEN

AMY

The vodka tonic hits the back of her throat with a sharp burn of pleasure. She almost didn't come out tonight. Her reflex is always to say no when her housemates ask. So much so that they rarely ever bother any more. She has more of a relationship with her textbooks than with any human being.

The past two years have been tough. Amy is passionate about medicine and she loves her course, but the schedule is punishing and she's always exhausted. Tonight, the lure of her duvet almost won, but then her mum's number flashed up on her phone and she couldn't face answering it. She knew if she stayed home her mum would keep calling until Amy couldn't bear it any longer and picked up.

Ever since her sister left home, her parents have been unbearable. It's not that they talk about Michelle at all, or even seem upset that she's gone – in fact if she's ever mentioned at all, it will be an under-the-breath comment about what a selfish and thoughtless person she is. It's just that now they focus all their considerable energies on Amy. Calling every night, wanting a blow-by-blow progress report on everything she's doing. It's so claustrophobic. It's reached the point where she dreads her phone ringing. She knows she's lucky to have their support. That their pride in her is something she should be glad of. But their scrutiny only adds pressure to her life. She's become their sole focus.

It's been over a year since Michelle left, and aside from the odd text message to say she's fine, Michelle doesn't keep in touch at all. Amy has to leave at least half a dozen messages before receiving a reply. Sometimes she wonders why she bothers to keep trying. It stresses her out every time her sister ignores her. But then she remembers Michelle's cheeky smile and sharp wit. The way she used to look up to Amy when she was younger.

Michelle won't answer any questions. She simply says: I'm fine, don't worry. And that's it. Their parents don't even get that much. After that first week of panic when Michelle left home, they've pretty much disowned their youngest daughter. At least she's kept the same phone number, even if they don't know where she is, or what she's doing.

So, tonight, to take her mind off the guilt of ignoring her mum's calls, she jumped into the shower, changed into a pair of faded jeans and her favourite black top with the slashed sleeves, and joined her housemates, Nat and Chloe, on a night out to the Rose and Crown. The drinks here are cheap on a Tuesday, so it gets inundated with students, as she discovered while trying to make her way through the five-deep crush to the bar.

And now here she is being spoken to by THE most gorgeous man she's ever seen in her life. Not model-gorgeous, but he's tall and broad-shouldered with slate-grey eyes, wavy brown hair and a smile that hits her right in the solar plexus.

'Need a hand with those?' he asks as she attempts to carry three drinks in two hands back through the packed pub.

She can actually manage just fine, but she realises she'd like a reason to keep talking to him. 'Um, thanks. That would be great, actually. Aren't you on your way to the bar though?'

'I was, but I don't think I can face it.' He tips his head at the mayhem.

'I know what you mean,' Amy replies. 'It's taken me half the night to get these.'

He lifts two of the drinks from her slippery grasp, leaving her with the vodka tonic, of which she takes another large gulp.

'Have you got a table?' he asks.

'Are you joking?' She smiles. 'My friends are over by the dart board at the back.'

He follows her through the crowd and she has a momentary panic that perhaps he's only done it to steal her drinks. He doesn't look like a thief, but then maybe he relies on his good looks to trick people into handing them over. She glances anxiously over her shoulder.

'Don't worry, I haven't done a runner with your drinks,' he says, reading her thoughts with a cheeky twinkle in his eye.

'No, I didn't think that, I was just checking you hadn't got caught up in the crowd.'

'Yeah, yeah.' He laughs.

They reach the spot where she left Nat and Chloe, but they're not here. Maybe they went to the loo.

He puts the drinks down on a small shelf attached to a column.

'Looks like my friends have gone AWOL,' Amy says, glancing around.

'You a student?' he asks.

'Yeah, you?' Amy sips her drink, aware that he's empty-handed.

'Second year of Hospitality. I'm at catering college.'

'I'm a second year too.' She's glad she wore her favourite top and bothered to wash her hair. 'Doing medicine.'

'Wow, that's impressive.'

'It would be if I wasn't in a state of panic every day.'

'Oh. Sorry to hear that.' He rubs at the faint stubble on his jaw and she imagines trailing her fingers along the same line.

There's a charged pause and the rumble of conversation

fades away for a moment. She takes a sip of her drink and comes back to herself. 'I don't know what's happened to my friends. You should probably have one of their drinks. I can always get them another one.'

'What are they?' He peers at the two glasses dubiously.

'One's pear cider, the other's a vodka and coke.'

'I'm more of a craft beer man, but I could do a pear cider. I think I'm secure enough in my masculinity to drink a half pint.' He picks up the glass and clinks it against mine. 'Cheers.'

Amy echoes his cheers and they each take a sip.

'Your eyes are amazing,' he says. 'Are they green?'

Her heart sputters. She swallows. 'Technically hazel, but sometimes they can look green.'

He leans forward to kiss her lips and her eyes close as she kisses him back. It doesn't last long, but she's already smitten.

'What's your name?' he asks.

'Amy. Amy Nelson.'

'Hello, Amy, Amy Nelson. I'm Seb, Seb Fletcher.'

TWENTY

LILIAN

Of all the times for Caroline to come into the kitchen, it had to be while Kim's shooting her mouth off about Amy. I'm absolutely sick to my back teeth of all this drama.

'So you'll do that extra delivery for us on Monday?' I ask Kim, desperate to be rid of her so I can troubleshoot whatever's now going on back in the kitchen.

Kim shoves her hands into her fleece pockets. It's chillier in the storeroom than it is outside. 'No problem. Seven a.m. suit you?'

'Perfect. Thanks again, Kim. It's lovely to have you back.' I wait for her to leave, but she hesitates at the back door.

'I'm sorry if I put my foot in it earlier about Seb and Amy. I didn't realise he'd got remarried. I'm such a big mouth.'

'Don't worry,' I reply. 'As you know, things ended quite badly between them, so Seb doesn't like talking about it. Thankfully, he's since met Caroline and things are finally looking up.'

'Oh, well that's so nice. Really happy for them both.'

I realise that what I'm telling Kim is actually true. Things *are* looking up for Sebastian. Perhaps I've been too hard on my new daughter-in-law. At least she's taken his mind off Amy's treachery. Given him a new start. And she didn't complain when I took her off service and put her in the kitchen – that shows character and a willingness to muck in.

I also found out that it wasn't Caroline who took the petty cash. Sebastian was right to be annoyed with me for leaping to conclusions. I asked Felix about it earlier and he said he'd borrowed the cash to take on the stag night as he could only withdraw £200 from the cashpoint. Thank goodness I didn't accuse Caroline outright.

Perhaps I need to stop looking for issues where there aren't any. If only I knew her heart was in the right place, and that her intensions were good, then I could relax and welcome her into the family with open arms. But it's tougher than I thought to give her the benefit of the doubt, especially where my boys are concerned. I guess you could say, *once bitten*…

'Well, I'd better be off.' Kim gives an awkward wave and closes the door behind her.

I take a breath and steel myself before walking back into the kitchen.

'I'm sorry, but it's not my story to tell,' Felix says to a scowling Caroline. 'Like I said, you'll have to ask Seb yourself.'

'What's not your story to tell?' I ask Felix.

They glance over at my return.

'*Amy*,' Felix replies, giving me a look that says, *Help get me out of this*. He takes his phone from his pocket and starts swiping at the screen.

'I *will* ask Seb,' Caroline replies. 'But while I'm here, Lilian, maybe you can tell me what's going on? Who is this Amy? And why did Kim ask about her? Were she and Seb an item before I came along? If that's the case, I don't mind – I mean, everyone has a past. I just don't understand why it's such a big deal. Why you won't tell me anything. Did she used to work here too?'

'Oh my goodness, all these questions!' I say brightly, clapping my hands. 'She's just an ex, nothing to worry about, but *now* isn't the time to be chatting about personal matters. I need to help Felix get ready for this evening.' I actually don't have to help Felix at all. In fact, I was looking forward to a long hot shower followed by a couple of hours with my feet up before I have to be back out in the bar and restaurant. But this whole Amy debacle has put paid to that. I'm not going to be able to relax upstairs while Caroline thinks we've got something to hide. Why Seb didn't tell her about his ex, I'll never know. It's ridiculous to keep these kinds of things quiet. We live in a small town where everyone gossips. In fact, it's a miracle it hasn't come out before now.

'So, when *is* a good time to talk about it?' Caroline persists, her eyes hardening.

'Later,' I declare.

'Well, Felix was about to make me a hangover cure,' she says, not budging. I'm sure she's hoping to wheedle some information out of him. But that's not happening.

'I'm sorry,' I say, giving her an equally hard stare, 'but there's far too much to do here right now.' I open the fridge and take out a bowl of pre-made pasta just to make myself look busy. 'Why don't you go back upstairs. Drink plenty of water. You're probably just dehydrated.'

She glares from me to Felix for a long moment and I prepare myself for more questions. But eventually she relaxes her gaze. 'Fine. I'll speak to Seb, then.'

Felix gives her a curt nod and turns to me, asking about how the lunch service went.

Caroline lets out an irritated huff and finally leaves the kitchen

'Better give Sebastian a heads-up,' I hiss.

TWENTY-ONE

CAROLINE

As I walk back up the stairs to the flat, I realise I'm shaking. Sweat prickles on my forehead and I'm wobbly on my feet. Lilian was probably right about me being dehydrated. I also got a shock hearing Kim ask, 'How's Seb getting on, after Amy?' It was so strange to hear him mentioned with her like that, as a couple.

I pause at the top of the stairs, psyching myself up to speak to Seb about it. I still find it very odd that while I was talking to him online for six months, he never once mentioned 'Amy', even when I asked him about his past relationships. He talked about a couple of serious exes and a few flings, but never a single mention of Amy. I'm now desperate to find out what happened between the two of them. What caused them to break up? Why do he and his family never speak about her? Where is she now?

I'm not in the best state to have this conversation, but I don't have much of a choice. I march into the living room to find out what's going on. The room is empty.

'Seb!' I call out, leaving the room and peering into the kitchen. He's not there either. Neither is he in our bedroom or our bathroom. I knock on Lilian and Brian's bedroom door but there's no reply. I'm pretty sure he's not in there either, but I open the door anyway and step inside.

Their room is slightly more compact than Seb's and smells of a mixture of Brian's shaving cream and Lilian's perfume. Funny how I already know their individual smells. The realisation makes me feel a bit odd. Their bed is a small double as opposed to our king-sized one, and the walls are a little shabbier than in our room, the woodwork faded from white to cream.

'Seb?' I say his name even though I know he's not here.

All I need now is for Lilian to find me snooping in her bedroom. That would really not go down well, especially after she saw me going through the desk drawers in the back office earlier. The thought of her walking in on me here almost makes me want to laugh hysterically. I back out of the room quickly and close the door, my pulse racing.

Where the hell is Seb?

My phone pings. It's a message from him:

Hey, Cal, so sorry but I've had to go to Blandford with Dad to help him pick up some supplies. Won't be too long. Love you xx

My body sags, the tension draining away. I'd prepared myself for... not quite a confrontation, but not mild conversation either, and now there's no one left to ask. Unless...

I have another glass of water, nip to the loo, grab my parka and creep back down the stairs away from the kitchen and towards an unusually empty bar where I see Tarik stacking clean glasses.

He looks up and smiles. 'Hey, you're Caroline, right? I don't think we've been properly introduced.'

'Hi.' I flash him my friendliest smile and I can see he appreciates it.

'Congrats on getting hitched,' he replies.

'Thank you.'

'Can I get you a drink or anything?'

'Thanks, but I'm just on my way out.' I take a couple of steps towards the exit and then stop. 'Actually, don't suppose you've got a forwarding address for Amy? Seb still has some of her stuff that he wants to get rid of, and you know he doesn't like to dwell on all that, so I thought I'd do it for him.'

Tarik gives me a look that lets me know he doesn't believe a word I'm saying. 'Look,' he says, 'you don't need to worry about Amy. She wasn't a patch on you.'

'I wasn't—'

'I can tell Seb's... well, he's really into you.'

'Oh, thanks, but I'm not worried. I'm—'

He shakes his head, dismissing my protestations. 'Just some friendly advice – don't go stirring up all that stuff again. Seb was in a bad way for ages until he met you. Just enjoy being together. No point in rocking the boat, eh?'

'I'm not rocking any boats.'

'Fine, but don't expect me to go dishing any dirt behind Seb's back, okay? He's my boss and he's also a good mate.'

'Got it,' I reply, annoyed at myself for being so unsubtle in the first place. 'Okay, well, in that case, can you point me in the direction of Kim's place? You know, the supplier. She was here earlier. We hit it off and she said I should pop round for a cuppa, but I forgot the address.'

Tarik raises a dark eyebrow, clearly not buying this story either.

God, I'm useless today. I remind myself never to let myself drink that much again. My hangover is impairing my judgement.

Despite Tarik's scepticism at my elaborate tale, he answers my question anyway. 'Kim and Mike live at the other end of town at number three Darracott Lane, just past the post office.'

'Thanks, Tarik. See you later.' I bob my head and sidle out

the front door quickly, suddenly worried that Lilian or Felix might make an appearance.

It's absolutely freezing outside. At least it's not raining, but the icy wind is flying down the road, snatching my breath and stinging my eyes. As I take a moment to get my bearings, my gaze snags on a cyclist coming out of the pub car park. It's Hugo.

I wave and he cycles over, his blonde hair tied back under a cycle helmet, his cheeks and fingers red with the cold.

'Where are you off to?' he asks. 'That was a bit awkward back there, wasn't it?'

'Do you know who Amy is?' I ask.

'Best not to ask,' he says. 'I've been sworn to silence.' His words are dramatic, but his expression is playful.

'You can tell me.' I give him a flirty smile. 'Promise I won't tell anyone.'

He opens his mouth to reply just as the pub door opens behind us. We turn to see Tarik standing in the doorway. He eyes both of us for a moment and glares at Hugo. Turning his gaze back to me, he says, 'Just wanted to add that I'm not sure if their house has a number on it, but it's pink, so you'll spot it straight away.'

'Oh, uh, thanks,' I reply.

'All right, Hugo?' Tarik asks.

'All good,' he says.

Tarik doesn't make a move to go back inside so the three of us are standing in awkward silence. Finally, Hugo speaks. 'Well, I better head off. Got another shift in about three hours.'

'Hold on a sec,' I say.

But he's already cycling off down the street.

'See you later,' Tarik calls out before returning inside.

I frown, wondering what just happened there. Did Tarik really come out just to give me extra directions? Or was he making sure Hugo kept his mouth shut? Or maybe I'm just tired, hungover and paranoid.

I glance up and down the street, trying to remember which way to go. I think the post office is at the other end of the main street. So, great, I'll be walking directly into the wind then. I bow my head and battle my way along the road beneath the hazy street lamps. It's busier than I thought it would be, with bundled-up pedestrians out shopping or grabbing a late after-noon drink in one or other of the bars and cafes, and cars sloshing through half-frozen puddles, their headlamps cutting through the darkening gloom.

The road and pavement narrow and the crowds thin out as I finally approach the end of the town. I have so many questions flying around my head. Questions that nobody seems to want to answer. Ever since I arrived here, things have felt off-kilter. The optimism I felt back in Byron, when it was just me and Seb, has now deserted me. I don't have a good feeling in my gut. In fact, right now, I have a feeling of pure dread.

But I can't let that stop me.

On the opposite side of the road, I notice a young couple kissing in a shop doorway, out of the wind. His arms encircle her and she's on her tiptoes, her face tilting up to his. I suddenly feel envious of them. Of the simple innocence of a kiss in a doorway. She pulls away and leans back against the wall and I realise I recognise her.

It's Mariah. And the man she was kissing is Tom Chancellor.

TWENTY-TWO

CAROLINE

I stop where I am for a moment, transfixed by the sight of Mariah and Tom together. At their passionate embrace. After seeing them at the club last night, I thought they hated one another. Well, I'd been sure that Mariah at least had no interest in him at all. I must have been wrong. Maybe they're an item and were having a bust-up. Maybe she was angry with him for grabbing my backside. That makes more sense. I bow my head and hurry past, not wanting them to catch sight of me. I've got more important things to worry about right now.

I stride past the busy post office, skirting a queue that's spilled out onto the pavement. Up ahead, I spot Darracott Lane on the opposite side of the main road. It's a tiny little street, barely more than a tarmac track, with a pavement so narrow they needn't have bothered.

Up ahead on the right, I see the only pink house in the lane, like a dinky little doll's house squashed between two equally pint-sized cottages. Before my courage deserts me, I stride up to the front door, lift the scarred black knocker and rap twice.

The door opens almost immediately, and I'm pleased to see Kim standing there. Her front door leads straight into the living room where I see a man sitting watching TV while bouncing a baby on his lap. Confusion flits across Kim's face for a moment and then recognition dawns. 'Oh, you're Seb Fletcher's wife, right? Hi.'

'Hi, yes, I'm Caroline.'

'Caroline, that's it! You'll have to excuse me, I've only just got in from work and my brain's a bit fried. First week back after maternity leave. It's been a bit of a shock to the system.'

'Kim! You're letting all the warm air out!' the man calls out.

'Sorry, do you want to come in?' she asks me, standing back and stifling a yawn.

I feel a bit guilty, knocking on her door on a Saturday when it's obvious she's tired, but I won't keep her long. 'Do you mind? I just need a quick word, if that's okay?'

'Yes, sure.'

I step over the threshold and she pushes the door closed behind me.

'Your cottage is so cute,' I say. 'Love the colour.'

'Thanks.' She smiles. 'Mike, this is Caroline, Seb Fletcher's wife. Caroline, this is my husband, Mike.'

'Hi.' He looks up at me with a friendly but confused expression on his face, but I don't want to get into explaining my and Seb's whirlwind relationship right now, so I just say, 'Hi' right back.

'Let's go into the kitchen, yeah?' Kim doesn't wait for me to agree, but walks through the lounge, past a narrow staircase to a generous contemporary kitchen-diner at the back, with slate flooring and bifold doors.

'Oh, it's lovely,' I gush, wanting to get her on side, but also meaning it.

'Thanks. We extended out the back before Spencer came along.'

'You've done an amazing job.'

'Tea? Or maybe something stronger? It's almost five o'clock.'

'Nothing for me, thanks.'

'Have a seat.' She gestures to a pale wood table with curved-back wooden chairs. I pull one out and sit while she goes to the kitchen area and puts the kettle on. 'I'm gasping for a cuppa,' she says. 'I'm making tea for me and Mike. Sure you don't want one?'

'I'm fine, thanks. Sorry for barging in on you like this, but your comment about Amy earlier came as a bit of a surprise.'

She stops where she is. '*Surprise?*'

'Yeah. No one's mentioned her to me. Like, ever. I take it she and Seb were a serious item?'

Kim's face falls and her throat bobs. 'Um. Oh, gosh, look, maybe we shouldn't be talking about this. The Fletchers are my friends and also clients of ours. I'd hate them to think I was gossiping behind their backs.'

'I don't think it's gossiping if I'm his wife. And isn't this something that's common knowledge anyway?'

She shakes her head. 'It's just that if I start talking about Seb, and then you tell him you heard these things from me, well, it could all start getting misconstrued, and I don't like drama or—'

'Oh no, absolutely. I totally understand. No, all I wanted to know is where Amy went. Is she still local?'

'I wouldn't recommend trying to contact her, if that's what you're thinking. Best to leave well alone. I mean, it's your call, your relationship, but confronting your partner's ex might be a bit...' She pulls a face.

'Oh no, you misunderstand. I just want to know if they parted on bad terms. Is she local and likely to come back and cause trouble?'

'Well...' Kim reaches up to a shelf for a couple of chunky pottery mugs. 'I shouldn't think so. Seb got a divorce after she went off with someone else.'

'A *divorce!*' I blink. 'He's divorced? So they were *married?*'

'Shit.' Kim puts the mugs on the counter and rubs her cheek. 'See, I've already gone and put my size six wellingtons in it.'

I swallow down bile. My mind is racing at the news I've just received. *Divorced.* 'When did all this happen?'

She puffs air noisily out of her mouth. 'Well, okay, might as well tell you what I know. I guess it can't hurt as I'm only saying what everyone else knows. Seb's a lovely guy but I can't believe he didn't tell you he was married before. I'm sorry to have been the one to tell you. Sure you don't want that drink?'

'No, no thanks. Maybe a glass of water?'

She runs the tap and pours me a glass.

'So when did all this happen?' I prompt. 'The break-up, I mean.'

'Hm, let me see... It was before Easter, so must've been about March time.'

'March this year?'

'That's right.'

'So really recently then.'

Kim nods sympathetically, handing me the glass before heading to the fridge.

'I tried to get Hugo or Tarik to talk to me, but it's like they've all been sworn to silence or something.' I take a few gulps of the ice-cold water.

She nods, reaching into the fridge for the milk. 'Well, they work there. They're loyal. Everyone loves Seb, you know? What am I saying? Of course, you know, you married him, right?' She laughs. 'Anyway, Hugo had a bit of a thing for Amy so I wouldn't take anything he says too seriously.'

'*What?*'

'Oh, there was nothing untoward,' she adds. 'It's just, she had a lot of charisma. Everyone was a little bit in love with her, Hugo included. But Amy and Seb...' Kim gets a dreamy look on her face. 'They were like this golden couple. Both so beautiful and charming.' Kim claps a hand over her mouth. 'Sorry, I didn't mean... I mean, obviously it wasn't true or they'd still be married. And *you*, you're obviously absolutely perfect for him. I mean, look at you!' She gestures to me with both hands, trying to make up for her faux pas.

'Don't worry, it's fine,' I reply, shaking away her apology, my heart beating wildly as she details Seb and Amy's seemingly perfect relationship. 'So, what else can you tell me?' I push.

Kim leaves the tea things and comes over to sit opposite me. 'I know this must have been a shock, love, but I really don't want to say any more. I think the best thing you can do now is go home and talk to Seb, yeah?'

I sigh. 'Can you at least tell me if Amy is still living locally?'

'The last I heard, she'd left the area. But that's just hearsay. I can't be sure. Anything else I tell you will just be rumours and speculation. Like I said, go and talk to your husband. I've found the best way to treat a marriage is to be open and honest, talk about stuff, yeah? Communication is the key.' She takes my hand and gives it a squeeze.

For some reason her sudden motherly kindness makes my eyes mist with tears. I tell myself it's the hangover making me emotional. I scrape my chair back, get to my feet and give her a brisk smile to hide my inner turmoil. 'Thanks, Kim. I really appreciate you being honest with me.'

She shrugs. 'I hope you sort things out.'

'Sorry I put you in an awkward position.'

'That's okay. I'd probably have done the same in your shoes. Take care, love.'

I leave Kim's cosy house for the dark, chilly street and start making my way back through town and up the hill towards the pub. I only hope that when I get there, I'll find answers to the myriad questions bouncing around my brain. That I won't find the same evasive responses from my husband that I've had from everyone else.

TWENTY-THREE

MICHELLE

Michelle stands on the balcony with her iced coffee. Right now, she can't decide whether to stay home and read or go for a hike with a few of her work colleagues. Although it's so hot right now. Maybe she'll stay here for now and then go for a solo walk later.

She picks up her phone from the white metal patio table and bangs out a reply that she's sorry but she can't make it today. She ends it with a sad-face emoji, but inside she's smiling contentedly at the thought of a whole day to herself.

She notices a missed voicemail and hopes it's not anyone trying to persuade her to come, but then she sees it's from her sister, Amy.

Talk about a buzzkill.

Any time there's a message from her family, her whole body tenses up with a mixture of anger, irritation, guilt and self-pity. Of all the emotions it triggers, that last one is the most annoying.

She feels bad because she hasn't actually spoken to Amy for over a decade and they did, once upon a time, used to be close. Amy was a gentle soul, a hard worker and a kind person. But her biggest flaw was not sticking up for Michelle when their mum and dad would come down on her. She didn't have the backbone to tell her parents how unfair they were being. Amy just wanted to keep her head down and get on with life. Which was great for her, but not so great for Michelle.

Every time their parents railed at Michelle, asking why she couldn't be more like her older sister, Amy would stay mute. Oh, she might come out with a weak one-liner in an attempt to soften her parents, but generally she simply took their generosity and praise, and left Michelle to take the criticisms.

The final nail in the coffin came when Michelle was seventeen. Their parents had happily put Amy through medical school, but then refused to help realise Michelle's dream of going to art school because apparently it was throwing money away. Michelle was supposed to live out her parents' idea of how to live her life, or they would withdraw their support.

It wasn't that she had expected financial assistance from them as her right, it was the fact that they favoured Amy over her. They always had. She suspected it was because they were disappointed she was a girl. They already had a daughter. Michelle was supposed to have been a son. Of course, they would have denied it if she'd accused them, but you didn't have to be a rocket scientist to work it out. She suspected their son's name had already been picked out too – Michael, after her grandfather.

Michelle had wanted them to see how unfair they were being in forcing their own desires onto her. In trying to mould her into another version of Amy. Amy had tried – half-heartedly in Michelle's opinion – to play peacemaker, but they all ended up having a huge fight and saying some awful things to one another. It had twisted her up inside until she couldn't stand it any longer and finally had to leave for her own sanity and self-esteem.

After an initial panic from her mum, both her parents had quickly accepted that she wasn't going to be returning home, and they swiftly cut her out of their lives. Never getting back in contact after that first month. If Michelle had had the courage to delve deep enough inside herself, she would have found disap-

pointment at their willingness to give her up so easily. But she didn't let herself go there. No. As far as she was concerned, it was better to put it all behind her and focus on a new life without them.

She remained in touch with her sister via text message, but rebuffed all offers to meet up in person. It was too painful to think about rehashing the past. Especially since both their parents had since passed away. Her mother from ovarian cancer seven years ago, and their father from a heart attack the year after that. Michelle hadn't gone to either funeral. Their parents had left everything to Amy. To her credit, Amy had wanted to split the proceeds with her, but bitter pride hadn't allowed Michelle to accept.

Normally, it takes Michelle at least a week to look at her sister's messages. They sit there in her phone unopened and accusingly, like someone tapping her repeatedly on the forehead. It's unusual to receive a voice message though. The last one was when Amy invited Michelle to her wedding – she didn't attend. The one before that was when her father died. And the one before that was after her mother's death. Each time she'd replied with a text, feeling sick about it, but unable to bring herself to have such huge conversations with Amy who – let's face it – was now a virtual stranger.

Right now, Michelle's first instinct is to do the same as always and ignore the voicemail for at least a week. But its intrusion has already ruined her day off. What could it be about? Bad news? Good news? Oh, this is hopeless. The wondering will drive her mad.

With a steadying breath, Michelle presses play on her sister's message:

'Michelle, when you get this this can you please call me back.'

Michelle is shocked by the emotion in her sister's thick, tearful voice.

'I know we don't talk any more, but I just... I didn't know who else to call. I don't know what to do. I really need to speak to you. I need my sister. Can't we just please put the past behind us and be there for each other? I've gone and done something really stupid and everything's... well, it's all just falling apart and I don't know what to do. Michelle, can you call me back.' There's a gulping pause, and then she says, 'I love you. Call me. Please.'

The message ends. It feels as if all the air has been sucked from Michelle's lungs. A silence falls over her like a cloak, muffling the traffic sounds below and the birdsong in the trees. Michelle sits heavily on the closest patio chair, letting the sound of her sister's voice echo in her ears. The voice of home wrapped up in a thousand conflicting emotions.

After a moment, she replays the message, wondering what on earth it could be about. Her sister said she's done something stupid. What could that be? Amy isn't the type of person to do stupid things. She's the sensible one.

She places her phone on the patio table and stares at it before picking it up again. Her finger hovers over the call button. Her heart is pounding. She feels a tightness in her chest and a lightness in her head. She can't do it right now. She can't speak to her sister and allow all those bitter feelings to resurface. She's spent the past twelve tears burying them. Making a new, happier life for herself.

No matter what's going on with Amy now, it's no longer Michelle's concern. She swallows down bile. Amy has it all – parents who loved her, were proud of her, a career as a respected GP, a handsome husband, money in the bank. Michelle has had none of those things. She's had to carve out a life with zero support. She doesn't want to be this angry person, but she can't help it. This is the reaction she has every single time her sister calls. Perhaps now is the time to change her phone number and cut ties completely. That would stop all this unnecessary upset.

But she can't forget the desperation in her sister's voice. What should she do?

Michelle picks up her phone and starts to text:

Change of plan. Count me in. Did we decide on a time and place yet?

A nice long hike with her work colleagues should help put her sister out of her mind.

TWENTY-FOUR

CAROLINE

I'm in the lounge sipping a peppermint tea when Seb finally returns from Blandford. It was hardly 'popping out' to pick up supplies; he's been gone over two hours.

'I'm so sorry, Cal,' he says, striding across the living room and bending down to kiss me. 'I didn't realise it would take so long.' His lips are cool and dry. His face shadowed with flitting emotions. I find I'm already looking at him differently.

Part of me wonders if he left the pub on purpose. If maybe his mum had given him a heads-up that I was about to come asking about Amy. But he seems genuinely sorry that he had to go out, so perhaps I'm just being paranoid.

'That's okay,' I reply.

'Sorry. It hasn't been a very good day off, has it?' He shrugs off his coat and plops down next to me on the sofa.

'Did you speak to your mum or Felix?' I ask, shifting slightly away from him so I can see his face. Examine his reaction to my questions.

'Did I speak to them?' He frowns. 'When?'

'This afternoon, before you went out with your dad. Or after you got back.' I don't take my eyes off his face.

'Uh, no, don't think so. They're working. I briefly saw Mum downstairs when I got back, but we didn't speak. Why?'

I swallow and lick my lips. 'Why didn't you tell me you were married?'

Seb blinks once, twice. His shoulders sag and he covers his mouth with his fingers.

I wait for him to reply.

The silence drags. He gets to his feet and starts pacing the lounge. 'I was going to tell you.'

'Might have been nice to tell me before *we* got married,' I say, looking across at him.

He comes to a halt by the TV. 'Would it have made a difference?'

'To me marrying you? No, of course not. But I do think it's the kind of thing you should tell your girlfriend, or fiancée or *wife*.'

'Who told you?' he asks, his eyes narrowing.

'One of the suppliers mentioned Amy earlier.' I leave Kim's name out of it, not wanting to cause her any trouble.

'Which supplier?'

'Honestly, Seb, I'm a bit pissed off that you're more concerned with who mentioned your ex-wife's name than you are about the fact you lied to me.'

'I didn't lie!'

'Come on.' I tilt my head to the side. 'A lie by omission is still a lie.'

'Fine, you're right.' He walks over to the window and stares out at the dark street beyond.

'How did it end?' I ask.

'Do we have to talk about it?' he asks, turning back to me.

'I think we kind of do, yes.'

'It was such a horrible time in my life that the only way I could cope was by blocking it out. By pretending it never happened.'

'That doesn't sound very healthy.' I pick up my mint tea and take a sip. It's almost stone cold.

'Maybe not. But the whole thing blindsided me. We had what I thought was a great marriage, and then, one day...' His voice breaks and he wipes his eyes with the back of his hand.

My heart is racing and my head has gone swimmy. Listening to him talk about her like this is... I don't even know what it is.

'She left me for someone else.' He spits out the words. 'Didn't even do me the courtesy of talking it through with me. Just left. Apparently, she fell in love. Which is funny, because I thought she was in love with *me*.'

'So do you still love her?' I ask.

'No!' he snaps. 'God, no,' he says more softly this time. He comes back and sits next to me. Takes my hand and covers it in both of his. 'Caroline, you're the best thing that's ever happened to me. I promise you. I thought I was in love with Amy. I thought I was happy with her. But when I met you...' He puts two fingers on my chin and turns my head to face him. 'We connected on a whole other level. I feel like I'm my true self around you. There's no pretence, no trying to be cool or acting or any of the games people play when they first meet. With you and me, it's real.'

I swallow and chew the inside of my cheek. 'I just... I can't help feeling like the rebound wife. Like she left you, and then a month later you started talking to me and I took your mind off the pain.'

'No, you have to believe me, it's not like that at all.'

'I'm not saying you rebounded intentionally. But, well, you have to see where I'm coming from.'

'I know. I know how it looks. That's partly why I didn't want to say anything. But you have to believe me that, right now, I'm glad she left me. I'm glad we're divorced. Because if she hadn't gone off with someone else, I'd never have met *you*.'

'So you don't miss her at all?'

'I mean, we were together for over a decade so, being completely honest, yes, there's a part of me that misses her. But not in a way that I wish she'd come back. More in a habit kind of way.'

I nod. 'So, where is she now?'

'I don't know.'

'You don't know?' I frown.

'She left and I divorced her and that was that.'

'But you must have an address; some idea about what she's doing now and who she's with.'

'Nope, and I'm not interested in finding out. And the last thing I'd want is you having some kind of confrontation with her. I mean, I wouldn't go chasing after any of your exes. Even if I might be curious about them.'

I nod. 'So, who did she go off with?'

'I don't know.'

I wrinkle my nose. 'How can you not know? You were married all that time and then she leaves you and you don't even know who she's with? That makes no sense.'

'Look, Cal, I've told you everything now. That's it, the whole truth.'

'It just doesn't make sense,' I repeat.

Seb is shaking his head. 'Why are you giving me such grief about this? I mean, I know I didn't tell you about her, and that's totally my bad—'

'Ya think?' I snap.

'I just said so,' he replies. 'I've admitted I should have told you. I'm in the wrong here. But I've told you everything now, so I don't know what else there is to say.'

'Hmm.'

'What?'

'Seb! There's years of being together that you haven't told me about. Am I supposed to just say, "Oh well, thanks for telling me about your hidden ex-wife, let's forget about it", and move on?'

'But it's not important any more. You're what's important now. Why can't we just forget the past and move on with our lives? This is exactly why I didn't want to tell you about her in the first place. It just makes everything complicated and sordid, instead of beautiful and romantic.'

'For goodness' sake, Seb! I'm not thrilled about talking about it either, but you can't just airbrush out the bad bits! We need to talk about it if we're going to have any hope of a decent marriage.'

'Fine. We met in Plymouth while she was at university studying medicine and I was at catering college, we married seven years later. She was a GP at the local surgery. She didn't want kids, I did. We argued about that a bit, but otherwise we were pretty happy, she met someone else, she left me, we got divorced.' He rattles off their history like it's some annoying laundry list. '*Happy?*' His eyes are suddenly flinty, his mouth sullen.

I inhale. 'No, Seb. Right now, I'm not happy at all.'

'Great. Perfect.' He stands up and runs a hand through his hair. 'I don't know what else you want me to say.'

'I just want to know about it, that's all. What's so wrong with that?'

He mutters something under his breath.

'What did you say?' I stand up too, wanting to get this conversation back on track, but unsure how to calm him down. I'm not going to agree to just drop it because he's uncomfortable. He owes me a discussion about this.

'I said I'm done with this.'

'Well, I'm not,' I reply.

'For Christ's sake!' he cries, making me jump. 'Why can't you understand that I don't want to talk about this? Not now. Not ever!' He walks around in a circle and comes to a stop. 'I'm going out to clear my head,' he says, more quietly this time, but his tone is ice cold.

'You're leaving?'

'I'm just. Going. To clear. My head.'

I grit my teeth and sink back down onto the sofa. 'Fine.'

He nods and walks out.

My heart is pounding and I'm short of breath. That went as badly as it could have, and I'm still no closer to finding out what actually happened.

I'm almost certain Seb is keeping something from me.

But I have no idea what.

TWENTY-FIVE

LILIAN

.

As I walk from the kitchen to the bar, I hear raised voices from upstairs. I stop where I am and cock an ear, listening. Perhaps I imagined it. The pub is heaving tonight, so it could well have been someone in the bar. But, no. I recognise Sebastian's voice. He's angry.

My stomach churns at the thought of the pain my youngest son has gone through. And then I feel the burn of anger that this girl, this *stranger*, has brought it all to the surface again with her questions. What do Sebastian's past relationships matter? If you're prepared to marry someone after three weeks of meeting them for the first time, then you have to expect that you're not going to know everything about them. Goodness, you're not even going to know 10 per cent of who they are, who they were and everything in between.

I'm startled by a bang, and look up to see Sebastian looming at the top of the stairs. He's just standing there, breathing hard. He lifts his head slightly and spots me. I see him sigh and start to walk down the stairs, his whole body heavy with the weight of the world. I want to wrap my arms around him and make things better, but I keep myself in check.

'Everything all right?' I ask.

'Just going out to get some fresh air,' he says morosely.

'Want some company?'

'No thanks.'

'Is Caroline cross about Amy—?'

'Just leave it, Mum.' He glares at the wall, flicks a scowl at me and heads for the bar.

I bite my lip and let him go, though it breaks my heart to see him back to his old sad self. This is the downside of working in a family business and all living together. We get a ringside seat to everyone's personal life. Every cross word and grumpy mood. We see it all. We experience it all.

It's moments like this when I want to pack it all in and move to an island where no one knows me. But I know it's a fleeting thought. If it came down to it, I could never leave my family. I love them too much.

I gaze up the stairs, where I know Caroline will be. No doubt moping around the flat after her bust-up with Sebastian. The restaurant needs me, but I'm itching to go up there and find out what's going on. See what she's said to upset him. This doesn't bode well for their marriage. But maybe that's not a bad thing. I don't think she's the right girl for him. I sensed something off about her from the start.

Maybe I'm being a little unfair. After all, Caroline has just discovered he was married once before. I suppose that's quite a big deal. I think the best thing I can do right now is to go up there and try to smooth things over so that she's calm by the time Sebastian gets home.

I sigh and trudge up the stairs. When I reach the door at the top, I almost feel an urge to knock to let her know I'm coming in. That's ridiculous. This is my home. I'm not knocking! Instead, I open the door and call gently down the hallway.

'Caroline? Are you up here? It's Lilian.'

There's a moment's silence, and then she replies from the living room. 'In here!' she calls in a small wavering voice.

I take a breath and march confidently down the hall and into the lounge where I see her sitting in the lamplight, hunched over on the sofa. From her voice, I'd assumed she was crying, but she looks up, white-faced and dry-eyed.

She doesn't speak, so I suppose it's up to me to start this conversation. 'Everything all right?'

'Yeah, fine,' she says without emotion. 'I was just going to have a shower.' She looks like she's about to get up. I don't want her to walk away until I've managed to calm the situation.

'Shall we have a cup of tea first?'

'Thanks, but I've just had one.'

'The early days of marriage can be hard,' I say, taking a seat opposite.

She gives the briefest eye-roll, but doesn't look at me.

'You heard about Amy?'

'I did.'

'It's been hard for Sebastian. She left him for someone else. He was heartbroken and humiliated. Although he probably wouldn't admit it.'

'Yeah, he said he didn't want to talk about it.'

'So maybe give him some space? Let him tell you in his own time?'

'Or maybe you could tell me.' She gives me a challenging stare.

'Well, it's not really my place...'

'That's what everyone keeps saying. But if it's not anyone else's place, and Seb won't tell me, then *what*? Am I just supposed to say, "oh well" and move on? Keep being a loved-up newlywed while this huge thing is just brushed under the carpet?'

'There's nothing to tell, Caroline. You know about Amy now, so what else do you want from him? You want him to go into the nitty-gritty of how she was unfaithful and treated him shabbily? He's spent months getting over her. Why would you then want to rake it all up again? I thought you loved him!'

'No offence, Lilian, but you're his mother. You're not exactly going to be objective when it comes to your son, are you? You're not here to see how I am, or what's best for me. You're here to make me see his side. To smooth things over so that he doesn't have to deal with an angry wife. But I am angry. And you being here and trying to tell me to "forget about it" isn't going to change that.' Her voice is rising with every word. She's working herself up into a state again.

I know I should agree with her, tell her I can see her side and try to get her to calm down, but I think she's behaving like a bit of a brat. Instead of comforting Seb at having gone through a hard time, she's making it all about her. 'I think you need to look at it from his point of view, Caroline.'

'What?!' She rises to her feet.

'It was a horrible time for Seb, and no one wants you unearthing it all again. No wonder the poor boy's upset. Show a little sensitivity.'

'I don't have to stay here and listen to this.'

'Actually, Caroline, you do. If you want your marriage to work, then you need to show some compassion for his situation.'

'What about compassion for my situation?'

'As far as I can see, your situation is pretty damn good! You've landed yourself a handsome, smart, successful husband. You've ended up with a roof over your head and a profitable, secure family business.'

She chokes out a disbelieving laugh. 'Are you actually calling me a gold digger?'

'If the cap fits.'

'You're absolutely unbelievable. You think I like it here in this claustrophobic unfriendly pub in the middle of a shitty winter? I left a well-respected job and loyal friends in one of the most beautiful places in the world to come here. I love your son, but I don't think I should have to put up with the nonsense I've put up with so far. You've done nothing but treat me like a wet-behind-the-ears skivvy, and we all have to put up with Mariah treating me like crap and setting me up to fail because – poor thing – she's in love with Seb, so let's all tiptoe around her, never mind how I, Seb's actual wife, feels.'

'Have you *quite* finished with your pity party?'

'And Nicki's a misery guts,' she continues with her tirade. 'Probably because she's had to put up with you as a mother-in-law for the past however many years she's been married into this family.'

'What's going on up here?' Brian walks into the lounge, his face creased with concern. 'I can hear you two downstairs in the bar!'

'This little harridan has upset Sebastian, and now she's having a go at me. I don't know how they talk to people in Australia, but here in the UK we behave in a far more civilised manner.'

'What, by repressing your feelings and pretending things aren't happening? By being passive-aggressive and pretending to be this holier-than-thou matriarchal saviour? Give me a fucking break!'

'Okay, Caroline, that's quite enough,' my husband says in a tone he used to use on the boys when they were teenagers.

'Thank you,' I reply, feeling grateful I have Brian to stick up for me. To have my back in such an upsetting situation. 'You see what she's like?' I tell him.

'Lilian, you're making things worse,' he snaps at me. 'Why don't you go back downstairs. Take over the bar for me.'

I can't believe he's spoken to me like that in front of *her*. I scowl at him. 'In a minute. First, I need to—'

'Please, Lilian. *Now.*'

He usually defers to me in these family situations, so I'm

shocked and annoyed at him telling me what to do. He'd better not be taking her side. 'Brian, can we talk in the bedroom for a moment?' I need him to understand what's going on here, but I don't want Caroline passing judgement on our conversation.

He shakes his head. 'Not right now. The pub needs one of us, and I'm not leaving you two alone up here.' He squares his shoulders and gives me a steely glare.

'Fine, I'm going.' I cast a disparaging look at Caroline. 'But don't think this is over.'

'Of course it's not over,' she drawls, folding her arms over her chest. 'I wouldn't expect anything less from you, Lilian.'

'Did you hear that?' I look at my husband, who gives Caroline a disappointed shake of his head before ushering me out of my own living room.

TWENTY-SIX

CAROLINE

I'm literally shaking after speaking to my absolute witch of a mother-in-law. And now it looks like I'll also have my father-in-law to contend with. Although at least he sent Lilian packing.

'What's all this about, then?' Brian asks gently, rubbing his chin. He sits on the arm of the sofa and gestures to the one opposite.

I do as he asks, and take a seat, but I'm perched right on the edge, ready to take flight if he starts having a go at me. I take a few steadying breaths. Seb had the right idea, going out for some fresh air. Maybe if I'd gone out too, I'd have been spared his parents getting involved. Although, this does give me an opportunity to try to get some information out of Brian if I can.

'Is this to do with Amy?' Brian asks.

I give a brief nod, my fingers twisting in my lap.

'You do realise that none of what happened with Amy is Seb's fault. I know as his dad I might be biased, but he was a great husband. She was the one who broke his trust.'

'So why didn't he just tell me about her?'

'I'm sure he was going to tell you. But you've hardly been together two minutes.'

'And Lilian was so rude to me, like it's all somehow my fault!' I hear the petulant tone in my voice, and resolve to speak more calmly. I want Brian to respect me. To like me. He seems like a reasonable person. More reasonable than Lilian, anyway.

'You'll have to give my wife some time. She was very upset about what happened with Amy and now... well...' He holds his hands out. 'She's protective of Sebastian. She's worried about him.'

'About him being with *me*, you mean.'

'Now, did I say that?'

'No. Sorry.'

'You'll know what it's like if you ever have children.'

'That's not something I'm in any hurry to do,' I snap.

Brian chuckles at that. 'Don't blame you. I love my sons, but once you have kids, everything changes.'

'So... *Amy?*' I ask, trying to draw the conversation back. 'What's the story? Did she move away? Or is she local? My arrival here has already put people's back up. Do I need to prepare for an angry ex to show up too?'

'I'd say that's very unlikely,' he replies. 'We don't even have a forwarding address for the lass. I'm fairly certain she's moved on with her life. You should put her out of your mind and concentrate on you and Seb.'

'I just wish he hadn't lied to me about her.'

'Well, I suspect he was caught up in the romance of meeting you. He didn't want to say anything to put a dampener on your relationship, did he? I think he was looking for a clean slate, a fresh start with none of the baggage that can taint it.'

'But that's not real life, is it?' I say.

'No,' he replies sadly. 'No, you're right. It's not.'

'And Seb might want a fresh start, but it feels like everyone else here is determined to hate me before they even get to know me properly.'

'I don't think that's true,' he says.

'Nicki doesn't like me.'

'Don't take that personally. She's caught up with her own problems. New baby, Felix away for weeks. She's been down in the mouth with all of us. I think now that Felix is back, she'll cheer up a bit.'

'And don't even get me started on Mariah,' I say.

'Well, that's an easy one to explain...'

'Oh. Yeah. Felix told me she's got a crush on Seb.'

'There you go,' Brian says. 'It's not the case that everyone hates you. Not at all. She's just realised it's not going to happen with Sebastian. She's licking her wounds.'

'If Mariah's so in love with Seb, how come I saw her kissing Tom Chancellor earlier?'

Brian raises an eyebrow. 'Tom Chancellor?'

I nod while Brian pulls a face. We both laugh.

'I'm glad Mariah's moving on,' he says. 'But I'm not sure he's the right boy for her.'

'Not sure he's the right boy for anyone, to be honest,' I reply with a shudder.

'Hmm.' Brian doesn't comment any further, but I still have an uneasy feeling about Mariah and Tom. There's definitely something that doesn't quite add up there.

TWENTY-SEVEN

LILIAN

I'm the last one in the pub. Even Brian's gone up to bed. Cloth in hand, I make my way around the tables and bar surfaces, looking for stray crumbs or spillages, and making sure there are plenty of clean beer mats. I'm taking my time going through the usual locking-up routine in the pub tonight, having decided to do a few spot checks. My staff are good at their jobs, and I rarely find fault with their standards, but it doesn't hurt to double-check every once in a while. Also, if I'm honest, I'm delaying going back upstairs.

My confrontation with Caroline earlier has shaken me more than I care to admit, and I'm furious with Brian for not unequivocally taking my side earlier. For trying to be the reasonable one, thereby making me look like a dragon. What I needed from him was to back me up. For us to show a united front in front of her. His calmness made me look stupid. Like some overprotective parent who mollycoddles her children, when that's not the case at all.

If my husband knew what had really gone on, he wouldn't have been quite so reasonable. But I don't suppose that's Brian's fault. It was my choice not to give him all the facts, and now I have to live with that.

The surfaces are all gleaming to my satisfaction. Even those hard-to-reach nooks and crannies are all free from dust and crumbs. Although, I realise that part of me wants to find fault with something tonight, just so I can give rise to the anger that's still simmering behind my ribcage.

I move on to checking that the bottles, ice bins, draught taps and soda guns have all been cleaned and sanitised, and the snacks have been refilled. I notice we're low on cashews and am about to make a note of it when I hear the back door in the kitchen close with a loud thunk. My shoulders relax. I can now admit to myself that the real reason I've been down here is to await Sebastian's return from wherever he stormed off to earlier. And now, hopefully, this is him back home at last.

I open the bar door and peer out into the hall where I'm rewarded with the sight of Sebastian leaving the kitchen.

He sees me straight away, his eyes widening a fraction. 'Mum, you're still up.'

'Just doing some checks. Where have you been, Sebastian? We've all been quite worried, you know. A text or a call wouldn't have gone amiss.'

'Sorry,' he replies gruffly. 'Went for a walk, and ended up at Nicki's. She made supper while I looked after Teddy. Then Felix came back so I thought I'd better come home.' He looks quite miserable.

I have to restrain myself from going over and putting my arms around him.

'Didn't mean to have a go at you earlier, Mum. I was upset, you know?'

My heart eases at his apology.

'I was pissed off that Caroline found out about Amy like that. Honestly, I was always planning to tell her about my first

marriage, but there was never any right moment. I suppose I
didn't want to burst our honeymoon bubble.'

I nod. 'Well, at least now she knows, you can both put it
behind you.'

'I hope so.'

'Of course you can. It's a brand new start, isn't it, and if
Caroline can't understand that, then—'

'Mum,' he warns.

I hold my hands up. 'You're right, sorry. I just worry about
her bringing up all these painful memories again. You know it's
not good for your mental health. You're recovering from a mini-
breakdown. You need less stress, not more. I don't know why on
earth you had to get married so soon after your divorce...' I stop
myself before he gets irritated with me again. 'Oh well, that's
done now. But if Caroline's going to be part of this family, she
needs to stop stirring things up.'

'Mum, just try not to worry about me and Caroline, okay? I
know you're protective after what happened with Amy, but you
don't need to be. I'm fine now. Maybe it would be better if me
and Caroline got our own place close by. Gave you and Dad
some space. It can't be easy having us here all the time, living on
top of one another.'

I'm caught off guard by his suggestion. 'Sebastian, this is
your home, and I never want you to think that you can't live
here. Or that you're in the way. You're absolutely not.'

'But, Mum, Caroline needs to feel like this is her home too,'
he says. 'And if that's too hard for you – which I understand –
then it would be better for all of us if we moved out.'

'Let's not make any rash decisions,' I say.

'Anyway,' Sebastian says, 'let's not talk about that now.
Happy birthday.'

'What?'

'It's after midnight, so it's officially your birthday.'

I realise he's right. 'Oh, yes, I suppose it is. With all the drama, I'd completely forgotten about it.'

Sebastian walks over to plant a kiss on my cheek. 'We should probably go upstairs to face the music,' he says sheepishly.

'Hmm, you're right, we should. You go up first. I'm just going to finish switching everything off down here.'

'No, it's fine, I'll help and then we can go up together,' he replies.

I nod, realising he's delaying going upstairs too.

We go around the pub in a well-worn synchronised routine of clicking off lights and triple-checking locks.

Finally, when everything is quiet and dark and we can do no more, we concede defeat and head upstairs.

TWENTY-EIGHT

MICHELLE

Michelle had hoped the hike would have taken her mind off Amy's call, but it absolutely didn't. The sun was too fierce, she was thirsty, her boots were too tight and the whole time she felt as though she was in a fever dream. The walk did give her some measure of clarity, though. She realised that, no matter what's gone on in the past, right now her sister needs her.

Okay, so maybe Amy hadn't given her the support she needed back when Michelle needed her, but Amy had been young and caught up in her gruelling studies. Maybe she really had wanted to help, but couldn't because Michelle hadn't allowed her get close enough. She had desperately wanted Amy's support, but she just didn't want to admit it. She'd been too angry and proud to let her in.

So, now, back from her hike, she unlaces her terrible boots, has a long cool glass of water, and heads into her bedroom to return her sister's call.

Strangely, and somewhat worryingly, Amy's number is no longer in use. She tries it several times, but each time she receives the same blank tone and message saying the number has not been recognised.

Michelle can't remember a time when she hasn't been able to get in contact with her sister — if she'd wanted to, which she never has. No, Michelle has always taken it for granted that if she needed her, Amy would be on the end of that line. But now, for the first time ever, she's not there...

TWENTY-NINE

CAROLINE

Seb creeps into our bed sometime after midnight. At the same time, I can hear Lilian moving about next door, the low murmur of her and Brian talking. I have my back to Seb and I made my breathing heavy and regular so he thinks I'm asleep. Part of me hopes he'll try to wake me up so we can have a proper conversation about what happened earlier. About him storming out on me. But I'm so exhausted that it's probably best if we leave things until tomorrow. I wonder what his mood is like. Has he mellowed at all since earlier? Or is he still angry? Within five minutes of getting into our bed, he's snoring heavily.

I'm annoyed at how quickly he was able to fall asleep when I've been lying here in a stew of emotion for hours. My irritation only makes me feel even more wide awake. I roll onto my back and glare up at the ceiling. A street lamp throws a long yellow rectangle of light through the window and across the room. Not for the first time, I wonder what the hell I'm doing here in this posh country pub in the middle of winter, miles away from my sunny home. Maybe I was crazy to marry Seb. To come here to live with his family without ever having met them. It hasn't exactly gone smoothly so far.

In fact, each day seems to have brought a brand new drama or disaster.

Right now, lying here next to my new husband, I don't think I've ever felt so alone.

I close my eyes and try to let my breathing slow. To relax. To fall asleep. But my brain feels like bubblegum being chewed really quickly. Worries and insecurities shoot through my body with no release. I wish I could talk to someone. Offload all these pinballing thoughts instead of keeping them all locked up tight.

I'd thought that Seb would take my side in everything. That he'd be loyal to me. Our online connection had been so powerful. He'd told me that from now on it would be me and him against the world. I'd revelled in that. But today, it just seems like it's *me* against the world. With Seb as part of 'the world'. It isn't a good feeling. Not at all. And his silence tonight has only reconfirmed that our connection isn't as strong as I'd thought. Now that we're back here in England with his family, his loyalties have shifted.

I need to shift them back.

After an hour of lying here with my brain on overdrive, I realise that I may as well put my insomnia to good use.

Slowly, I sit up and peel the covers back. Seb is still out for the count. I slide out of bed, pull on a pair of joggers and a sweatshirt and walk around to his side of the bed to check that my husband is still sleeping. He is. Maybe I shouldn't be doing this, but if I can't get answers from Seb or his family, then I need to get them for myself.

Carefully, I lift Seb's bunch of keys from his bedside table. I freeze as they jangle and clink together. But Seb remains unmoving. His face slack with sleep, his eyelids fluttering as he dreams. I clutch the keys tightly and creep out of the room, pulling the door almost closed behind me. I pause in the hall, keeping an ear out for any sounds from Lilian and Brian's room, but there's nothing.

Before I can change my mind, I walk carefully down the hall, unlock the front door to the flat and tiptoe down the stairs, wincing every time they creak. My heart is pounding now. I have no idea what I'll do if one of them wakes up and finds me creeping around down here. I know the bar, restaurant and kitchen are all alarmed at night, but the hallway and office are clear as, apart from a small amount of petty cash, Lilian and Brian keep the day's takings upstairs.

I walk quickly along the corridor, my bare soles freezing on the cold tiles. The office is locked, so I try a few of Seb's keys – listening out periodically in case anyone comes along – until the right key slots in and turns with a satisfying click. Despite the night chill of the place, sweat breaks out on my upper lip and prickles the back of my neck. I walk into the room, switch on the light and pull the door closed behind me, letting out a breath of relief. Unless Seb wakes and wonders where I am, I should hopefully remain undiscovered. If he does come down, I won't try to hide what I'm doing. I'll tell him straight.

I start off with the desk drawers, carefully easing each one open. I ignore the petty-cash drawer, the invoices and the stationery, instead concentrating on any other paperwork. I lift out each sheaf of papers and go through every sheet. There are letters of complaint, letters of thanks, checklists, marketing materials, but nothing of any interest to me. The shelving unit to my left contains books, a few local trophies, and some ornaments. There's a two-drawer filing cabinet in the corner behind the desk, but I don't hold out too much hope at finding what I'm looking for in there. I guess I'll check it anyway.

The cabinet is locked, but I quickly find the small key that unlocks it on Seb's key ring. Opening the top drawer first, I flinch at the noise it makes, rattling the silence horribly. I pause and listen, but all seems quiet beyond the closed door. Inside the cabinet, I see that each hanging file is labelled alphabetically. There are bank statements, paid invoices, order forms and other pub-related paperwork. I close the drawer and slide open the one beneath. My heart gives a little skip. This one looks more promising. There are more bank statements, utility bills and various insurances, but rather than relating to the pub, they're all personal to the Fletchers. Right at the back, there are four files for each member of the family – Brian, Felix, Lilian and Sebastian.

I lift out the green file labelled '*Sebastian Fletcher – Personal*'. It contains medical information, educational qualifications, car insurance and the document I was looking for – his divorce papers.

I sit at the desk, lay the papers in front of me and take a breath.

After a quick scan through, I see that the initial petition stage was back in April of this year, and the final order came through just over six months later. So, only last month. Which maybe explains why Seb then wanted to fly out to see me in Australia – his divorce had just come through. But for him to then want to marry me straight away is crazy. I'm getting the feeling it was simply a reaction against Amy's infidelity. If that's even what really happened.

As I read through their joint statement of why the marriage broke down, it all seems very vague and there's no specific reference to adultery; they just cite irreconcilable differences. But they've both signed it, so it must have been something they both wanted. Annoyingly, the address at the top of the page is the pub's address. There's no other address for Amy. Perhaps she was still living here when they petitioned for the divorce.

I lean back in the chair and rub my eyes, suddenly feeling heavy with exhaustion. There's nothing here that's telling me any different to what Seb's told me. Maybe I'm looking for darker issues where there are none. But I'm still puzzled as to why they wouldn't have cited adultery. If that was the reason they split up, then surely that would be written on the divorce form.

I slot the papers back into Seb's file and replace them in the cabinet, closing and locking it. I should go back upstairs. I don't want to push my luck by staying down here longer than I need to. I switch off the office light, leave the room and lock the door behind me. As I walk back up the stairs to the flat, I realise that I want to confront Seb about it, even if that means I'll have to admit to snooping. Now is probably a bad time to bring it up as Seb and I are already on shaky ground after our argument. Plus it's Lilian's birthday, so today will be all about her.

But if not today, then soon. Because I need to know about the wife who came before me. And why Seb lied.

THIRTY

LILIAN

I awake to breakfast in bed and a beautiful bouquet of hand-tied pink lilies from my husband.

'Happy birthday, darling. Lilies for my Lilian,' he says, as he always does on my birthday.

'Thank you, Brian. They're beautiful.'

'Not as beautiful as you,' he replies.

I've always woken early. I'm one of those people who can spring out of bed with a day full of energy. But recently, my mornings have been groggier and slower than usual. I hope it's not age catching up with me. I have a sneaking suspicion it's more stress-related than anything to do with getting older. How did I wake up this morning as a sixty-eight-year-old? I still feel as though I'm in my thirties.

'Felix made your favourite,' Brian says, placing the tray next to me on the bed covers. 'Eggs Benedict and smoked salmon on a toasted muffin.'

'Mmm.' I cast my eye over the plate. 'What a treat.'

'And a nice hot cup of tea.' Brian leans down to give me a kiss. I kiss him back, sleepy but content for now. I know there are pressing family matters to attend to outside this room. But all that can wait a while.

'What's this?' I ask, looking down at a small neatly wrapped oblong package next to the plate.

'Open it and find out.'

I smile and place a hand on my heart, suddenly overcome with love and gratitude for this wonderful man who's been by my side for over forty years.

I undo the ribbon, and turn over the package to loosen the Sellotape, but it's too well wrapped, so I find an end and tear through the floral paper instead. Inside is a black plastic box with gold edging. I lift the lid to see a gold chain with a square-cut emerald pendant.

'It's beautiful, Brian! You shouldn't have.' I blink, feeling ridiculous as tears sting my eyes. Everything has been so horrid and stressful recently, that it's wonderful to feel so cherished.

'Here, let me...' He takes the necklace and I lean forward as he places it around my neck and confidently does up the clasp. He gazes at my throat where the pendant sits, cool against my warm skin. 'Beautiful,' he declares.

'Thank you,' I say.

'Are you getting emotional, Lil?'

'What? No. I'm still waking up. My eyes are scratchy.'

'Hm.' He smiles and squares his shoulders. 'Right, well, I'd better go downstairs and get things started in the bar.'

'Why don't you stay and have breakfast with me?' I ask, not ready for him to leave. 'There's far too much here for me to eat by myself.'

He pats his stomach. 'Tell you the truth, Felix already did me a full English. But I'll make a coffee and bring it in. Sit with you a while.'

I nod, move the tray up onto my lap and start slicing into the muffin.

Breakfast is over all too quickly, and the day slides into the usual business of setting up, followed by lunch service. Even though it's my birthday, I don't like taking time off. I'd only worry if I was out. Anyway, it's nice to bustle around while friends, family and staff all wish me a happy birthday and make a fuss, presenting me with gifts, treats and drinks. The star of the show is my emerald necklace that everyone has commented on, complimenting Brian on being such a loving and attentive husband. I can't help glowing with a little smugness at my good fortune.

The only fly in the ointment is my surly new daughter-in-law, who's in the kitchen with a face like a wet weekend. She wished me a happy birthday, but her whole manner is subdued. I acted like I didn't notice – I'm not about to let Caroline ruin my day.

THIRTY-ONE

CAROLINE

As I nip out of the kitchen to go to the ladies, I see Mariah heading down the corridor towards me with a scowl on her face.

'Hi,' I say, wondering if the scowl is for me, or whether she's just in a bad mood.

She rolls her eyes and walks past me toward the kitchen.

'What's your problem, Mariah?' I ask, regretting it as soon as the words leave my lips. I have enough issues without adding her name to the list.

I needn't have worried as she ignores me and bashes her way through the swing door into the kitchen. I shake my head in exasperation and head to the toilet. On my way back out, I have the misfortune to pass her again.

'My problem is,' Mariah says, picking up on my earlier comment, 'that I don't believe you really love Seb. I think you're using him.'

I almost laugh in her face. Instead I let out an incredulous cough. 'And what makes you say that?'

'It's obvious,' she says airily. 'You're supposed to be married and I never see you together. He's all over you, but you look like you're trying to get away from him. It's a joke!'

'Not that it's any business of yours,' I say quietly, trying to be mindful that she's supposedly in love with my husband, 'but I'm not really into public displays of affection. I like to keep my private life private.'

'Sure, whatever,' she replies.

'Anyway,' I counter, 'I saw you kissing Tom Chancellor in town yesterday. What's all that about? I thought you hated the guy. Are you seeing one another now? When did that start up exactly?'

Mariah swallows and looks down at her feet before lifting her head back up and giving me a defiant stare.

'Because,' I continue, 'I'm just wondering if maybe you and Tom set me up on purpose last week.' I'm relieved to be finally voicing my thoughts, even though my hands are trembling at this unexpected confrontation.

'What do you mean?' she snaps. 'Look, I've got to get back out there and do some work or Lilian's gonna go off.'

'I *mean*, did you arrange for Tom to grope me, just to create drama on my first day? To make me react and get me into trouble?'

'Piss off, course I didn't.' She takes a step away from me towards the restaurant.

I take a step after her. 'I don't believe you.'

'Believe what you want.'

'You never mentioned you were seeing Tom,' I persist.

'That's cause it's none of your business.'

'And yet Sebastian and I are somehow your business. Anyway, at the club, you told me you couldn't stand Tom.'

'So?' She rolls her eyes again but I can see she's not as unbothered as she'd like me to think. Her neck is mottled red and she's picking at her fingernails.

'*So*, why would you kiss him if you don't like him? I think you and he have been having a laugh at my expense.'

'God, Seb really knows how to pick them,' she mutters.

'*Them?* Are you talking about Amy?'

'*What?*'

'Seb's ex-wife.' I clarify, watching her carefully for a reaction.

Mariah swallows and blinks rapidly.

'Do you know what happened to her?' I ask. 'Did you play some part in driving her away? Are you trying to do the same to me because you want Seb for yourself?'

'What are you even on about?' She screws up her face. 'I never met the woman. Didn't start working here till after she left. I heard she did a runner though. Left Seb broken-hearted. He said he'd never be able to get over her.'

This is obviously an unsubtle dig at me. Trying to make out that Seb doesn't feel for me what he felt for Amy, when I know that's not the case at all. Seb has told me often enough that I'm the love of his life. That he's never felt this way about another person. Unless... maybe he's been lying to me.

'Look, Mariah,' I say, realising I need to bring up the elephant in the room. 'I heard you've got a crush on Seb, and I'm sorry about that. I had no idea you liked him. How could I? I was in another country when he and I got together. But we don't have to be enemies. I don't want there to be any bad feeling. I know what it's like to crush on someone who doesn't return the feeling.'

Her face flames and she takes a step towards me. 'A *crush?* You don't even know the half of it!'

I blink and frown. 'Well, why don't you tell me.'

'It's true, I did like Seb. But he also liked me back.'

'O-kaay, so what are you saying?'

'I'm saying that we slept together. More than once.'

I stare at her, open-mouthed, trying to work out if she's telling me the truth or simply trying to get a rise out of me. 'I don't believe you.'

She gives me a sly smile. 'Believe what you like.'

'So if he was sleeping with you, why did he marry me?'

'Who knows? Maybe because I told him that the best way to get over a bitch like his ex-wife was to get under another one.'

Before I know what I'm doing, my hand shoots out and my palm connects with the side of her face.

Mariah clutches her cheek. 'You slapped me!'

I realise I shouldn't have done that, but she's been goading me ever since I got here.

'What's going on?' A voice from behind startles me.

I turn, not quite believing that Seb has chosen just this second to step out of his office into the corridor.

'Did you see that?' Mariah cries, her eyes flashing with hatred. 'Your psycho wife just slapped me!'

'Maybe that's because she's making up lies about the two of you,' I reply. My palm is tingling with pain and my whole body is shaking. 'She said you slept with her!'

Seb stands outside the office with a hangdog expression on his face.

I shift my gaze from him to a triumphant-looking Mariah.

'So you *did* sleep together?' I ask him.

'Look, Caroline—'

'Well that's just great,' I reply. 'You might want to go in the kitchen and help your brother, because my shift has suddenly just ended.' I march up the stairs towards the flat. My breath is coming in short gasps, my heart racing, hands trembling. I stop halfway up and turn, glancing back over my shoulder to see the two of them together, heads close, whispering. Seb is facing away from me, but Mariah looks up and catches my eye, a smug smile snaking its way across her face.

THIRTY-TWO

LILIAN

I must admit that by the time the lunchtime rush has died down, I'm more than a little tipsy. The thought of an afternoon nap feels very enticing and I wonder if I can sneak away upstairs for half an hour.

'Right, Lil,' Brian says, rubbing his hands together. 'Tarik, Mariah and the gang are going to hold the fort down here for an hour or so while we pop upstairs for a birthday tea.'

'Oh, Brian, that's not necessary.'

'Necessary? It's your birthday. Felix baked fresh scones and we're having a proper cream tea. Just the family.'

I take a breath and try to conjure up some excitement at the prospect. Now, if it were just Brian and the boys, that would be wonderful. But the thought of being in close proximity with Caroline is making the eczema on my elbows flare up.

'Come on now, Lilian,' Brian murmurs in my ear. 'Let's treat this little shindig as a clean slate, eh?'

His words sink in, and I realise he's absolutely right. The only way for my family to be happy is for all of us to put in the effort. As the matriarch, I need to lead by example. To be magnanimous and loving. To put past hurts behind us and bring everyone together. Gosh, I really am a bit drunk. 'You're absolutely right,' I reply, planting a kiss on my husband's clean-shaven cheek. 'I love you, Brian Fletcher.'

'Course you do,' he replies with a wink.

We all troop upstairs to the living room which has been decorated with balloons and a happy-birthday sign strung over the fireplace. The wall lights and table lamps cast a cosy glow across the room in the gloom of the wintry afternoon. Brian extends the little-used main dining table that sits in the corner while I take out my mother's cream embroidered tablecloth from the sideboard drawer and spread it over the top. Seb comes in with a stack of extra chairs from downstairs and slots them beneath the table.

'Mum, you sit there,' Felix says, directing me to the head of the table.

'Let me get the kettle on first,' I reply, taking a step towards the kitchen.

'I'll do that,' Nicki says, passing little Teddy to Felix.

'I need to sort the scones,' Felix replies, kissing his sleeping son's head and looking back expectantly at his wife who shrugs and disappears into the kitchen.

'Give him here,' I reply, taking my gorgeous grandson onto my lap. He's warm and heavy, reminding me of my boys when they were this age. I realise that I don't spend nearly enough time with my grandson. These early years fly past so quickly. I still can't believe my sons are grown up and married. It doesn't seem real.

As I watch my family flit in and out of the room with the tea things, I notice that Caroline and Sebastian still aren't talking to one another. He keeps trying to catch her eye, but she's purposely avoiding his gaze. Silly girl. She should try to fix things instead of sulking.

Soon, the table is laid with tea, sparkling elderflower water, mini sandwiches, crisps, snacks, fresh scones, clotted cream and strawberry jam. Sebastian uncorks a bottle of champagne and fills our glasses. I sip mine, enjoying the crisp sharp bubbles on my tongue as they blur the edges of my thoughts.

Nicki turns off the lights as Felix walks in with a huge chocolate-buttercream-covered birthday cake topped with a gold-and-white sixty-eight candle flickering and fluttering, casting strange shadows across my family's faces.

'*Happy birthday to you...*' Their singing fills the air as Felix approaches with the cake held theatrically high.

Nicki comes over and scoops the still-sleeping Teddy out of my arms. Caroline shifts to the side, making room for them, but as she does so, she knocks Felix's arm with her elbow. His hand tilts and I watch in disbelief as my beautiful birthday cake slips off the gold cake board and glances off the table, sliding down my cream-trousered leg and onto the living room carpet with a dull squidge.

There's a collective gasp followed by a beat of horrified silence. Caroline's cheeks are flaming red, and I can't be sure but I think I catch the faintest hint of a smirk before it's gone again.

Before we have time to react to the disaster, I realise the birthday-candle flame has brushed my mother's tablecloth. With a small scream, I almost fall back off my chair as the table in front of me catches light with a violent whoosh.

'Mum!' Felix cries.

'Lilian!' Brian rushes over. He shakes off his jacket and throws it over my arm.

As he does so, I feel a bright pain on the skin of my wrist.

Felix douses the rest of the fire with the jug of elderflower fizz. And throws my lovely tartan wool blanket over the lot, patting it down.

'Oh!' I cry, realising my whole body is trembling. There's a horrible smell of burning hair and flesh in my nostrils.

Brian helps me to my feet and gently moves me out of the

way of the ruined table. 'Come and sit on the sofa. Let me have a look at that arm.'

'I'm so sorry,' Caroline says, shaking her head. 'I can't believe I...' Her voice trails off.

Teddy is suddenly awake and screaming.

'Nicki,' Felix's voice cuts through the noise. 'Do you think you can—'

'I'll take him in the kitchen,' Nicki mutters, disappearing through the door. I notice she didn't even ask me how I am.

Brian and Sebastian are seated either side of me and Felix pulls up a pouffe to sit on while Caroline hovers awkwardly by the table. Brian gingerly lifts his jacket off my arm. We all gasp as we see my charred blouse that's stuck to the skin on my wrist. There's a red sticky patch of blistered skin, the sight and smell of which makes me feel a little light headed.

'Ohh,' Felix and Sebastian cry in unison.

'Think we better get you to A and E,' Brian says.

Caroline comes over and examines my wrist. 'Get your mum a big glass of water, Seb.'

'I'm not thirsty,' I snap.

'It's for dehydration,' she says, her voice steady and calm. 'And we need to bathe that in cold water. Brian, can you get her bracelet and rings off, in case her arm and fingers swell.'

I reach out to touch the biggest blister, but Caroline grabs my hand.

'Don't touch,' she says. 'Don't want to get an infection. Brian, if you fetch the car, I'll bathe her wrist, then you can take her to the hospital.'

'Shall I get some ice?' Seb asks, his face pale and tinged with green.

'No ice,' she replies, taking control of the situation.

She's absolutely right in what she's saying. I'm up to date with my first-aid training and, by the sounds of it, so is she. My husband and sons are all standing uselessly, staring at me for confirmation. 'Well, don't just stand there; listen to the girl,' I say croakily.

Everyone jumps into action and I'm led carefully into the bathroom by my new daughter-in-law.

Caroline was the cause of all this – she knocked the plate from Felix's hand – and I'm sure I saw her smile after it happened. But now she's being nice as pie. She's helping me in an efficient and kind way. Much as I would aid someone with this kind of injury.

The question is, did I imagine her previous snide smirk, or is she playing some kind of twisted game? Was she really trying to hurt me?

THIRTY-THREE

CAROLINE

I turn on the shower and let the hot water do its best to pound away today's drama. After the aborted birthday party, I helped Felix clean up the living room and dining table while Brian and Seb took Lilian to the hospital. She didn't have to wait too long to be seen. It was a superficial burn so they fixed her up, gave her some painkillers and sent her home.

Despite Felix's attempts at conversation, I couldn't concentrate as my mind was teeming with everything that had gone on today. From Mariah's revelation that she and Seb were once a thing, to Lilian's cake disaster. I do feel quite ashamed that I lashed out at Mariah. I think everything's starting to get on top of me. I need to reboot my relationships with everyone, but I'm so on edge that it's almost impossible. As the water cascades over me, I wish I could stay like this and not have to emerge to deal with them all.

'Thanks for helping Mum this afternoon,' Seb says after I finally wrench myself from the en suite shower and enter the bedroom, drying my hair with a towel. He's sitting on the edge of the bed watching me.

'Of course,' I reply tersely.

'The doctor said your actions probably saved her a lot of pain.'

'Well, it all happened so quickly.'

'I didn't really see what happened,' Seb says. 'One minute we were singing happy birthday, the next...' He throws his hands up. 'All hell breaks loose.'

I finish towel-drying my hair and dump the towel in the linen basket with a stab of resentment. Of annoyance. He still hasn't apologised after our argument last night and he hasn't mentioned the fact that he slept with Mariah. I'm wondering if I know anything real about Seb at all.

'So what did happen?' he asks.

'What do you mean?' I turn to look at him.

'Mum said you knocked Felix's arm.'

I exhale in disbelief at his implication. 'That's because I was moving out of the way to let Nicki and Teddy through.'

'Oh, okay, sorry.'

I pull on my work T-shirt. 'You're not actually saying you thought—'

'No, no, not at all.' His eyes are wide with worry that I might think he's accusing me of something terrible. 'It's just that Mum said—'

'Your mum thinks I shoved a cake in her lap and set fire to her arm?' I stare at my husband, all thoughts of an easy resolution evaporating.

'No, don't be daft. Course not.'

My heart is racing and my palms are clammy. I still can't quite believe what's gone on today. Plus, the whole birthday debacle makes everything else so much harder.

'Even before that happened,' Seb adds, 'you didn't look like you were having a particularly good time. You looked... well, you looked miserable.'

'It's hard to enjoy myself when we're still fighting.' I sit on the bed and pull on my jeans.

'I'm not fighting,' he replies wearily, getting to his feet and walking over to the window. 'That thing with Mariah happened before we even met. It was after she first started working here. Amy had just left and my head was all over the place. It should never have happened, but it shouldn't affect the two of us. It's way in the past. As soon as you and I started chatting, I put a stop to it.'

'Maybe, but it's still another thing that you didn't tell me. I get that we both have pasts, but she works with me, for goodness' sake. I would have thought I at least deserved a heads-up from you so I didn't go flaunting our relationship in front of her.'

'I know, I'm sorry. It's just... it's embarrassing.' He turns back to face me. 'No one else knows what went on. My parents just think she's got a crush on me. Mum would go mad if she knew I'd slept with one of the staff.'

'I wonder why,' I reply, rolling my eyes. 'It's not like it's going to cause any drama or anything.'

Seb gives me a sheepish smile.

I'm not about to let him off the hook quite so easily. 'Like I said, I'm not expecting you not to have a past, I just don't like having these nasty surprises keep popping up. It's upsetting, not to mention it makes me look like an idiot.'

'I'm sorry,' he says, coming over and taking my hand. 'I really am. But I'm also disappointed that you let it spill over into Mum's birthday. She works so hard, and this was supposed to be an afternoon where we could all show our appreciation, and give her a bit of a pamper. She doesn't get a fuss made of her very often.'

'It's not my fault Felix dropped the cake.'

'I'm not talking about the cake, I'm talking about... your... your general moodiness.'

I bristle at his accusation. 'Can you blame me? Aside from

what happened with Mariah, you stormed out on our argument yesterday, and didn't get back until after I was asleep. Then, this morning, you went out on some birthday errands without even asking if I was okay. Am I supposed to just forget about the fact that you're divorced and never told me?'

'Whatever our differences might be at the moment, I love you, Cal, and I genuinely didn't mean to do anything to hurt you. Can we please, please make up? It's so horrible falling out with you. My stomach's in knots. I've barely eaten anything all day. And what with poor Mum's accident...'

I grit my teeth and try not to think uncharitable thoughts about Lilian. I suddenly pity Amy having to put up with her for twelve long years. Although, at least she didn't have to work with her too. 'Was this the room you shared with her? With *Amy?*' I ask.

Seb doesn't reply, just shakes his head and lets out an exasperated sigh.

'You lived here all those years?' I persist. 'Why didn't you get your own place together?'

'We didn't need to. We were fine here.' He shoves his hands in his jeans pockets.

'In this room?' I walk back into the en suite to run a comb through my damp hair.

'What's wrong with this room?' he asks, following me.

'Nothing. But, there's not much privacy, is there?' I tie my hair back off my face and return to the bedroom.

'There are four walls. A door.'

'You know what I mean.'

'Yes, I think I do. You don't like my parents.'

'No, it's not that at all. I just... I guess I've always been used to my own space. It's a bit of a shock living so close to family, you know?'

Seb's shoulders droop. 'I'm sorry, Cal. You're right. I think I've been insensitive.' He shakes his head. 'You're not used to family life.' He comes over and pulls me into a hug, but I'm still too tense to reciprocate properly. 'Or, maybe growing up in foster care, your experiences haven't been good.'

I don't reply.

'I promise you, we'll save up to get our own place as soon as we can, okay?' He leans back a little and looks down at me.

'I still can't believe you all lived together for years and your ex-wife was fine with it.'

Seb runs a hand through his hair. 'Caroline, can we just leave the past in the past and just enjoy being together?'

'But how could you have asked me to live here in the same room without even mentioning that it's where you slept with your first wife?'

His jaw tightens, but he doesn't reply.

'So you're really not prepared to talk to me about it?' I push.

'I don't see the point in talking about something that's over.'

'But I'd like to know what happened. I'd like you to open up about what your marriage was like. If you don't want to talk to me, then what's the point in having a wife? A partner? I want us to be one of those couples who don't have secrets. Who confide in each other, support each other.'

'I don't have any secrets,' he replies flatly.

'You said she cheated on you,' I reply.

'She did.'

'Look, you're not going to like this,' I say, tensing against his imminent anger.

'Like *what*?' His face darkens.

'Last night, I couldn't sleep so I went downstairs into the office and found your divorce papers.'

My husband turns his back and walks away, his hands clenching and unclenching by his side.

I press on, heedless of his reaction. 'The papers stated you both filed for a no-fault divorce. So did Amy really go off with someone else, or were you both to blame? Is there something you're not telling me?'

I'm not sure if Seb is shutting down even more or preparing to go ballistic. He's over by the window again, his whole body rigid.

I hardly dare breathe.

After a few moments, he sighs and turns around, leaning back against the windowsill. 'The only reason we did a no-fault divorce is because I didn't want to drag it out. I could have cited adultery but, to be honest, I didn't even care what it said on the papers. I just wanted it over.'

I nod slowly, realising that what he's saying is entirely plausible.

'Plus, after Amy left, I had no way of getting in touch with her. She changed her number, took herself off social media and didn't leave a forwarding address. This was the only way we could get divorced without a load of hassle. She handed in her notice at work. Moved out and moved on... I can't believe you went looking for our divorce papers. Do you really not trust me?'

I hesitate. 'It's not that I don't trust you. It's more that you don't want to open up to me. You've been so guarded. Since I found out about your ex, I feel like I've had to drag every little thing out of you. Like I'm your enemy rather than your wife. Mariah's the perfect example. When we were in Australia, you seemed so open and happy. You promised me that we'd be a real partnership. But since I got here...'

'I know it hasn't been the best start.'

I bite my inner lip to stop the retorts flying out. I need to calm down, my evening shift starts soon.

'Look,' he says, coming over to sit by me on the bed, 'all I know is that once I started talking to you online, that was it. I was almost glad that Amy had left me, because if she hadn't then I would never have met you.' He takes both my hands in his.

I gaze into his grey eyes, wondering if he's telling me the truth this time, or if he still has secrets to hide. And if he does, will I be able to discover them?

THIRTY-FOUR

CAROLINE

'Night!' Hugo calls as he pushes his way out through the back door of the kitchen.

'See you tomorrow,' Felix replies.

'Night,' I echo listlessly.

'Okay, what's wrong?' Felix puts down his cleaning cloth and fixes me with a look.

'Hmm? Nothing.' I turn away and take the last of the dessert bowls over to the sink to rinse.

'*Nothing*, she says. After spending the whole shift in near silence with a face like thunder.' He says the words teasingly.

Despite his gentle tone, I flinch, still in turmoil after my earlier conversation with Seb.

'Is this about what happened with Mum's cake today?' he asks. 'Because you know that was an accident, right? And you more than made up for it with your Florence Nightingale routine afterwards.'

'It's not about that, but thank you for being so nice.' I turn off the tap and start stacking the bowls into the dishwasher.

'Well? Are you not going to tell me? Should I be minding my own business?'

'It's nothing,' I insist. I don't think I have the mental energy to go over everything with Felix tonight. Not after the day I've had.

'Right,' he says, folding his arms. 'Stick the dishwasher on and leave the rest.'

'It's okay, I've almost finished.'

'Exactly. A few bowls won't make a difference.'

'But—'

'No, come on.' He starts untying his apron.

'What? Where are we going?'

'The bar.'

'I think it's all closed up.'

'Exactly. We're going to have a drink in peace, and you can tell me what's been going on to make you so miserable.'

'What about Nicki?' I ask, not wanting her to find any more reasons to dislike me.

'Oh, she'll have gone to bed hours ago. Don't worry, a quick drink won't make a difference. She's almost always sound asleep after my evening shifts.'

'If you're sure...'

'I'm sure. So, what's my brother done?'

I shake my head. Felix is so easy to talk to, but I'm not sure it would be right to moan to him about my husband.

'You can tell me. I've known Sebby since he was born.' Felix grins. 'If there's a problem to figure out, I'm the perfect man to help.'

I push out my reservations and figure what the hell. Maybe Felix can shed some light on things. Or maybe not. But either way I could do with a quiet drink and an excuse not to go back upstairs just yet.

I follow my brother-in-law into the pub and he slides behind the bar while I settle myself on one of the leather bar stools.

'So, Caroline, what's your drink of choice?'

'Seriously, right now I could murder a hot chocolate.'

'Nope,' Felix replies, gesturing to the line of optics.

'Fine, I'll have a whiskey and coke. But I'm only having one. I have to work tomorrow.'

'Okay, okay. I'm working too.'

I watch him pick out a glass and add a double measure of whiskey. I reach over the bar to add my own coke, topping it right up to the brim. He pours himself a double shot of the same, but only adds a splash of coke. We cheers and each take a swig. Despite being heavily diluted, the drink manages to go straight to my head.

'So?' Felix asks.

I give him a bemused look, although I know very well that he wants me to confide in him about my relationship with Seb. I'm still hesitant to blab about my private life, but as Seb's having an issue opening up about his ex-wife, perhaps Felix will be more forthcoming. I make a decision not to mention Mariah's brief fling with Seb. He told me no one knows about it, and I don't want to create more drama over something that's over and done with. And anyway, I have other, more important things on my mind.

'You're obviously upset about something,' Felix says, pulling up a stool from the far corner. He sits off to one side so we're facing diagonally across the bar.

'Look, I don't want to moan about Seb behind his back. We're newly married, we're still figuring shit out.'

'Of course. I just wanted you to know that you can always talk to me if you need to. We're a close-knit family. I'm pretty sure Nicki slags me off to Seb. But that's fine by me. Gets it all out of her system.' He flashes me a grin.

I'd already clocked that Nicki and Seb were close, and I'm not entirely sure how I feel about that in light of the other revelations. 'Thanks.' I take an overlarge gulp of my drink and think *Oh, what the hell.* I stare into my glass and start talking. 'Okay, well, I'm worried because Seb doesn't want to talk about Amy at all. I found out this huge piece of news that he has an ex-wife, and he doesn't think it's a big deal that he didn't tell me about her. Not only that, he wants to act like that part of his life never even happened.' I look up to see Felix gazing at me with sympathy in his eyes.

'I guess he just wants to put the past behind him.'

'That's what he told me, but I'm his wife, I should be able to talk to him about this stuff.'

'Do you talk about your exes with him?' Felix asks.

'No. But I would if he asked me about them. And anyway, Amy isn't just an ex. They were together for over a decade.'

Felix is quiet for a few moments. He takes my almost empty glass and refills it. I open my mouth to protest, but then close it again. My brain is nicely soft around the edges. The effect of the alcohol combined with a deep exhaustion and not much food, is that I'm airing all my worries without actually feeling worried, which is a nice change. It feels as if I'm looking down on everything from a great distance.

Felix sets my glass in front of me and tops it up with coke. He looks pensive for a moment. 'I think that, as well as being shocked by Amy's infidelity, my brother also felt humiliated by it. I mean, in case you hadn't noticed, Stalbridge is a small town. Everyone knows everybody else's business. Seb hated the gossip and the pity. He wanted to move as far away from all that as possible.'

I nod and take a sip. 'I guess that makes sense.'

'He's in love with you, Caroline. He also wants to impress you. To feel like you love him back just as much.'

'I do!'

'Yeah, well, Amy broke his trust. Made him second-guess himself. I think the reason he asked you to marry him so quickly was to test you. To see if you loved him just as much. To see if you were prepared to commit.'

'That's the strange thing, though,' I muse. 'I'd have thought after being burned once, he wouldn't have been in any rush to get married again. I certainly wouldn't.'

He shrugs. 'Seb's a romantic. Look, I probably shouldn't say this...'

I snap my head up and look at Felix, alerted by his tone, by his reluctance to tell me whatever it is that's on his mind. '*What?*'

'No, it's nothing. Don't worry.' He averts his gaze.

'You can't say that! That's not allowed. You have to tell me now.'

His rubs at his jaw with his thumb and fingers. 'Okay, but look, you can't say anything to Seb.'

'Why not?'

'Because.'

'I can't keep secrets from my husband.'

'Okay, forget it.' He slides off his stool and tops up his drink with ginger ale.

'Felix!'

He doesn't reply.

'Okay, I promise,' I say, relenting, wondering if it's a promise I'll be able to keep. I should have crossed my fingers behind my back.

'So...' He sits back down. 'Back when Seb and Amy were married, Amy actually made a few passes at me.'

'No!' I gasp.

'I turned her down, of course. It was really awkward and so, well, I was incredibly relieved when she left him.'

'Did you tell anyone? What about Nicki? You must have told *her*.'

He shakes his head. 'No. You're the first and only person I've told.'

'Why? Why didn't you tell Seb at the time? Why would you tell *me*?'

'Because I want you to know that that's the kind of person Amy was.'

I realise my palms are sweating and my pulse is racing. I've had too much to drink. I feel a little out of control. Reckless.

'She wasn't right for him,' Felix continues, unaware of the turmoil this news is causing me. 'I'm also pretty sure she was unfaithful to my brother all the way through their marriage. Maybe he had an inkling what was going on but chose to ignore it. I wanted to tell you, because now you know that she was never the right person for Seb. You are.'

I swig my whiskey, trying to take in what Felix is telling me. I'm not sure if this makes things better or worse. 'When did she make a pass at you?'

He shrugs. 'A few times over the years. It's not really important.'

'But, honestly, shouldn't you have told Seb? Warned him what was going on.'

'Maybe.' He chews the inside of his cheek. 'I was probably being selfish, but he's my brother. Telling him something like that... it could have ruined our relationship. I couldn't do it to him. To us.'

I nod, but my head is spinning. I stare at my almost empty glass, regretting having had so much to drink. 'So, you're saying that she made passes at you while she was married to Seb, and then she eventually left him for someone else. But no one knows where she is now?'

'That's about it. I think the best thing you can do now for you and for Sebby is to forget the past and enjoy your new life together. Honestly, what's the point in raking over all that crap?'

'I mean, of course I want to move on with my new life. But it's difficult when the man I've just married has kept this giant secret from me. I feel duped, you know?' My words are slurring. I reach over the bar and add coke to my empty glass.

Felix reaches across to take it. 'Let me get you another shot in that.'

'No!' I keep hold of my drink. And then more softly, 'No. I've had enough. I've had too much, actually.'

He leaves the glass and raises his hands in surrender. 'Okay, okay.'

'Got any crisps or peanuts? I need something to soak up the alcohol.'

He slides some dry-roasted peanuts my way. I tear open the packet and shove a handful in my mouth. I crunch, chew and swallow, but my head is still so fuzzy. 'I just... I feel like there's more to the whole Amy story, you know? If I could just speak to her and find out why she stayed in the marriage so long if she wasn't satisfied.'

He gives me a strange look. 'There's nothing to find out. Honestly, I'd tell you if I knew anything. And you already know Seb – he's the biggest softie out there. The girl was just trouble from the start. She broke his heart. You've been the best thing to happen to him since she left. Since ever, actually. I'm really happy he found you, Caroline.'

I jump at a creaking sound to my right.

'What's going on here, then?' Brian has walked into the bar in a pair of navy checked pyjamas and a grey cardigan. He's frowning at the two of us drinking together.

'Hi, Brian,' I say, trying to sound sober.

He gives me a tight smile.

'Hey, Dad. Just having a post-shift debrief,' Felix says. 'Want one?' he gestures to the bar.

'No, I'm ready for bed.' Brian sounds uncharacteristically grumpy, but I guess it's not surprising given the day he's had. 'Hope you're not drinking away the profits.'

I hold up my glass. 'Coke,' I say, omitting to tell him that I've already knocked back about four whiskies.

He nods but doesn't smile this time. 'You should be getting back to Nicki, Felix,' he says. 'It's past midnight.'

Felix replies, but I'm not concentrating on what he's saying. My mind is in turmoil. I don't know if it's the stress of today, the whiskey, or Felix's story about Amy making a pass at him, but I realise I can't go on like this. I'm no nearer to finding out anything about Seb and Amy's marriage. If I don't push harder, I don't think I ever will. I've reached an impasse. No one's talking, no one's taking me seriously. I think I need to get Felix to open up. And there's only one way I can think of to do that.

Brian says goodnight, with a last reminder to make sure we switch everything off and tidy up.

The pub falls silent as his footsteps fade.

'I think Dad's right,' Felix says with a yawn. 'I should be heading back.'

'Felix...' I begin.

He downs the rest of his drink and starts rinsing the glass in the bar sink.

'Felix,' I say a little louder to make myself heard above the whooshing of the tap.

'Hm?'

'There's something you should know.'

'Oh yeah?' He looks up sleepily, his expression growing serious when he sees my face. He turns off the tap and puts down the glass, giving me his full attention.

My pulse pounds and my mouth is dry as I prepare to speak.

'What is it?' he prompts.

'The thing is,' I begin. My heart thumps in my ears. I know it's a risk to tell him, but I'm running out of options. I clear my throat and look him dead in the eye. 'There's something I haven't told you. But it's a secret, so you have to promise you won't tell anyone.'

THIRTY-FIVE

LILIAN

Where has Brian got to? I peel back the covers with my good arm and swing my legs over the side of the bed. My wrist still feels as though it's on fire despite the doctor dressing it and loading me up with pain relief. The only thing that seems to have done is make me feel slightly sick and very woozy. This is *not* the birthday I'd been looking forward to.

I've been asleep since I got back from the hospital and now I'm feeling quite disoriented and strange. I woke when Brian came upstairs to get ready for bed, but then he left and he's been gone for almost twenty minutes. I take a sip of water and replace my glass on the bedside table. My new necklace sits next to a bottle of painkillers, the emerald glinting beneath my bedside lamp, its gold chain heaped in a small, tangled puddle.

I get to my feet, pull a dressing gown over my nightie and shuffle out of the room to see where my husband can have got to.

'Brian,' I croak, heading down the hall towards the living room. I can see from here that the kitchen is in darkness, so he's obviously not in there. I peer into the lounge. It's a mess – my birthday decorations look sorry for themselves in the empty room lit only by a single table lamp. I should turn it off, but I don't have the energy. I'll ask Brian to do it when I find him.

I think back to earlier today when I was last in this room. The warmth of being surrounded by my family. Being pampered and treated. And then the shock of the cake falling, the mess it made, followed by the flames on my arm. I twitch as I remember the pain, realising that the more I think about it, the more it hurts. I may have acted calmly at the time, but the whole incident shocked me more than I care to admit. I can still smell the scent of burning hair and flesh.

I shudder, turn away and head back the way I came. It was Caroline who knocked the cake from Felix's hand. I know that it was probably an accident, but I can't help thinking that there's a possibility that it wasn't. Not that I think for one minute she wanted to set me on fire. More likely, she just wanted to ruin the cake. Ruin my day. Perhaps that was why she was so keen to help me afterwards – she felt guilty about the inadvertent fire. Or maybe I'm simply tired and paranoid. Caroline and I haven't got off to the best start, but surely she's not that malicious...

Seb's bedroom door is closed. I pause outside, listening. There's no sound from within so I keep walking to the end of the hall, open the front door and peer down the stairs. The lights are on down there, so somebody's still up, unless they forgot. Perhaps my husband's double-checking things.

'Brian!' I call softly.

I hear footsteps approach and seconds later the reassuring figure of my husband appears at the foot of the stairs. 'Lil, what are you doing up?' He sighs and makes his way heavily up the stairs towards me.

I back up to let him through the door, and wait while he closes it.

'Aren't you going to lock it?' I ask.

'No. Caroline's still down there.'

'Still? What's she doing?'

He sighs. 'Having a drink with Felix.'

'*What?*' My mind starts racing to places it shouldn't.

'Shh, come on.' Brian heads back to our bedroom and I follow. 'How's your arm?'

'Sore, but I'll live.' Brian helps me shrug off my dressing gown. I wince as it brushes my bandage. 'Tell me it isn't just the two of them down there.'

Brian takes off his dressing gown and hangs it on the back of the door next to mine. 'It's fine. I told Felix to head home now.'

'But what are they doing down there in the first place? It's at least half an hour after closing.'

'It was just a quick after-work drink, Lil, don't worry.'

'And I suppose Sebastian's in bed waiting for her to come up?' I slip back under the covers, shivering.

Brian slides in next to me. 'You're freezing. Here, come close, let me warm you up.'

'Careful of my arm.'

'Don't worry.' He starts rubbing my good arm. 'Put your feet on my leg.'

I do as he says, enjoying the warmth emanating off him. 'I'm worried about that girl, Bri. I think she's trouble.'

'You should put her out of your mind and try to get some sleep.'

'I know. I know you're right. But after what Sebastian went through with that hussy, Amy... Honestly, I don't think he has any sense when it comes to women.'

'Give the boy some credit,' Brian replies gently. 'He and Amy were together for... how many years was it?'

'Twelve,' I grunt.

'Yes, twelve. So they must have had some good times too. It's just unfortunate it didn't work out. But now he seems happy with Caroline, so shall we just give her the benefit of the doubt?'

I take a deep breath, trying to dislodge the bitterness stuck in my throat. 'Fine. But will you just do me one favour?'

'Anything for my sweet Lilian.'

I roll my eyes, but grace him with a smile. 'Could you just go back down and check on them? Tell them you want to turn everything off now, then you can come back up with Caroline. I won't be able to sleep otherwise.'

Brian presses his lips together in a reluctant frown. 'All right, all right. For you, I'll go and poke my nose in where it's not wanted.'

'Thank you.' I lean over to kiss him. 'And thanks for today, even though it didn't quite turn out the way we wanted.'

'I'll make it up to you. We'll have another birthday tea when you're feeling better.' He sits up and gets out of bed.

'No birthday cake this time, please.'

He chuckles. 'No birthday cakes ever again after today.'

Brian leaves the bedroom, and my anxieties ease a little, knowing he's going to break up the little party going on downstairs. My heart goes out to Sebastian. I hope he's asleep and not tossing and turning in bed waiting for his wife to come back up. I'd like to warn my youngest son to guard his heart against Caroline, to tell him to watch out in case she's got her sights set on Felix. But I can't do that. The last thing I want is to cause any animosity between Sebastian and Felix. To damage their close brotherly bond. No. I can't tell Sebastian my suspicions. There's only one person I need to speak to about this situation – Felix.

THIRTY-SIX

MICHELLE

Back home from work, Michelle sinks onto her bed and closes her eyes. Just for a moment. It's been the most unsettling few days. Ever since receiving that distressing call from her sister and then discovering that Amy's number is no longer in use, Michelle hasn't been able to concentrate on anything. She's been making silly mistakes at work, and all the hours in between have been a blur.

Today, on her break, Michelle found the contact details for her sister's husband's pub, the Royal Oak. It's where they live together in some twee Dorset village. Michelle found the place online back when Amy first announced her engagement, but hasn't looked at it since.

She leans back against the headboard, clears her throat and calls the number, her heart thumping. This is the first time in years she actually wants to speak to her sister. She needs to find out what had her so upset the other day. She needs to know she's okay.

After a couple of rings, an older woman answers. 'Royal Oak, how can I help?'

'Uh, hi, can I speak to Amy Fletcher please?'

There a pause before the woman replies. 'Who's calling?'

'This is Amy's sister, Michelle.'

There's an even longer silence on the end of the line. And then the woman clears her throat. 'I'm afraid Amy no longer lives here.'

Michelle wonders if Amy and her husband have moved out together. Or maybe they've split up, and that's why she was so upset. 'Oh. Do you have a forwarding address or landline number for her?'

'No. Sorry.' The woman sounds impatient, like she's about to end the call.

Michelle sits up straighter on her bed and speaks quickly. 'Did her husband move with her, do you know? Or is he there? If he is, can I talk to him please?'

The woman huffs. 'Look, I'm not being funny, but how do I know you're her sister? You could be anyone.'

Michelle's momentarily thrown. 'Why would I pretend to be Amy's sister? Who are you, anyway?'

'I'm Amy's mother-in-law and I don't think she'd appreciate me giving out her personal information over the phone. She said she was estranged from her sister.'

Michelle exhales. 'Fair enough. How about if I come in person and bring ID with me?'

Another pause.

'Hello?' Michelle says after a while.

'I don't want any more drama,' the woman says. 'If you must know, Sebastian and Amy have split up. They're getting a divorce because she went off with someone else and left him heartbroken. Satisfied?'

It takes a few seconds for the information to sink in. 'That doesn't sound like the kind of thing Amy would do.'

'How would you know?' the woman snaps. 'Amy said you

haven't spoken in years. That you didn't even attend your own parents' funerals.'

'Wow.' Michelle's momentarily stunned by the sheer rudeness of the woman.

There's a sigh, and then, 'I apologise for the outburst, but you have to understand, your sister treated Sebastian very badly.'

'Okay,' Amy gulps. 'Was this recently? It's just, I had a voicemail from her, and she sounded quite upset. And now her phone number's out of service.'

'It was very recently, and things are still quite raw,' the woman replies. 'We've tried to get in touch with her too but, like you said, the number's out of order. She obviously doesn't want us to call her. After everything that's happened, I'd prefer it if you didn't call here again. My son's very upset by all this and the last thing he needs is to hear from Amy's sister.'

'Sorry, but if you could just let me know where she is...'

'She left no forwarding address. And, to be honest, we'd all be happier if we never saw her again. Now, I'm going to say this once, and I want you to listen hard...'

Michelle raises her eyebrows, but she doesn't reply.

'Are you listening?'

'Yes, I'm listening.' She grinds her jaw at the woman's condescending tone.

'Do not call here again. Do not come here. Do not attempt to contact my son. I will not have him upset again by Amy or by any member of her family. Do I make myself clear?'

Michelle inhales, biting back all the retorts that are hovering on her lips. 'Crystal,' she eventually replies, pitying Amy for having had such an awful mother-in-law. 'But before I go, can you please just tell me where you think she might have gone. Some clue so I can at least try to—'

'I've told you everything I know,' the woman replies, and ends the call.

Michelle stares at her mobile, feeling breathless and some-

what blindsided by the whole interaction. The problem is, she still doesn't have any answers.

So what should she do now?

How will she be able to track down her sister if her husband's family won't even talk to her?

THIRTY-SEVEN

CAROLINE

'A *secret*?' Felix frowns at me across the bar. 'What kind of secret?'

It feels as though everything in the room is holding its breath. I swallow and decide to just come out and say it.

'I'm Amy's sister.'

There's a moment's silence.

'What did you just say?' Felix jerks his head back. 'That's a weird thing to joke about.'

I swallow. 'It's true. I'm Amy's sister.'

'Shut up, no you're not.' He gives a nervous laugh. 'I've seen a photo of the two of them together. Her name's Michelle and they haven't spoken in years. She looks nothing like you.' His voice trails off as a tinge of doubt creeps in. 'Anyway, she moved abroad...' His mouth falls open. 'Oh.'

What have I done?

What. Have. I. Done?

'My real name is Michelle Nelson,' I say, feeling actually physically sick now. I shouldn't have told him. I shouldn't have told him. Why did I do that? Because I'm an idiot who's had too much to drink and didn't think it through. I wonder if I could get away with saying I was joking? I taste sour whiskey and coke in my gullet. The lights behind the bar are too bright. The air around us is still and silent. The smell of furniture polish, disinfectant and beer stings my nostrils.

Understanding dawns across Felix's face. 'Oh my God, you're actually serious. You're her sister.' His face reddens and then pales. He blinks and swallows. 'Does Seb know?'

I shake my head slowly.

'Bloody hell, Caroline. I mean, *Michelle*? This is crazy.' He massages his forehead with his fingertips and turns away. Turns back again. 'But your hair, your face... you don't look anything like her photo.'

'What can I say? I was a dorky kid back then. I left home, went travelling, lost weight, dyed my hair. Forget how I look, I don't even *feel* like the same person I was back then.' I realise I'm suddenly completely sober.

'*Why?*' Felix cries. 'Why would you do this to Seb?' He shakes his head. 'I don't believe this. I don't understand.'

'My sister's gone missing. I'm worried to death. I needed to find out what's happened to her. I don't know if maybe her new relationship might be toxic or dangerous. I haven't heard from Amy for months. Not since she left Seb. I need to know she's okay.'

Felix is open-mouthed again. He takes a breath. 'So you're telling me you married my brother just to find out where your sister is? That makes no sense. It's insane. Why would you do that?'

I realise I've absolutely definitely and completely made a mistake in telling Felix who I really am. And now it's too late to undo it. I stupidly thought he would be an ally.

'You used him!' Felix cries.

'No, no. Look, it may have started like that, but we did fall in love. I'm completely committed to him.' That's not exactly true, but Felix doesn't need to know that. I was so stupid to think he'd be on my side. I overestimated our friendship. I should have waited longer to come clean. Should have tried harder to discover the truth without revealing my identity. Now I've blown it. The question is, will Felix help me or will he ruin everything? I shake away my doubts. Once he's had time to realise I did this with good intentions, he'll come around.

'I think you'd better tell me exactly what's going on here,' Felix says, his bronze eyes glittering. There's no sign of my friendly brother-in-law in this man. No. I've become the enemy now.

I get up off my stool and walk around the bar, composing myself, working out how to phrase things so that Felix won't hate me even more. How do I explain that I gave myself a pseudonym and befriended Sebastian Fletcher online? That I studied his posts and comments on Facebook and Instagram, then made myself into his perfect girl.

I had a loose idea that if I gained his trust, Seb would open up to me about his ex-wife. He had wiped every single reference to Amy from his social media history, but I was certain that he'd eventually bring her up in conversation. Only he never did. Even when I asked him outright about his previous relationships. It was as though she never existed. I couldn't bring up her name myself, because then he'd want to know how I knew about her.

The whole getting-to-know-him process took far longer than I'd anticipated, but I wanted to make it feel real. To get him to trust me completely. It was a balancing act. I had to remain a little bit aloof so I didn't come across as needy, yet keen enough that he wouldn't be put off. Obviously I can't tell Felix this pure unvarnished truth. I have to soften it so he'll see I had no choice. I need to get him onside so he'll tell me more about where he thinks Amy might be.

I walk back over to the bar, but I don't sit down. We're both standing now, both facing one another. Tense. He's angry. I'm determined.

He doesn't speak. Just gives me a look that says, *Well?*

I look up at the ceiling for a moment, at one of the oak beams that's probably been there for hundreds of years absorbing everything that's gone on at this bar. The dramas and celebrations. Mundanities and heartaches. Confessions and revelations. I shift my gaze back to my fake brother-in-law. 'I just wanted to find my sister,' I say. 'That's how it started. She sent me this panicked voicemail saying she'd done something stupid.'

'A voicemail?' His eyes narrow. 'Have you still got it?'

'Well, yes, but—'

'Can you play it?' he asks.

'What, now?'

He nods.

'I suppose so.' I pick up my phone from the bar, scroll through to the message and press play.

As Amy's voice fills the space, I swallow down my emotion, blink back tears. I wish for the hundredth time that I'd called her back straight away. That I hadn't let an ancient family squabble keep me from having a relationship with her. Over the years, we've played out this stupid dance where she continued reaching out to me and I continued rebuffing her. She never gave up on me. Which is why I owe it to both of us to find out where she is and make up for all the wasted years.

'Michelle, when you get this this can you please call me back.

'I know we don't talk any more, but I just... I didn't know who else to call. I don't know what to do. I really need to speak to you. I need my sister. Can't we just please put the past behind us and be there for each other? I've gone and done something really stupid and everything's... well, it's all just falling apart and I don't know what to do. Michelle, can you call me back.

'I love you.

'*Call me.*

'*Please.*'

I stare at my phone and watch as it times out to a blank screen. I wonder again where my sister can be. Perhaps she's just down the road, or maybe she's moved away for a fresh start. Has she given up on me? Has she finally decided to pay attention to my years of rejection. Has she stopped trying to be my sister?

'Right,' Felix says.

I lift my gaze to him once more. 'So, now you've heard it, you can see why I had to come here. I tried calling her back, but that number's not in use any more. Well, you already know that.'

'Why didn't you just come here as yourself?' he asks. 'As Amy's sister. I find it unbelievable that you went to all these lengths. *Marriage.* All this deception. What was the point?'

'It's not like I wanted to do it this way. Before all this, I called here so many times as myself. When I spoke to your mum, she said she wasn't prepared to give any information out over the phone. So I told her I'd come and visit in person. Well, that didn't go down well at all. She told me in no uncertain terms that I wasn't to come here and I should never call again. I wasn't put off. I called here again so many times. I spoke to your dad, Seb and various other members of staff. I explained that I was Amy's sister, but they all told me the same thing – that she'd gone and there was no forwarding address. So what was I supposed to do?'

Felix doesn't reply.

'Anyway, after that, I called the UK police, but they wouldn't do anything. Said it wasn't a missing-person case and that it's common for people to lose contact. They suggested using a tracing agency and gave me a link to a website. I thought it would be easier to do it myself.'

'I've just realised you're not even from Australia.' He chokes out an incredulous laugh. 'You're a good actress, I'll give you that. You're still using your fake accent, even now!'

I grit my teeth at his tone. 'Not really. I've lived there so long, I talk like a native. I guess I might be laying it on a bit thicker than usual.'

He shakes his head. 'I still can't believe it. How did you get Seb to marry you?'

'I didn't. I mean, that wasn't part of my plan. I only wanted to chat to him online and get him to tell me where Amy went and who she's with. But, so annoying, he didn't mention her at all. It was his idea to fly out to see me. I was completely against it at first. It's one thing to talk to someone over the internet, but a whole other situation to meet face to face. The thought terrified me.'

'But you did it anyway,' Felix says, curling his lip.

'Yeah, I did. If I wanted to find my sister, I didn't really have any other choice.'

'Right. And your flatmates, what about them? Did they know what you were doing? Were they all in on it too?'

'No. I timed Seb's visit for when my flatmates were away so I wouldn't have to explain anything about my name change. Then, before they came back, Seb and I went camping for a week.'

'Quick question...' Felix puts a finger on his chin. 'I take it you've slept with Seb?'

I swallow and push down a flare of anger. I shouldn't be surprised at all these questions, but I hate the way he's talking to me like I'm some disgusting criminal, when I'm just worried sick about my sister. 'Actually, no, I haven't.'

'*What?*' he sneers. 'I don't believe that. You're married to him.'

'Not that I need to explain it to you, but right from the start I told Seb I wouldn't sleep with him before marriage. Then, when we got here, I told him that I didn't want us to do anything in your parents' flat because it felt too awkward.'

'Convenient. I've seen you kiss him, though.'

I shrug.

'Well, my brother is one patient man. Not sure I would have been able to wait as long.'

I roll my eyes. 'He's not exactly happy about it... but I do have limits. Sleeping with my sister's ex-husband crosses that boundary.'

'But marrying him doesn't?'

'We're not really married, Felix. I paid an actor friend to be the registrar and print out a marriage certificate with my fake name. I flew to the UK on a separate flight so Seb wouldn't see my real passport.'

'Wow, you really worked it all out, didn't you? I thought you said you loved him!'

I realise I've revealed too much for Felix to believe that's true. 'I think he's a really good person,' I offer lamely.

Felix chokes out a bitter laugh. 'So you've gone from telling me you love him, to saying he's a good person. There's a bit of a gap between those two statements, don't you think?'

I have no response to this. Felix is right. I don't love Sebastian.

'How did you see all this playing out in the end?' he asks. 'Were you just going to leave my brother high and dry with no explanation? Were you just going to disappear, leaving him with a broken heart, *again*?'

'I honestly don't know.'

'Well, that's great.'

'I just want to find my sister, that's all. Surely you can understand that? What if it was Seb who'd gone missing? You wouldn't just shrug your shoulders and say, *Oh well, I'm sure he'll turn up.*'

'Yeah, I'd want to find him, but I'm pretty sure – no, I'm one hundred per cent sure – I wouldn't fake-marry his ex-wife to find out the truth!'

I flinch at his raised voice, paranoid that he's about to bring the rest of the Fletcher clan rushing downstairs to see what all the noise is about. I need to pry as much information out of Felix as I can. This could be my last opportunity. 'So what about this guy she went off with – who is he? What's he like?'

'I have no idea.'

'So you never met him?'

'Nope.'

'You must have a name at least.'

'Nothing.' Felix is clearly angry at my questioning, but I don't care.

I let out a frustrated growl. 'What if this person's taken her against her will? How do you know he's not dangerous?'

'That's a bit dramatic.' He shakes his head. 'Look, Seb and Amy had a toxic marriage. They'd been having problems for ages. She didn't even tell Seb to his face that she was leaving him. She told Mum.'

I grasp on to this nugget of information. 'Amy told Lilian that she was leaving Seb? What did she say exactly?'

'I don't know, something along the lines of she'd fallen in love with someone else, she was leaving my brother for good and don't try to contact her, etcetera, etcetera.'

'Can you ask your mum exactly what Amy said before she left?'

'No.' He wrinkles his nose.

'Why not? I can't ask her for obvious reasons.'

'Because as far as our family's concerned, it's all ancient history. I'm not upsetting my mum all over again. She took it really hard when Amy left. Anyway, more importantly, Seb needs to know the truth about who you really are after I overheard you both talking in the bar last night.'

'No,' I reply. 'You can't say anything. Not yet. Not until I've found her. If he knows who I really am, he'll never talk to me again.'

'I have to tell him. He's my brother. There's no way I can keep this from him. No way in hell.'

'Please, Felix.' I reach across the bar and place my hand on his shoulder. 'I'm begging you. I promise I'll tell him in my own time. It'll be better coming from me. You know it will. If it comes from you he'll be devastated. He'll feel so betrayed. If I tell him, I can do it gently.'

'You're deluded if you think you can let him down gently. He'll be gutted whoever tells him. He's besotted with you.'

'I know it'll be rough, but I need some more time. Unless you know where she is?'

'I know as much as you do,' Felix replies. He leans his elbows on the bar and rubs his eyebrows. 'I'm exhausted, I'm gonna have to go to bed.'

'You won't tell anyone about me? Not Seb, or your parents. Not even Nicki. Please.'

'I won't say anything tonight, but I can't guarantee what I'll do tomorrow. This is all just...'

'Promise me you'll at least give me a heads-up beforehand.'

He glares at me. 'Fine.'

'Thank you.' My heartbeat slows a little at his reluctant agreement. Even though I'm not at all convinced I can trust him to keep his word.

What have I just done?

THIRTY-EIGHT

LILIAN

I ring the doorbell and wait under the chilly porch, trying to ignore the burn of my throbbing wrist. I had an absolutely terrible sleep last night, kept awake alternately by the pain and by uncharitable thoughts about my new daughter-in-law. Speaking of daughters-in-law, my other one has just opened her front door.

'Oh, er, hi, Lilian.' Nicki greets me wearing a coat, scarf, gloves and woolly hat. Teddy is behind her, equally bundled up and strapped into his pushchair. 'Come in,' Nicki says, although the expression on her face looks like this is the last thing she wants me to do.

'Are you off out?' I ask, stating the obvious.

'I'm supposed to be meeting Kim for a coffee and playdate with her son Spencer. They've got one of those ball pits at the back of Claire's Bakery.'

'Really?' I give a shudder. 'You know those things are riddled with germs.'

'He'll be fine,' Nicki replies. 'It'll build up his immunity.'

I don't voice my opinion that it's not Teddy's immunity I'm worried about. He'll be sniffly for a couple of days at most, it's the rest of us who'll suffer if we all get struck down with flu over the Christmas season. 'Don't let me keep you,' I say instead. 'I'm actually here to see Felix.'

'Oh. Everything okay?'

'Yes, fine, just pub stuff.'

'Okay, well, he's still in bed. He was late in. Sounds like you had a busy one last night. Oh, I almost forgot, how's your arm?'

'Not too bad. They've dressed it and dosed me up with painkillers.'

'You poor thing. That was so scary. I actually feel a bit responsible. I think I might have jostled Felix as I was carrying Teddy out of the way.'

'No, no, it wasn't you.' The memory of Caroline knocking into Felix flashes into my mind.

'Oh, well, as long as you're sure. Anyway, don't stand out there in the cold. I'll come out and then you can come in.'

We switch places and I kiss my grandson goodbye. 'Have a lovely morning,' I call after them.

She raises a hand and walks off briskly, the buggy's wheels rattling over the icy tarmac. I close the front door and sigh, not looking forward to this conversation one bit. Brian tried to insist I stay in bed this morning, but I'm not going to laze about while everyone else is busy. Who am I trying to kid? The only reason I was up so early is because I know I won't get a moment's peace until I've spoken to Felix. Even then, I made myself wait until a decent hour to come over.

I cast an eye over the dusty, cluttered hallway, peer into the dank, messy lounge and try to resist the urge to start cleaning. Even if I wanted to risk Nicki's annoyance, it would be tricky with my damaged wrist.

I head upstairs and hover outside their slightly ajar bedroom door, raise my fist, pause for a moment and then knock twice. I wait, but there's no reply. Through the crack, I see the room is dark. I push slightly and make out a large hump in the centre of the double bed, beneath a crumpled duvet. This room is as messy as the rest of the cottage. I take a breath and tell myself it doesn't matter. They have a young baby, of course they don't have time to keep things nice.

'Felix?' I call gently.

'I'm sleeping,' he calls out groggily, annoyed.

I head down to the kitchen. There are no clean mugs, so I wash up a couple with my good hand and make us both a strong coffee. This room is a health hazard. I'm surprised at Felix, as he keeps the pub kitchen immaculate. Well, I suppose he doesn't have a choice. The health inspector would close us down if it was a tenth as bad as this kitchen.

I locate a biscuit tin which contains a rich tea biscuit and half a chocolate-chip cookie. They'll have to do. I take my offerings up to the bedroom and place them on Felix's bedside table.

'Felix,' I say firmly. 'I made you a coffee.' I stand by the window and inch one of the curtains back.

'What? Mum, is that you?' He inhales and sits up with a loud yawn. 'What time is it?'

'Just after nine.'

He stretches and arranges a pillow behind his head. 'Did you say coffee?'

I point to the bedside table.

'Great.' He leans over to pick up the mug and then turns back to me. 'Why are you here anyway? Is everything okay? How's your arm?'

'Fine, it's fine. I'm here because I wanted to have a chat.'

'At nine in the morning?' He feigns a scared look. 'Did you put these biscuits here?'

'I got them from the kitchen but I can't vouch for their freshness.'

He dunks the rich tea into his coffee and shoves the whole thing in his mouth.

'Felix,' I begin. 'Dad told me you were in the bar with Caroline last night.'

He stops chewing for a moment and gives me a disbelieving look. 'Mu-um.'

'Well, I don't think it's appropriate,' I continue, annoyed at how prim I'm sounding.

'We work together,' he says. 'We had a quick drink afterwards, that's all.' Something flashes across his face. A frown or a shudder. Like he's remembering something.

'*What?*' I pounce. 'What was that look for?'

'What look? Nothing. Just, you're right, that biscuit was stale. Ugh.' He blows on his mug and takes a cautious sip of hot coffee.

'Felix, I know you. Tell me what's going through your mind.'

'Mum, you've just woken me up. What's going through my mind is that I'd like to go back to sleep for another half hour.'

'Promise me you won't get too friendly with Caroline. These Australians are very flirty, you know. You're married with a baby now. You need to take responsibility for your family and stop acting like you're single.'

'Jeez, Mum.'

'I mean it, Felix.'

'I know you do. But I haven't done anything wrong.'

'Nicki missed you terribly while you were away. You should be spending all your free time with her and Teddy. Make her dinner, take her out. Have drinks with *her* in the bar after work. Not with your brother's wife!'

'All right, all right. Point taken.' He rubs the bridge of his nose.

I blow on my coffee, feeling a little bad at having woken him up to give him a hard time, but if I don't say it, no one else will. 'I don't *like* having these conversations, you know. I don't *want* to interfere in your life, but—'

'Yes, yes, I know. You don't have to say any more, okay?' He closes his eyes and takes a deep, long-suffering breath.

'Good. Just make sure I don't.' I stare at my handsome son, hoping I've said enough. All I want is to avoid any more drama. Is that too much to ask?

THIRTY-NINE

MICHELLE

'We're running low on the sea bass,' Felix calls over. 'Only four left.'

'Okay,' I reply, picking up table thirteen's order of one pea risotto, one parmesan gnocchi and two baked trouts. I've been reinstated on service this evening as Lilian is still out of action after yesterday's birthday mishap.

Of course, I'm pleased to be out of the kitchen at last and back with the customers where I feel most at home, but it's meant that I haven't been able to get a minute alone with Felix. He and Hugo have been joking around all day, and it's obvious that Felix is avoiding me, pretending that nothing's wrong. Not allowing even a millisecond of eye contact between us. I'm desperate to speak to him now that we're both sober. To know what his intentions are after my revelation last night that Amy is my sister.

Does he plan to tell Sebastian? Has he told Nicki or – even worse – his mother? I don't think he can have, as no one has said anything untoward to me today, but I can't relax. I feel like my clothes are crawling with ants and every time I think about the rest of the Fletchers finding out who I really am, I want to throw up.

I almost bolted last night. There were a few moments where I was tempted to pack a bag and leave. But now that I'm here, it would be pointless to go without at least trying to get some more information about Amy's whereabouts. Finding my sister is pretty much all I can think about.

I knew my true identity would have to come out some time, but I'm still no nearer to finding Amy and I'm terrified Seb and his family will refuse to talk to me once they know. If that happens, what chance will I have of finding my sister? Perhaps I'll have to go to one of those tracing agencies. Only trouble is, I now have zero funds in the bank, as I spent everything on my plane ticket. At least Felix hasn't said anything to anyone yet. The fact that he's stayed quiet overnight might mean he's decided to keep my secret. If he can just stay quiet long enough for me to discover some useful information, that would be great. Maybe he'll even help me find out where she's gone.

Meanwhile, Seb and I seem to have called a truce. We had breakfast together this morning and he was relieved that I wasn't pressing him about Amy. He thinks I've let the matter drop when, in reality, I'm thinking about my next course of action. It's hard to talk to him when we never get any proper alone time. He's working all day, and I work most evenings. I told him to get an early night tonight and not worry about waiting up for me. I think he was relieved. He looks as exhausted as I feel.

Added to all this inner turmoil, I'm having to work along-side my biggest fan, Mariah, who's gone back to being her rude self today. I'd thought that after our blow-up yesterday, we might have got over our differences. Obviously, I was mistaken. I know I shouldn't have slapped her, but I did it in the heat of the moment. I let her wind me up and I shouldn't have.

'Try not to break anyone's wrist today,' she drawls as she leaves the kitchen.

I'm already tense, but her snide comments aren't helping. Plates in hand, I follow her out into the corridor. 'Can't we just be civil, Mariah? I already apologised for slapping you. You did call me a bitch, you know.'

She stops, turns, looks me up and down with a sneer before turning away and sashaying back into the restaurant.

I suck air in through my teeth and tell myself to let it go. I've enough to worry about without adding Mariah to my list of problems. I deliver table thirteen's order with a friendly smile, take a drinks order from a sweet elderly couple at table eleven and make my way back to the kitchen.

The rest of my shift speeds past in record time. The restaurant and bar are packed as usual, so there's no more time to think about anything, let alone worry or strategise about what I'm going to do next to find my sister.

The minute Hugo leaves for the night, Felix turns to me with a cold expression on his face. 'I think we need to talk,' he says. 'There are things you need to know.'

I nod and, despite his frosty demeanour, my spirits lift. His words give me hope that he might actually have some information for me. I'm glad at least that he's not ignoring everything, like Seb's doing.

'We better wait for everyone else to leave.' He removes his apron, takes it through to the back and shoves it into the washing machine with the rest of the dirty linen.

I stand in the doorway watching him. 'We can meet in the bar, but I'm not having anything to drink tonight,' I reply, still queasy from last night's whiskey.

'Not in the bar,' he says, straightening up.

'Okay, so where? Here, in the kitchen?'

'We need to be away from the pub,' Felix replies, refusing to catch my eye.

'Away from the pub?' I query. 'Why?'

He gives a bitter laugh. 'Mum has this crazy idea that there's something going on between the two of us.'

'*What?*'

'Yeah, after Dad saw us having a drink last night, he told Mum. She put two and two together and came up with fifty-eight.'

'Oh,' I reply. 'Well, that's not good.'

'No. So once she's gone up, we'll need to leave separately. Can you drive?'

'Uh, yes. But I don't have a car and...'

He closes the washer door and presses the start button. 'Here.' He takes a set of keys from his pocket and detaches a car key. 'You can drive mine. It's the navy Ford Kuga parked out the back. I'll take the works van.'

'Fine, but where are we going? It's almost midnight. Every-where's shut. Unless you want us to go clubbing?' I raise an eyebrow to let him know I'm joking.

'Don't worry about that. I know a good place.'

'I don't know why we can't just talk here—'

'Fine, you can explain to my mum and Seb why we're spending time outside work together—'

I raise my hands. 'Okay, point taken.'

Now that Felix has had a chance to digest who I really am, I wonder what he's going to do about it. What decision he's come to. I pray I've chosen the right member of the Fletcher family to help me find Amy, but I know I shouldn't get my hopes up.

I guess I'll find out tonight.

FORTY

LILIAN

As I wait for the kettle to boil, I peer out of the upstairs kitchen window watching the last of tonight's customers get into their cars and drive away. I hear the satisfying thump and judder of the main bar door below as Brian pulls it closed and slides the bolt home. I always feel a stillness settle over the building at this time. A calm sigh after all the hustle and bustle.

Brian insisted I take today off to recover, but I'd much rather have been working than sitting around up here feeling useless. Plus, all these enforced hours of rest have meant I've had far too much time to think about things. Not that thinking has helped. In fact, I'm more anxious than ever.

I reach for the tea caddy, take out a rooibos teabag and drop it into my favourite bone-china mug. I'm starting to wonder if trying to maintain the family business might actually be becoming more trouble than it's worth. If maybe Brian and I shouldn't have retired years ago and be spending our time gardening or travelling, let the boys sort out their own futures. The two of us have worked our socks off to ensure the boys have a secure home and income, but right now our children seem to be doing their darndest to ruin things.

Maybe I'm being a little harsh on them. After all, it's outside influences upsetting the apple cart. Felix and Seb just need a little helping hand now and then to pull them away from disaster and set them back on the right track. And the thing is, I love having us all here together. Our extended family unit, supporting one another. It's a rare thing these days to have three generations under one roof. Brian and I have always felt proud and privileged that our children wanted to stay, that they love us enough to want to forge their lives alongside ours rather than pulling away. Added to which, I don't think I'd be very suited to retirement. Along with my family, the pub is my life.

I pour boiling water into my mug and pause as I hear the crunch of gravel outside. I squint down to see a man trudging across the car park under the glow of the security lights, but I can't quite make out who it is. My distance glasses are in my car – I really should order a spare pair. There are no customer vehicles in the car park. Perhaps whoever it is has stashed a bicycle somewhere out there. The man stops by our dark-green works van, glances left and right and eases himself into the driver's seat.

Who's that then? Brian or one of the boys? Surely not. Where would they be going at this hour? I have my suspicions and I'm not going to be very happy if I'm proved right. I stride across the kitchen, switch off the kitchen light and rush back to the window. The van is still there, unmoving, its headlights still off.

I'm not going to skulk up here wondering. I sweep up my phone and keys from the kitchen counter and head towards the flat door, only stopping to grab the first coat that comes to hand from the hall cupboard – my smart black wool coat with the thick velvet collar.

I hurry down the stairs, along the corridor and into the dark, deserted and silent restaurant. I make for the nearest bay window and kneel on the burgundy velvet window seat, which gives me the perfect vantage point to see any comings and goings from the driveway that leads to the car park at the rear.

It feels strange, lurking down here on my own like this. As though I'm an intruder in my own home. I hear footsteps in the bar next door. Must be Brian or Tarik going through the end-of-night routine. It's still and quiet out front, the sky a whiteish grey, which probably means more snow is on its way.

I hope I didn't miss whoever it was driving away while I was coming down the stairs. Leaving the restaurant, I head back along the corridor, then switch off the security light before letting myself out of the side exit and locking the door behind me. I catch my breath at the chilliness of the night. The sky is full of snow, giving the darkness an eerie, luminous quality.

Picking my way carefully around the side of the pub, I'm just in time to see the van's headlights wink on. I hastily step back into the shadows and watch as it reverses before trundling away across the car park. I can only make out one silhouette on the driver's side, so thankfully my theory that it could have been Felix and Caroline leaving for a romantic tryst was incorrect.

Nevertheless, I hurry across the gravelled area, hugging the line of the building, and ending up by the laurel bush next to Felix and Nicki's cottage. I watch as the van cruises towards the exit and turns right, away from town.

Perhaps I should follow...

Moments later, I hear footsteps heading this way. I duck behind the laurel bush and watch to see who it is. My heart drops when I see the willowy figure of Caroline walking nervously across the car park, her blonde waves cascading over the shoulders of her parka. She's coming this way. Is she heading to Felix and Nicki's cottage? Surely not.

She pauses by Felix's navy Ford Kuga, glances behind her and then in my direction. I shrink back against the foliage. The lights on Felix's car blink twice with an accompanying beep. She settles into the driver's seat and starts up the engine. She pulls out of the car park and turns off in the same direction as the van.

Do they think I'm stupid?

'Felix, what are you doing?' I mutter under my breath.

Well, I'm not going to just sit by and watch my family implode because of some girl who thinks she can flutter her eyelashes at my sons and play us all for fools.

I don't stop to think. I hurry back to where my VW Polo's parked. I'm on so much pain medication that I'm not even sure I'm fit to drive, but I'll give it a damn good go. By the time I drop into the driver's seat, I'm shivering hard.

I can't believe Caroline and Felix are having an affair. Poor Sebastian. I was absolutely right not to trust Caroline. I wipe a tear from the corner of my eye, take my driving glasses from the glovebox and start up the engine. I'm so furious with Felix I could throttle him.

It's just like last time.

FORTY-ONE

MICHELLE

Felix's van turns off the main road and takes a few successive winding turns. As I follow him, I feel sick with anxiety that he might want to tell Seb my real identity. I do feel bad for putting Felix in this awkward position. It's not great for him to have to keep this monumental secret from his brother. It also doesn't help my state of mind that I'm trying to get to grips with navigating these narrow country lanes. I haven't owned a car for years – too expensive to run – and I've never driven in the UK before. Not sure if I'm even insured to drive here.

I realise I'm going to have to come clean with Seb very soon. To tell him who I really am and that we're not legally married. I owe him that much, but I'm dreading the conversation. From what I know of him – his fling with Mariah excluded – he seems like a good person. A rash, impulsive, emotional, messed-up person, but good, nonetheless. He doesn't deserve to be hurt all over again.

My hope is that once Seb knows who I am, he might take pity on me and open up about Amy. Give me a clue as to her whereabouts. Even if he tells me where she is simply to get rid of me, that would be fine. I can't let myself think about the possibility that he's as in the dark as I am. That no one knows where she is. Finding my sister is more important than anything. Even if her radio silence is because she doesn't want anything to do with me any more, I need to know she's okay.

I peer through the windscreen into the gloom. All I can see is the red smear of the van's tail lights and the encroaching hedgerows on either side of road. I have absolutely no idea where we are. It feels like the middle of nowhere. The road is steep and it feels like we're climbing. I hope Felix pulls over soon. I'm exhausted and, to make matters worse, snow has just started whirling down, flakes flinging themselves against the windows in white splats.

Eventually, the road plateaus and the van turns off down a single-track lane, its right indicator flashing. I follow into what looks like a car park with a grassy area at the far end. I bump over uneven gravel and park a short distance from the van in front of a swathe of grass that's rapidly disappearing beneath a carpet of white. The car lights illuminate a single wooden bench and what looks like a deep valley beyond. This looks like some kind of viewpoint.

I turn off the engine, get out of the car and slam the door, shivering as an icy breeze laden with snowflakes sweeps over me. It's far too cold to sit on the bench so I head over to van with the intention of sliding into the passenger seat next to Felix. However, he's out of the van before I can reach him. He's left the headlights on so they throw an arc of light straight ahead, making it look as though the snowfall is contained within the light, like a giant snow globe.

Felix looks different somehow. Bulkier. He turns and gives a single wave and it's then that I realise this man isn't Felix at all.

'Hello, Caroline.'

It's Brian.

'Oh.' I'm taken aback, unsure what to say or do.

'Don't worry,' Brian says gently, drawing closer. 'Felix told me all about who you really are.'

'Oh. Right.' My stomach lurches. I feel wrong-footed. So much for Felix keeping quiet about my revelation. I can't believe he broke his word and blabbed without telling me. Brian must think I'm a terrible person to have lied to his son like that. I wonder if Felix has told anyone else. I'm sure he'll have told Lilian. And what about Seb? My brain is racing at what this might mean. The optimistic part of me is hoping Brian might have some information for me.

'I suppose I should call you *Michelle*,' he says. 'Nice name that. Reminds me of a Beatles song. *Michelle my belle*. Do you know the one I mean?'

'Um, yes, I do.' A long-buried memory flashes to the front of my brain, of my dad singing it to me when I was little. I blink away tears and tell myself they're a result of the stinging wind.

'Let's sit.' Brian gestures to the bench ahead of us.

We approach it from opposite ends. He sits on the left while I perch on the right. The seat is already blanketed with snow and I feel the damp cold seep upwards through my jeans. I feel like we should be having this conversation cocooned in the warmth of one of our vehicles, but I'm reluctant to suggest it. I don't want to start making demands right now. Not when I need to get him on my side.

I clear my throat. 'I'm really sorry that I didn't tell you and Lilian who I am.'

He doesn't reply.

'Did Felix explain why I had to keep it to myself?'

Brian gives a single nod. 'He did, yes. Something about your sister going missing and you not being able to get in touch. You still could've told us, love. No need to have gone to such drastic lengths.'

'I already told Felix that I tried that already, but none of you wanted to talk to me when I called and introduced myself as

Amy's sister. That's why I had to try something else.' I cough as the cold air finds its way into my lungs. 'Can I just ask why didn't Felix come tonight?'

Brian turns to look at me and sighs. 'He was worried. It wasn't really fair of you to ask him to keep such a big secret from his family. He didn't want to tell me, but he needed someone to talk to. We thought it best if I came tonight instead. That way you and I can sort all this out without getting emotional. You know...' he says, staring at me with his head cocked. 'Now that I know who you are, I can really see the resemblance.'

I touch my cheek self-consciously. 'Really? Amy and I never looked alike as kids.'

'Well, you certainly do now. The spitting image, in fact.'

Despite my thick parka, I'm shivering quite violently. I thrust my hands between my thighs to try to try to warm them, my brain racing, thoughts whirring, wishing I'd never got into this awkward situation. If only I'd kept my mouth shut last night and hadn't told Felix my identity. But did I really have any other option? I need to find my sister, and I think at least one of the Fletchers might know the truth about where she's gone.

I clear my throat. 'So, now that you know everything, I was wondering if – well, I was going to ask Felix this, but I'll ask you – I was wondering if you might help me to track down my sister.'

He gets to his feet and rubs his hands together. 'Brrr. Chilly out here, isn't it?'

'Maybe we should get back in one of the cars,' I suggest longingly. The snow is falling so thickly now that I can hardly see Brian's face.

'Come and have a look at this view first,' he says, gesturing me over to the edge of the grass. 'It's an absolute belter. Course, it's a bit tricky to see in the dark, but while we're here, you may as well take a look. It's actually an old quarry.' He starts walking.

Reluctant as I am to spend any more time out here, I get to my feet and catch him up, figuring the quicker I look at the view and make all the right appreciative noises, the quicker we can get back into the warm and talk about finding my sister.

The van's headlamps light our way, but it's not exactly enjoyable trying to navigate this windswept snowy terrain. My trainer-clad feet are already ice blocks. 'Maybe we should come back when it's daylight,' I say with a nervous laugh. 'And not snowing.'

'A few more steps will do it,' he replies, putting a hand at my back to guide me.

I'm shivering like crazy and my teeth are actually chattering, like those wind-up teeth you can buy. I'm seriously starting to get a bad feeling about this. I stop abruptly. 'Honestly, Brian, I'm freezing. Not used to these UK temperatures.'

'Come on now,' he says briskly. 'You're an English lass, aren't you? All that pretending to be Australian doesn't count any more.'

'Right, but I've lived abroad for over ten years. I'm used to the heat. And anyway, I can't see a thing out here! Sorry, I'm heading back. We can talk in the car.'

Brian takes hold of my upper arm. 'Just a couple more steps and then you'll see.'

I give a confused laugh. 'Actually, Brian, you're hurting my arm. Can you let go please?'

He grips it tighter.

'Brian, what are you *doing*?' I try to shake my arm free, suddenly angry with him for manhandling me in this way. This bullish behaviour doesn't fit with his character. He's always been so mild-mannered and gentle. Not here. Not now. Outrage bubbles up through my body and I twist my arm violently, hoping it's enough to make him let go.

But it isn't. He's too strong. His grip unshakeable.

I experience a dark streak of fear, a sour taste in the back of my throat as he yanks me forward.

'That's it, almost there,' he croons, as though I'm a frightened pony.

I turn my head to look at him. His eyes are fixed on the cliff edge ahead. My guts churn as I realise this whole situation is getting out of hand. It's scaring me to the point of pure terror. 'Okay, that's it, let go!' I cry. 'I want to go back!'

'No,' he replies, his voice unexpectedly deep and loud in my ear. 'It's too late to go back. You have to keep going.'

And that's when I see it. I blink rapidly, unsure if my eyes might be playing tricks on me.

But they're not.

In his left hand he's holding a long, black-handled kitchen knife.

FORTY-TWO

MICHELLE

'Brian, what are you doing?' My head swims with fear and my knees go soft, but I can't allow myself to buckle. To sink into the snow and give up. I have to stay alert. I have to understand exactly what's going on here.

'Just take a few nice big steps towards the edge and it will all be over without any fuss.' Brian's still talking to me as if I'm a nervous pony.

'Are you crazy?' I cry. 'Why are you doing this? What have I done that's so wrong?'

He shakes his head and raises the knife a fraction.

I can't take my eyes off it.

'You lied to us, Michelle. You lied to Sebastian. He thinks you love him. He thinks you're his *wife*. We welcomed you into our home as our daughter-in-law and you betrayed us.'

'I'm sorry! I truly am. But surely you understand why I did it. Didn't Felix explain about Amy? About how I came here to find her.'

'He explained all too well.' Brian's face darkens.

'I get that you're angry. I would be too. But that's no reason to do *this*. Whatever this is! Are you honestly trying to *kill* me just because I misled you over who I am?'

'I'm afraid I don't have a choice, love.' His expression is one of genuine sadness and I realise that this man is not thinking straight.

'Of course you have a choice,' I reply, trying to stay calm, trying to get him to see reason. 'Does Felix know what you're doing here? How do you think Seb would react if he knew you were here trying to end my life?'

'Whatever I'm doing, I'm doing for their own good! Everything I do, I do for this family. The minute I found out who you really were and that you'd come here snooping around after your sister, well... I knew things weren't going to turn out well. Better to end it sooner rather than later. I can tell you now, I was furious with Felix back then.'

'*Furious?* Why?' The longer I can keep him talking, the more chance I have of figuring out a way to escape.

'I told him that he had everything – a beautiful wife and a precious son, why would he jeopardise all that? And how could he do that to his brother? I could have slapped him into the middle of next week. I told Lilian she was too soft on the boys. They always got their own way, see. It wasn't good for them. They never saw any consequences for their actions. Made them think they could do whatever they wanted without repercussions. Well, look where that's got us? It's led us here, hasn't it?' He gives me a regretful look. 'To the edge of a quarry in the middle of a snowstorm.'

'But what did Felix *do*?' I ask, genuine curiosity overcoming my fear for a brief moment.

'What *didn't* he do is more the question.'

FORTY-THREE

AMY

'Mum knows everything,' Felix hisses, running both hands through his dark hair

'What do you mean?' Amy has just let herself in the back door of the Royal Oak after a stressful day at work, only to be confronted by Felix dragging her into the storeroom. At first she'd thought he wanted to have a steamy encounter. It's been a while since they had sex in here and the thought makes her pulse race. But the look on his face says otherwise.

'She saw us a couple of nights ago when we were kissing in the bar.'

'Can't you deny it?' Amy asks. 'You know what your mum's eyesight's like.'

'I did. But apparently she walked in on us months ago when we were having sex in the cottage. You know that evening Nicki was out with her friends? Mum didn't say anything back then because she hoped it was a one-off. A mistake.'

Amy exhales, her brain making rapid decisions. 'Okay... So, maybe this could be fate.' She gives a hopeful smile and shrugs with a nonchalance she doesn't feel.

'Yes, I agree,' he replies.

Amy presses herself up against him. 'I'm so happy to hear you say that. It's about time we brought everything out into the open. I'm sick of hiding things.'

'What are you talking about?' Felix snaps, moving her away from him. 'I'm sorry, Ames, but we need to end things. As of right now.'

'End things?' Amy's skin goes cold. 'Why would we do that? Ending things makes no sense.' She places a hand on his chest. 'Not when we love each other.'

'Look, Ames, you know I love you. I do. But I'm a father now. I have Teddy to think of.' He removes her hand from his chest and goes into the kitchen, glancing left and right, to check no one's out there eavesdropping.

Amy follows him but he corrals her back into the storeroom. 'I'm sorry, Amy, it's over. For good this time.'

'No.' She bites her lip to try to stop her chin from trembling.

Amy has always been a sensible, caring, no-nonsense kind of girl. She married Sebastian Fletcher with an open heart, and never ever dreamed that she would cheat on him. But that was before Felix started paying her attention. That was before Felix kissed her. Before Felix touched her and made her feel like she was the only woman in the universe. And right now, the thought of a universe without Felix is one where she doesn't want to be.

'Look, what if I tell Seb tonight?' she suggests, trying to keep her voice from trembling. 'Once he knows the truth then we'll be able to get on with our lives. If you tell Nicki at the same time, we can get it over with quickly. Rip the plaster off. It's not fair to stay with our spouses out of some misguided obligation. You can still be an amazing dad to Teddy. Plenty of couples parent separately—'

'No, Amy! You're not understanding me. I am absolutely not tearing my family apart over this. Mum finding out, well, it's turned out to be a blessing. It's forcing us to stop. I've felt so terrible betraying my wife and my brother like this. If either of them found out, it would be a complete disaster.'

Amy's heart is smashing against her ribcage. She feels as though her guts are being twisted inside out. 'Felix, listen, it was you who wanted this from the start. You made me fall for you. You told me you loved me.' She can barely get the words out. She knows her desperate words are only pushing him further away, but she can't help herself.

'I do love you,' he says. 'But not enough to destroy my family.' He takes hold of her wrists. 'Think about it. About what it would do to Seb.'

'I have thought about it. Yes, he'd be upset. But he'd eventually get over it. He would move on. Find someone else.' She gazes into his dark eyes and tries to get him to look at her. Really look at her. But he won't.

Felix's gaze is somewhere over her shoulder. He gives her an agitated glance. 'If you won't think of Seb, then what about my livelihood? When Mum and Dad confronted me, they laid it all out in black and white. They said that if you and I pursued this, that it would more than likely be the end of the Royal Oak. Right now, Seb runs the place and I'm the chef. Mum and Dad are getting older – they can't do this without the two of us. The place would fall apart. Look, Amy, whatever's gone on between me and you, I still love my brother. He would never forgive me for this. Not ever. It would be the end of my family.' He gently eases himself out of her grip and takes a step back.

'You've given this a lot of thought,' Amy says, her voice now high and wobbling.

'I'm sorry,' he says gently.

'You're making the wrong decision,' she cries. 'You're choosing practicality over our long-term happiness.'

'I'm not. Coming clean will only make everyone miserable.'

'What about me?' she says, her voice catching in a sob.

'I'm sorry,' he repeats, more firmly this time.

'Maybe I'll take the decision out of your hands,' she says defiantly. 'If Seb and Nicki know about us, then you'll finally be free to choose who you want to be with.' Amy knows she's acting irrationally. She would never normally threaten something like this, but her brain feels hot with fear at the thought of losing him. Her whole body is sick with longing. How will she be able to live here with Sebastian while Felix plays at happy families with Nicki?

It will be impossible.

She won't do it.

FORTY-FOUR

MICHELLE

As I listen to Brian telling me about Amy and Felix's affair, I feel like I'm standing outside of my body. He hasn't explicitly told me the outcome of that awful situation, but my brain is slowly trying to piece it all together. The snow-laden wind is like needles against my skin, reaching inside and chilling my blood, freezing my heart. Everything feels as though it's happening in slow motion and I also feel as if I'm missing one important piece of the puzzle. That it's right there in the box waiting to be picked up and slotted into place.

Brian's steady voice rumbles on. 'Felix admitted he never loved Amy. It was just an unnecessary fling. But, still, she threatened to break up his family and his livelihood. You can't do that to someone and expect to get away with it. It's not right.

'I told Felix it wasn't just *his* livelihood he had to worry about! This affected all of us. I asked him what he thought Sebastian would do when he discovered the affair. I asked him if he thought his brother would ever want to work with him again. That knowledge would have crushed Sebastian. Course it would. And what about his mother? Everything my Lilian does, she does for the boys. For her family. We built this business up for our kids, for their families. And Felix just wanted to chuck it all in the bin. I told him he was a bloody idiot and he had to put Amy in her place. Tell her what was what.

'He couldn't even do that right. She was threatening to blab, wasn't she? So I told Felix that I supposed it was down to me to sort this out then, wasn't it? Well, he was happy not to know any details. Left it to me to deal with everything. But that's what you do for your kids, right? You look after them when they get into trouble.' He stares out over the abyss, his mind elsewhere for a moment.

Even though I'm almost numb with terror, I use this as an opportunity. It might be my only one. I tense my whole body and yank my arm out of his grip, twisting away as he stabs the knife towards me. I scream and back away along the edge of the cliff, but luck isn't with me. I stumble and fall on my backside into the snow.

Brian looms over me, a hulking great shape within a vortex of swirling snow.

'Please,' I whimper.

'You shouldn't have done that,' he says, crouching down and hauling me to my feet effortlessly. He's switched the knife to his right hand. He's trying to edge me backwards.

My gaze is riveted to the blade, and I'm also hyper aware of the cliff edge behind me. I can't tell how far away it is, and I'm getting vertigo just thinking about it.

'Nearly stabbed you then,' he says, 'and that would have spoiled things. Got to make it look like an accident. Like you fell, or maybe you ended it yourself. This snow is a godsend. It'll cover all our tracks nicely. We need to hurry along with this before the snow stops.'

As he calmly explains that he really does mean to kill me, another dark realisation sweeps over me. 'Did you...?' I swallow. 'What did you do to Amy?'

'Okay, that's enough questions.' He holds the knife at chest height now and jabs it towards me. 'I liked you when you first arrived, when I thought you were "Caroline from Byron Bay". But you've turned out to be just as selfish as your sister. You're both rotten eggs. Both destructive. You've come into our lives and caused havoc. I won't let you upset my Lilian with all your secrets. You won't break my family apart like your sister wanted to do.'

'What did you DO?!' I scream, letting my tears of dread and terror fall freely.

'All right, now. Calm down. I only did what I had to. What any husband and father would do to keep his family intact. Look, I knew that if you'd gone to these lengths to find your sister, well, you'd soon stumble over the truth. And I'm afraid I just couldn't let that happen.'

'Oh my God,' I weep. 'You killed Amy, didn't you? You killed her.'

FORTY-FIVE

LILIAN

I turn into the car park of the old quarry with a million accusations and recriminations on my lips. I'm so disappointed in Felix. I truly thought he would have learned his lesson by now.

After I discovered his affair with Amy earlier this year, Brian had strong words with Felix, who eventually saw sense and called things off with her. Sadly, she left Sebastian the very same day without a word of goodbye. Apparently, as well as Felix, she'd also been seeing someone else. She told Brian that she couldn't face Sebastian, so Brian encouraged her to leave to be with this other man. I was glad of it. Amy leaving cut down the chances of Sebastian finding out about her affair with Felix. It meant that my boys' relationship with one another could be saved. That our family could go back to being happy again.

But now everything is in jeopardy because of Felix and Caroline. I slowly navigate my Polo across the snow-covered car park, hardly able to see more than a few feet in front of me. Eventually, I reach two vehicles parked side by side – the pub van and Felix's Kuga. Both apparently empty.

Turning off the engine, I notice that the van's headlights are on. All I can see in the beam is flurrying snow. No sign of Felix or Caroline. I unclip my seatbelt and open the car door, gasping as icy air rushes inside. Stepping out into the snowstorm, I button up my coat and pull the velvet collar up to protect my ears. It's a proper blizzard now. I hope we don't get stranded here. As each second passes my fury with the pair of them is growing. And to think poor Sebastian is at home in bed, oblivious.

I walk gingerly over to Felix's car and squint into the dark interior, holding my breath, wondering if they might both be on the back seat. They're not, thank goodness. Next, I open one of the van's rear doors, but all I'm greeted with are a couple of empty crates. I close the door and battle my way around the van against the wind, peering ahead into the whirling grey gloom that's only dimly illuminated by the van's headlights.

I think I can make out the shape of a bench ahead of me and maybe a figure beyond that, but it's hard to tell. What on earth do the pair of them think they're doing out here? Having sex in a blizzard? I wouldn't be surprised if they were up to something ridiculous like making snow angels. Only, they'd better be careful; the quarry edge is so steep. One wrong step and I hate to think what would happen. A shiver turns into a deep shudder and a sudden lurch of worry.

'Felix!' I cry out, but my voice is snatched by the storm. 'Felix, are you there?'

A short scream over to my right catches my attention.

'Caroline?' My voice is quavery and ineffectual. 'Where are you?' I take a few careful steps, petrified at how close to the edge I might be stepping.

And now I see them. Caroline's face is white. She looks terrified. What's Felix doing? His back is towards me, but he looks like he's... Wait a minute, that's not Felix. That's...

'Brian!' I call out.

Suddenly, Caroline notices me. 'Lilian! Lilian, oh thank God. Help me! Please!'

My husband turns and as he does so, Caroline ducks beneath his arm. Brian twists around, and to my absolute horror, I see he's holding a lethal-looking kitchen knife that he's using to jab at Caroline as she tries to get away.

She halts, screams and twists around. Then sprints towards me, clutching her upper arm before veering away towards the cars.

'Michelle!' Brian roars. He turns, the knife still in his hand, and lumbers after her.

'Brian?' I cry. 'What's going on? Did she try to attack you? Why have you got a knife? Did you just call her *Michelle*?' I try to think where I've heard that name before.

'Stop her!' he yells at me as he thuds past, giving chase.

I experience a jolt of terror as I realise that Felix isn't here. 'Where's Felix?' I cry. I pull desperately at my husband's coat, accidentally causing him to skid and fall face down in the snow.

'Oh no!' I cry. 'Bri, I'm sorry, are you okay?' But while I'm checking on my husband, I'm mentally trying to digest what I just witnessed. Did Brian really just stab Caroline?

Brian scrabbles to get up. 'Don't let her leave, Lil!' he yells.

'What? *Why*?'

A car engine starts up, its headlights shining directly into my eyes. Caroline is back in Felix's car and is reversing away. All I can think about is what was she doing here, and did she harm Felix? I feel physically sick as I think about that sheer drop into the quarry. I feel so weak that I can no longer stand. Was Brian here trying to save Felix? Did she do something to our son? I'm down on my knees in the snow now, scrambling to get up. 'Where's Felix?' I gasp. 'Is he okay?'

He cries out in exasperation. 'You let her get away, Lil.'

'Felix!' I cry. 'Where is he?'

'*Felix*? Don't worry about him, he's at home,' Brian says.

'Are you sure?'

'Yes, yes.' He staggers to his feet, pulling me up with him. There's blood, snow and dirt on his face.

'We have to go after her,' he says. 'Right now.'

'No. You need to tell me what's going on, and I want the truth.'

I follow his gaze to Caroline's receding tail lights. He pulls a set of keys from his trouser pocket. 'I'll tell you later, but right now, we need to stop her.'

FORTY-SIX

MICHELLE

I can barely grip the steering wheel my hands are shaking so badly. They're numb to the bone. My whole body is stiff and freezing and my shoulder is on fire. Brian tried to kill me. But I'm still here. Still able to function despite the throbbing pain radiating down my arm. Thank God I'm wearing my parka. At least he only caught my arm. I hope to goodness the knife didn't go in too deep. The thought of it makes me woozy and nauseous. I have to pull myself together.

Despite my intense physical discomfort and an emotional pain that I can't even begin to process yet, I reverse across the car park, feeling the wheels skid out beneath me, but hardly caring. I'd never been so relieved to see Lilian. Her face showed utter confusion. I don't know what she's doing out here, or whether she's involved in some way, but I'm thankful she showed up. If she'd been a few minutes later, I could be dead.

Brian was going to kill me! He wanted me to go over the edge into the quarry. I swing the car around so that I'm pointing towards the exit, and I glance in my rear-view mirror to see if there are headlights behind me. None that I can see, but that doesn't mean he isn't about to come chasing after me. Think, Michelle, *think*. My brain is a cloud of fear and confusion.

I drive out of the car park and back onto the lane, trying not to go too fast, even though my instinct is to ram my foot to the floor and gun it as fast as I can. I have no idea of my location and I don't have the luxury of time to open Google Maps. All I know is, I need to get somewhere safe, where Brian can't find me.

I set off along the lane, and then start zigzagging left and right down dark, snow encrusted country roads. My sister's image is burned into my mind. Can she really be dead? Will I never see her again? Did Brian kill her?

I don't know how I'm even managing to keep the car on the road. It's a miracle I haven't wrapped it around a tree yet. But I'm still here. Still gripping the wheel and keeping my gaze on the way ahead. And all the while, my heart is in my throat, and I'm praying to God I won't see headlights coming up behind me.

FORTY-SEVEN

LILIAN

As Brian takes the van keys from his pocket, I'm desperate to get him to explain what's going on. He gives me an exasperated stare as blood starts trickling down his face.

'Bri, your nose is bleeding,' I cry.

He puts a hand to his upper lip and looks dispassionately at his bloodied fingertips. He's gazing down at the snow now, glancing around for something.

I follow his gaze to where it lands and see what he must have been searching for – the knife lying in the snow. I swallow down bile as I realise the blade is smeared with blood, falling snow starting to cover it.

I look up at my husband, at the blood still dripping from his nose. 'What were you doing out here?' I ask, afraid to hear the answer. 'Why on earth did you bring a knife?'

'She was stealing from us, Lil.' Brian bends and picks up the knife, shoves it clumsily into his coat pocket and eases himself up again. Its black handle is sticking out of his pocket, and I can't help thinking about the blood on its blade. About how it must be soaking into the lining of his pocket.

'I caught her taking money from the till,' he says gruffly.

'She denied it and ran. She took Felix's car. I came after her in the van.' He grabs my hand. 'Come on, we need to go after her. She doesn't know these lanes; we can still catch her.'

'Why are you lying to me, Brian?' I stare at my husband, at his dirtied bloodied face. At the shifty, desperate look in his eyes. 'You didn't follow her,' I insist. '*She* followed *you*. I saw you both leave separately.'

'No, Lil, listen. I'm telling you—'

'Stop it, Brian! Just stop it! You stabbed her! You don't stab someone for stealing. You confront them maybe, or call the police.'

He starts hobbling over to the van. 'We'll talk later. There's no time. We need to get hold of her. Stop her.'

'No! Tell me now. If you love me, Brian Fletcher, you'll stop right where you are and tell me exactly what's been happening here.'

He keeps walking so I stride after him, wrench the keys from his hand and shove them deep into my coat pocket.

'What are you doing?' he roars. 'Give those back!'

'Brian!' I cry. 'What's got into you? Just let her go. If she leaves she leaves. Now tell me what the hell's been going on!'

He lunges towards me, aiming for my coat pocket. 'I need those keys, Lilian. Just give them here or it will all be for nothing.'

I dodge out of the way, pull the keys from my pocket and hurl them towards the cliff edge. 'Now you'll *have* to talk to me.'

'Why did you...? Fine, we'll take your car instead,' he growls.

'No! She's gone, Brian. You won't catch her. She could be anywhere by now. If you don't want me to throw *my* car keys over the edge too, you'd better start talking.'

'Give me your keys, Lil.'

'No.'

'Please, you don't understand.'

'So explain.'

He roars in frustration and for the first time in my life I feel scared of my husband. I take a step back and wrap my arms around myself, shivering and feeling like this must all be some horrid nightmare.

Brian must notice the fear in my eyes because he stops. Just stands in front of me, panting. Suddenly, the fight in his body seems to deflate before my eyes. His whole frame droops.

He bows his head and puts his fingers to the bridge of his nose.

I pause, take a shuddering breath, and finally take a tentative step towards him. I pat his shoulder. 'Whatever it is, Brian, we can fix it together, all right?'

He moves his hands to his temples and shakes his head. 'It's too late,' he mutters. 'I'm sorry, Lilian. I tried. But it's too late.'

'Too late for what?' I ask.

But he shakes his head one more time and turns away, walking back the way he came. Towards the quarry.

FORTY-EIGHT

MICHELLE

I don't know how long I've been driving. Could be seconds, minutes, an hour. Everything hurts and my thoughts are a jumble of pain and devastation.

Amy is dead. She must be. My kind, beautiful sister is *dead.* It's too terrible to even contemplate. How can she be gone? My brain can't take it in. We didn't even get the chance to reunite. So many things I wish I'd told her, and now it's too late. The adrenalin that got me out of the quarry car park is leaching away. My body is icy, my mind sluggish. I should be sobbing right now but I can't even cry. I think I must be in shock. The whole thing is like a surreal nightmare.

After approaching and dismissing numerous spots to pull over, I see another layby up ahead and fear that if I don't stop at this one, I might collapse at the wheel. I only hope I'm far enough away from the quarry to be safe from Brian.

Terrified that I'm going to see headlights approaching any second, I slow the car anyway and risk pulling into the layby, my heart pounding.

I keep the engine running, just in case, and with trembling

fingers, I pull my phone from my coat pocket and call the police.

FORTY-NINE

LILIAN

'Brian, stop! Where are you going?' I watch him blunder off into the grey snowy gloom. My heart is pounding and I'm so confused I can hardly think straight. Is Caroline having an affair with Felix? Or is something else going on here? My breath is ragged and my lungs are burning with cold. Why did Caroline run off? Did Brian really stab her? I wish I hadn't taken my pain medication this evening. Everything is suddenly feeling fuzzy round the edges. I take a few steps forward, and a few more still, until I finally make out the shape of my husband. If he's not careful, he's going to go over the edge. 'Brian, stop!' I yell with all the force I can muster.

It works. My husband comes to a halt, but he doesn't turn around.

I walk over to his side, my feet sinking into shallow snow-drifts. I place a hand on his arm and gaze up at his face. 'What happened here tonight? What were you two doing?' For one crazy moment, I think that maybe Brian and Caroline were... But that's ridiculous. I shake away the crazy thought. My husband is the most loyal man I know.

'You should go home, Lil,' he says, his voice barely audible over the whistle and hum of the wind.

'Yes,' I reply, 'if you'll come with me. Let's get out of this blizzard and you can tell me what's been happening here.'

'Oh, Lil, it's too late for all that...' He looks over my head into the distance.

'Stop talking like that!' I snap, unused to this behaviour from Brian. I want my assertive, practical husband back, a man who knows what's what.

'I suppose I should tell you.' He turns to face me and his eyes are full of misery. Of defeat.

'What on earth has got into you?' I ask, snappishness masking my fear. 'And why did you lie to me just now?'

'Because... Well... I'm afraid I did something.' He takes a breath and squares his shoulders. 'Something that needed to be done.'

'*What?* What did you do?'

He inhales deeply once again and lets his breath out through clenched teeth. 'Amy didn't leave Sebastian.'

'What are you talking about? Of course she did! Has Caroline been filling your head with lies because—'

Brian holds up a hand to silence me.

I snap my mouth shut, not sure I want to hear what he's about to say.

'Amy didn't leave Sebastian. Because I didn't give her the opportunity.'

My heart pounds steadily, but so loudly and vigorously that it feels as though my whole ribcage is moving back and forth. As though my ribs are being plucked like guitar strings.

Brian continues, 'Amy was threatening to tell Sebastian about her affair with Felix. I know you were terrified about it all coming out. About the boys coming to blows and splitting the family in two. And the business collapsing. I didn't want to take the chance that she'd come clean. Felix didn't even love the girl. It was just a fling to him – stupid idiot. But she was head over heels for him, wasn't she? She was willing to destroy everything in order to have him.'

I want to ask Brian what he did. I want to tell him that no matter what it was, I'll be here for him and we'll get through this together. That's the kind of thing I would normally say. But standing here in the early hours of the morning in the middle of a blizzard, waiting for my husband to confess to something so inconceivable that I can't even let my thoughts go there, I find my throat has gone dry and my mind has frozen. There are no reassuring words for me to speak.

Brian purses his lips for a moment. 'I killed Amy out by the back of the recycling bins. I stabbed her with a kitchen knife then I took her out to the woods and I buried her.'

I cover my mouth with my hand and scream silently into my palm. My eyes feel as though they're open so wide they might pop out of my head.

Brian doesn't seem to notice my shock. He's still talking. The words pour from his lips like pus from a wound. 'Caroline isn't Australian. She tricked Sebastian into a relationship. And they aren't really married. Her real name is Michelle Nelson. She's Amy's sister.'

I hear the words he's saying but I can't seem to process anything beyond the fact that he killed Amy in cold blood. That he stabbed her with a knife. My husband. The man I've slept next to for over forty years. The respected publican who everyone knows and loves. *My Brian.*

'Michelle came to Stalbridge looking for Amy,' he continues. 'So, you see, I couldn't let her live either because she would have discovered the truth. I was going to make it look like an accident. Like she'd fallen off the edge of the quarry. It was a simple plan that could easily have worked. But now she's left. And she knows what I did. So, you see, Lilian, love...' He finally looks down at me. 'It's all over. I'm finished.'

'You killed Amy?' I whisper.

'I hoped I'd never have to tell you. I didn't ever want to see that look in your eyes, Lil. The shock.'

'You told me she'd left,' I say, my voice barely above a whisper. 'That she'd cleared out her and Sebastian's bank account.'

'I cleared out the account to make it more convincing. I found her pin and password written in her diary and transferred the money to her personal account.'

'What are we going to tell the kids?' I say, the very thought of it filling me with an unreal horror. 'Does Felix know what you did?'

'No,' Brian confirms. 'I told Felix the same story I told you – that I'd convinced Amy to leave and never come back. Nobody knew anything except me. Until today. Now *you* know, and so does Michelle.'

The burn on my arm is throbbing. It's so cold it feels like it's on fire again. I can't believe my birthday party was only yesterday. It feels like a lifetime ago. To think, my only worry then was if *Caroline* was good enough for my son. I've been such a fool.

Part of me wants to jump straight into wife mode. To fight for my husband. To make everything right. To fix it all. I could race to the car and scour the lanes to find Michelle. Beg her to stay quiet... We could offer to pay her. To... I stop my train of thought. There's no way Michelle will ever keep this to herself. She'll want justice. Rightly so.

I realise I'm crying, the snow merging with my warm tears. I'm crying for the loss of it all. The thing I feared the most is finally happening. But not because of some malign outside influence. It's because of a choice my husband made. The *wrong* choice.

The wind has dropped and there's a strange hush in the air. Just the darkness, the snow and this unwanted confession that's threatening to crush me under its weight.

For the first time in my life, I realise I have no idea what to do.

Brian's eyes light up for a moment and then instantly dull.

'What?' I prompt. 'What were you thinking?'

'I was wondering if maybe that stab wound I just gave her did more damage than I first thought. That maybe she's crashed the car. Or had to pull over... Maybe she's already dead... I wondered if we could take your car and look for her. We might still be able to salvage this, Lilian.' But he's talking without any real hope in his voice. He's not making any move back to the car.

A sudden disturbance at the far end of the car park startles me. Brian and I both turn our heads at the same time.

Cars.

Blue flashing lights heading this way.

The police are here.

Brian takes my good hand in one of his and gives it a squeeze. He bends and kisses my lips. I taste blood and tears. He straightens up and clears his throat.

I press my lips together to stop them from trembling.

'So, there we are, Lil. It's no good. Everything will come out now. You can tell them the truth.' He tips his head in the direction of the police cars. 'Don't try to cover any of it up. I just want you to know, I did it for us. For our family. To protect us. That's my job.' He pauses, swallowing. 'But I failed.' His eyes brighten with tears. 'I love you, Lilian. You've been the light in my life. I'm sorry I didn't do better. I really am.'

He turns and takes a couple of steps.

'What are you doing?' I cry, my voice strangled and sharp. I'm frozen in place by the shock of his confession. By the horror of everything that's unfolding.

Brian takes another few steps away from me. He quickly disappears from view as the whirling snow and the darkness swallow him up. I somehow manage to stumble after him, reaching out to try to claw him back, but all my hands find is the cold empty air. I gasp as my right foot slips into nothingness and I wobble backwards, realising with a dizzy lurch that I'm right at the edge of the quarry.

My husband doesn't cry out, but my heart cracks as I hear a muffled thud and then another and yet another. Each one more distant than the last. It's unbearable to think that he's gone. That I'm too late to stop him.

Despite what he's done, that man was my life.

I sink to my knees and silently cry out his name, forcing myself to look down.

But all I can see before me is blackness.

FIFTY

MICHELLE

Five days later

My boots sink into the dirty slush on the pavement as I walk along the high street, head down, hands shoved into my coat pockets. It's incredible to me that people are going about their everyday business as though nothing has happened. Well, I suppose for them nothing *has* happened. But for me... it's been hell.

Discovering that Amy is dead, that she's been gone almost eight months, makes me so unutterably sad. So *angry*. Mainly because I know that I'm the one responsible. I may not have been the one to kill her, but I wasn't a good sister. I didn't call her back when she needed me. I put my own petty issues before her well-being.

If I'd only returned her call straight away, I could have talked things through with her. Advised her. Told her to leave Sebastian Fletcher if she didn't love him. I could have asked her to jump on a plane and fly out to see me. We could have got a flat together. She'd have loved Byron Bay. She would have had no trouble getting work over there as a doctor.

I swallow down a surge of emotion. I don't know why I'm torturing myself with all the what-ifs. The truth of the matter is, I've been a shitty sister and I deserve to be devastated by her death. Knowing Amy's no longer in this world is such a monumental loss to me.

I accepted that my parents had died without reconciling with me; our relationship had never been great. I still don't feel they treated me well. Yes, I was the one to leave, but they washed their hands of me pretty quickly and never made any effort to bring me back into their lives. But to lose Amy... it still doesn't feel real. Even though we hadn't seen one another in person, hadn't spoken in years, just sent the odd text, I still felt like she was there with me. Thinking about me. Wishing me well in my life. Now she's gone and I don't have that one, constant person in my corner any more. Even if it was a distant corner on the other side of the world.

There is, at least, one spark of light for me in all of this; and that is that my sister never abandoned me. Before returning to the UK, I thought Amy had given up on me after my long silence. Moved away leaving no forwarding address and no contact number. I thought she'd finally cut me off. But the truth is that Amy hadn't given up on me at all. The truth was far worse...

As I approach the end of town, I find myself slowing, wanting to turn back. I haven't been back to the Royal Oak since the night of the snowstorm. I'm not exactly crazy about returning there now. But I'm swallowing my apprehension and doing it anyway.

I've spent hours talking to the police. Going over and over everything that happened that night and ever since my sister disappeared. Thankfully, the stab wound on my shoulder was nothing more than a surface cut. A paramedic dressed it for me when an ambulance and police car arrived at the layby where I was waiting in Felix's car. They took me to the hospital, where they treated me for shock and kept me in overnight.

So far, I've managed to avoid everyone else. Even though I know they've all been pulled in for questioning – the Fletchers and the pub staff, the neighbours and other locals.

Aside from my hours in the station, I've spent the past five nights holed up in a bed and breakfast at the other end of Stalbridge, too scared, upset and emotionally drained to have any kind of conversation with the Fletchers. Even though it's Lilian who's been paying for my accommodation – she offered, realising I have absolutely no money, and I've been too upset to reject her offer.

Seb has been calling and messaging constantly, but aside from sending back a short text asking him to give me some space, I didn't reply until this morning and then I somehow agreed to come and meet him in the pub. I told him I'd pick up my stuff. I don't even know what I'm going to say to him – *Sorry I lied? Sorry you're dad's dead, but he killed my sister? Sorry your brother cheated on you with your wife?* It's all so utterly awful. The thought of seeing any of them makes me queasy.

I still can't believe that Brian is dead. That he stepped off that cliff into the quarry. The same quarry he wanted *me* to fall into. Since that night, I've had several terrifying dreams about falling, but I always wake before I hit the bottom.

As I walk through the gate and along the path that leads to the entrance of the Royal Oak, my legs are gradually turning to jelly. I steady myself on one of the wooden porch pillars and try to get it together. I can do this. It's just a quick visit and then I never need to come back again. I can move on.

I push open the door and walk inside. The bar is virtually empty. Just an older guy sitting at the far end sipping a pint and leaning over a newspaper.

It all looks exactly the same. Why wouldn't it? Yet it *feels* so different. Like an alternate-reality version of the place I knew. I almost expect Brian to step up behind the bar and ask me how I'm doing. Instead, Tarik looks over and does a double-take that he tries to cover up by coughing.

'Caroline... uh, sorry, I mean, *Michelle*, is it?' His awkwardness is excruciating.

I walk up to the bar. 'Hey, Tarik. Yeah, it's Michelle. I guess you heard.'

'Uh, yeah. Sorry about... everything. You're here to see Seb, right?'

'Please.'

'He said for you to go upstairs when you got here.'

'Oh. Okay.' I suppose I should have expected that. I just hope that Lilian's not going to be up there too. I don't think I could face talking to them both at once. I'm not even sure I know how Lilian feels about me. Although she's been paying for my accommodation, so perhaps she doesn't blame me for Brian's death. Or perhaps she just doesn't want me staying here. Not that I would ever want to spend another night here.

'Caroline!'

I turn at a familiar voice, my heart sinking into my wet boots. 'Mariah,' I say, feeling my meagre reserves of mental energy draining rapidly away.

FIFTY-ONE

LILIAN

'Are you sure you won't come with me, Lil? It'll be good for you to get out for a bit of fresh air.'

I stare up at my younger sister blankly. Rose has aged badly. Put on a lot of weight. Hasn't made any attempt at all to be stylish. Her once chestnut hair is now streaked with grey and her skin is blotchy. But she still has the same sharp brown eyes.

'Lil?' she repeats.

'Hmm?' I look up from the armchair I'm slumped in. I don't even remember getting out of bed this morning. Or getting dressed. I glance down at myself to see that I'm wearing black jeans and a cream sweater. There's a large grease stain on the sleeve.

'You should come out to the shops with me. We can go for lunch after. It'll be nice.'

'No, I'm fine.' My voice is monotone. I don't sound like me at all.

'But—'

'I said I'm fine, Rose.'

Her shoulders drop, but she nods as she shrugs on an ugly

blue raincoat. 'I won't be long. We'll have lunch when I get back.'

I nod absently, not remotely interested in eating. Not interested in anything.

Ever since it happened, I haven't been able to think properly. Recent events have been a jumble in my mind. Michelle, Brian, the quarry, the police, Sebastian... *Amy*. It's all just one big lump of horror. The perfect life I thought I was trying to preserve has turned out to be nothing more than a lie.

As soon as the police finished questioning me, I knew I had to get away from the pub, from Stalbridge, where I was surrounded by nothing but idyllic memories that have all been tainted. I had a yearning to escape to a silent white room with nothing in it but a bed. No other furniture or adornments. Just a place where I could sit and stare until my mind went as blank as the walls. Instead, I've ended up at my sister's cramped and cluttered little terraced house on the outskirts of Poole. She lives alone with her two cats, so at least I don't have any other family members to deal with, and Rose isn't a big talker, thank goodness.

The front door bangs as she leaves to go shopping. A whisper of cold air rushes into the living room. Silence settles over the house and I let myself breathe for a moment. In and out. In and out. I haven't even cried yet. It's as though my body and emotions are frozen.

One of the cats comes in and jumps onto my lap. It's the tabby, imaginatively named Tabby. Overweight and content, she starts purring and licking a white paw. I stroke her head.

Amy's face flashes into my mind. Her warm brown eyes and gentle smile. When I first met her, I really felt as though she was the daughter I'd never had. I was thrilled for Sebastian that he had found this beautiful, clever doctor to be his wife. Later, I blamed her completely for the affair with Felix. I felt duped by her. I'd been furious. Outraged. But, if I'm honest with myself, I knew that it had been Felix who'd instigated it all. That he'd seen it as some kind of challenge to make his brother's wife fall for him.

In my heart, I knew Amy would have tried to resist Felix. It wasn't in her nature to cheat. She had loved Sebastian at the start. Had been dedicated to him. They were planning on starting a family together.

Felix hadn't cared about any of that. He's one of those men with such powerful charisma that he can have whoever he wants. He thinks it's a superpower, a blessing. When in reality it's a terrible, destructive curse that will never bring him happiness.

If it weren't for little Teddy, I would tell Nicki to get as far away from Felix as possible. Although, to give her some credit, she's a tough little cookie. I don't think she has any problem letting him know what she thinks of his behaviour. Maybe she's the only one who can stick by him without his behaviour destroying her self-esteem. I hope so.

I blame myself for a lot of it. If I hadn't been so determined for us all to live and work under one roof, then this would never have happened. I should have let my sons go off on their own journeys. Forge independent lives. I should have known that Felix would try to assert his authority over Sebastian. That he would try to prove he was the superior brother. He's always been that way, especially when they were younger – taking charge of games, flirting aggressively with Seb's girlfriends. I naively assumed he'd grow out of it, not that he would get *worse*. It makes me sick to think of Felix acting like the wonderful, protective older brother, when in reality...

I lift Tabby off my lap and set her down on the carpet. I ease myself out of the armchair and stand. My knees click and my back aches. I feel as though I've aged twenty years in five days.

I shuffle over to the front window and gaze through the net curtains to the grey street beyond and the row of brick houses opposite, each with their own families inside, living out their individual dramas and disappointments. Mothers, fathers, sisters, brothers, wives, husbands...

I can't let myself think about Brian. What does it say about me that I married him? A *murderer*. I can't even pass it off as a one-time dreadful mistake, because he was about to do the same thing to Caroline, or rather *Michelle*. To send her over the cliff and make it look like it was an accident. I shake my head and shudder. That poor girl. I treated her so shoddily when she arrived. She'd been searching for her sister and I had believed she was some kind of gold digger, or that she had married Sebastian to get British citizenship. I'm ashamed of myself. I know I'll need to speak to her at some point. To apologise. To make sure she's going to be all right. And I will do that. Just... not yet.

A movement through the window catches my attention. A young woman is leaving one of the houses opposite, with two little boys bundled up in coats and hats. They're charging up and down the front path while their mother locks the door. She calls out to them, but I can't hear what she's saying. Probably warning them not to run out into the street. She looks stressed. They don't appear to be taking a blind bit of notice.

I smile at their antics even as the tears start to slide down my cheeks.

FIFTY-TWO

MICHELLE

'Can we talk?' Mariah asks, her face unreadable. A few curls have escaped her ponytail and her face is pale. There are dark circles beneath her eyes and her T-shirt is wrinkled.

'Look, Mariah, I don't want any hassle. I'm just here to see Seb and then I'm leaving.'

'I promise it won't take long. I'm not going to cause any trouble. I just... I need to explain.'

I shrug exhaustedly and follow her over to one of the window seats. She sits on the edge of the bench and I take a seat opposite.

'I just wanted to apologise,' she says, looking down at the table and then glancing up quickly before returning her gaze downwards. 'And I need to tell you that you were right. What you said about me and Tom, I mean. Only it got out of hand and I... Oh, it all sounds so petty and stupid now after everything you've just gone through. I'm really sorry about your sister. It's... well, it's unbelievable, isn't it?'

'Thanks,' I reply, surprised and somewhat touched by her garbled apology.

'Would you let me explain what happened?' she asks.

'Go ahead,' I reply.

'Can I get you a drink?'

'No, I'm fine, thanks.'

'Sure? I can make you a coffee...'

'Honestly, I'm fine.' I don't want to drag this visit out any longer than I need to. I need to get out of here as soon as possible. Put it all behind me.

Mariah swallows. 'Okay, well, you have to understand that I really thought Seb and I might end up together one day. So when you showed up married to him... it was a shock.'

I nod and try to look understanding.

'Thing is, *Michelle* – it feels weird calling you that – thing is, though, I did ask Tom to touch your bum.' Her face flames as she admits this.

I don't comment, but her admission doesn't surprise me. I'd thought as much.

Mariah clears her throat and shifts in her seat. 'I only did it for a laugh to see how you'd handle it. I thought it would be funny to see you get annoyed with him. But I didn't realise it would lead to such a massive drama. After you hurt his wrist, he went mental at me. Told me it was my fault.'

'He's just a big bully,' I reply. Not adding that she was childish to have suggested the whole thing in the first place.

'I know,' she agrees. 'He blackmailed me into going out with him. Said he'd tell everyone that the groping was my idea if I didn't kiss him. Told me I'd probably lose my job if Mrs F found out. He wanted me to sleep with him too, but I told him to piss off.'

'Well.' I raise an eyebrow and take a breath.

'Aren't you mad? I'd be fuming if I was you.'

If I'd heard her confession last week, I would have been off the-scale furious. But, right now, it hardly registers. 'I'm not mad, Mariah. Thanks for the apology though. I appreciate you telling me the truth.'

'Yeah, well, I figured after everything that's happened. You didn't need all that hanging over you too.'

I get to my feet and so does she. I'm surprised and a little touched when she comes around the table and leans in for an awkward hug. I pat her on the back and straighten up.

'So, what are you going to do now?' she asks. 'You gonna come back to the Oak? To Seb?'

'I don't think so,' I reply.

'No. Well. S'pose I better get back to work.' She gives a half wave and I muster up a smile before she turns and heads back into the restaurant.

Tarik catches my eye and gives me a nod. I return the nod and head to the back of the bar, through to the corridor that will take me up the stairs to see Seb.

On my way through, I glance at the kitchen, wondering if Felix is in there. I'd rather not know. Head down, I quickly head up the stairs and knock on the apartment door, which is slightly ajar.

Sebastian is waiting in the hall. He opens the door immediately. His eyes sweep over me and he looks all at once relieved and devastated. His face is colourless, his eyes red-rimmed. He takes a step towards me and somehow falls into my arms. We hug and I realise he's weeping into my shoulder. Emotion bubbles up inside me but stops at my throat.

We stand like this for a while as I let him cry on me. Great wracking sobs that shudder through him, reverberating in my bones. I don't know what I was expecting from this meeting. But it wasn't this.

Eventually, he stops. 'I'm sorry,' he gulps. 'I really am so sorry. I don't know what just came over me. It's just... seeing you after everything that's happened.'

I don't offer up platitudes and condolences. Instead, I ask if we should go through to the lounge and sit down.

'Yeah, of course. Let's...' He gestures for me to go first.

'Mum's not here, in case you were wondering. She left last night to stay with her sister in Poole for a few days. Felix is still here though.' Seb gives a bitter laugh. 'He and Nicki had a blazing row, but she seems to have forgiven him, if you can believe that? Not that I ever will. The three of them are moving out soon. He's managed to wangle a new job up north. Good riddance.'

We're sitting on the sofa. Him at one end. Me at the other. Facing one another like bookends around an empty space.

'You know I had nothing to do with any of it,' Seb says, blurting out his innocence.

'I know,' I reply. 'I know you didn't.'

'I loved Amy. I trusted her. And all the while she was seeing my prick of a brother.' He exhales and shakes his head. 'When she left, I spent months trying to track her down, which was hard because after an initial couple of messages, she disconnected her mobile. And now I find out that it was Dad who sent those first texts. Texts I spent hours analysing, looking for clues in those words. My own father, lying to me like that.' Seb's nostrils flare. 'I'm glad he's dead. Because if he was still alive, I think I'd kill him.'

'How did you get divorced?' I ask. 'If she wasn't here to sign the papers.'

'Mum and Felix sorted it out.' He sniffs. 'Neither of them knew what Dad had done. Dad told them she'd left and wasn't coming back. Mum was relieved, as she knew Felix had cheated and she wanted to protect me from the truth. Save our brotherly relationship – what a joke! They forged Amy's signature. I was so upset by her "running off with someone else" that I barely registered any of it.'

I realise Seb is staring at me intently.

'You don't look anything alike,' he says. 'Although... I always thought it was a bit weird that your laugh is the same as hers.'

'Is it?' I look down at my hands, unsure what else to say to this man. A man I sold a dream to. A man I shared a bed with in order to try get to the truth. At least we didn't have sex. I'm glad about that.

'So, it was all a lie,' he says, his face pale as water, his grey eyes flat and dull.

I shift in my seat. 'I didn't want to hurt you, Seb. I just wanted to find out what happened to my sister.'

'But I loved you. It was all real to me. I thought we were married! Why did you have to take it so far? Couldn't you have just talked to me about Amy?'

I shake my head at having to explain this all over again. 'I tried, but you didn't listen to me. None of you did. When I was back in Australia, I called the pub so many times. I spoke to your mother, to the staff, I spoke to *you*. But you all told me to stop calling. To leave well alone. You said that Amy had left. You washed your hands of her. I asked your mum if I could come to see her. To speak to you all about Amy and where she might be. But she shot me down in flames. Told me never to call and never to visit.'

'I'm sorry,' Seb replies. 'I wish I'd been more receptive. But I was gutted. I thought she'd run off with someone else.'

'So then I called the police and told them Amy was missing. I explained what had happened, and they said the likelihood was that she didn't want to be found by me. They said there was very little they could do. She'd divorced her husband and gone off with someone else. There was no cause to think anything untoward had happened. I think the fact that I was calling from Australia didn't help.

'But I knew something was wrong. That phone message she left was a cry for help. And I didn't call her back in time. It was my fault. If I hadn't been so stubborn. If I hadn't held on to such a stupid, childish grudge, then maybe I could have stopped it from happening. I could have helped. Or at least *tried* to do something.'

'You can't torture yourself,' Seb says. 'You had no idea my

father was going to...' He shakes his head. 'I still can't believe it. That was my *dad*.'

'He fooled me too. Completely and utterly.' I think back to Brian's warm, easy manner. His way of making me feel so relaxed and part of the family. 'And Felix too.' Is that what he was like with Amy? Is that how he got her to trust him?

Seb clenches his fists. 'He's my older brother. I always thought he was so trustworthy. So likeable. He was the person I looked up to. The one person I could depend on. I was proud that he was my brother. *How could he do that to me?* He betrayed me. He betrayed Nicki. And then for Dad to try to fix things by doing that. It's sickening. Mum is... well, you can imagine, she's devastated. She must have aged a decade in the past week.' Seb is crying again, silent tears washing his cheeks.

I wish I could cry, but I still feel numb from it all.

I still can't believe that Amy is gone.

It's ironic that the made-up backstory I told Seb about having no family of my own, has become my reality.

Seb gets up and leaves the living room, comes back a moment later with a sheet of kitchen roll that he uses to wipe his face and blow his nose. He sits back down next to me, closer this time. It's hard for me not to feel something for this man. None of it was his fault. He was simply caught up in a storm of other people's making.

'The thing is, Cal— Sorry, *Michelle*, I'll never get used to calling you that. The thing is...' He takes my hand. His skin is warm and dry. 'Even after all of it, I still love you.'

I shake my head and chew the corner of my lip. My chin wobbles at his words. I can't even let the words sink in. 'Don't.' I disengage my hand from his.

'I can't help it,' he says. 'Even though you're not who you said you were. Even though you're Amy's sister. It actually doesn't matter to me.'

'It should matter,' I reply.

'I can't lie about how I feel,' he cries. 'All those months we chatted online. I opened my heart to you. I laid everything out there. I might not know the real you, but you know everything about me. *Everything.* Just think about the possibility of us.'

'It's too weird, Seb. After everything that's happened, how could we even make a normal life together? Your father killed my sister. He ended her life.'

'I know, I know. It's completely fucked-up. But I'm not him. I'm nothing like him.'

'I know you're not. But it doesn't matter. We got together under false pretences. I lied to you. How can you love me? You love the image of me that I showed you, that's all.'

'Caroline, please...'

I put a hand on his cheek and feel his warm tears sliding between my fingers. Then I get to my feet.

'Are you really leaving?' he asks, his voice choked. 'Stay a bit longer, please. At least let me make you a drink.'

'I'm sorry. I have to go. I need to head back to Byron and salvage my job. My apartment.'

'What about money?' he asks. 'You said you were skint.'

'I am. But a friend is lending me the ticket money – unless the pub owes me any wages,' I add with a dry smile.

'Oh, uh, yes, of course—'

'I'm joking.'

Seb chews his bottom lip. 'Apparently, there's quite a lot of money in Amy's bank account,' he says. 'It's due to come to me after probate, as she never changed her will and the divorce obviously wasn't legal. But in the circumstances I think it should go to you.'

'Oh.' It takes a moment for me to digest what he's saying. I realise I'm not sure how I feel about it.

Seb carries on talking. 'Most of it was inherited from your parents. So it's yours by rights.'

Money has never been a driving factor in my life, but I

guess having a little something would make my life easier. For now, I put all thoughts of finances out of my head. 'Look, Seb,' I say, changing the subject. 'If you want my advice, I think you should leave too. Start fresh somewhere else.'

'I can't leave my mum to deal with this place,' he says. 'Not after everything she's been through.'

'No, I don't suppose you can,' I reply. 'You're a good person, Seb.'

'Just not *your* person, right?' he says sadly.

'Just not your person,' I echo as a solitary tear rolls down my cheek.

I'm not crying for Seb. I'm crying for Amy. For my sister who got caught up in this dark, dysfunctional family's web. Seb is just as crazy as the rest of them if he thinks there could be any kind of future for the two of us. Not after what's happened. *No.* I can't trust any of them and right now all I want is to get as far away from here as I can.

The other side of the world might just about be far enough.

EPILOGUE

I watch Brian as he digs Amy's grave. As his rusty spade bites into the waterlogged ground. I didn't want to come tonight, of course I didn't. But when he asked for my help, I couldn't say no. After all, bodies are heavy. Easier to move with two people.

A half-moon briefly lights up the night as dense clouds race past. The woods are thick with rain that spatters onto new leaves as a cold wind blows through the branches.

She's lying face down in the mud. Brian turned her over, but I'd like to see her face one more time to satisfy myself that she really is dead.

When I discovered what Brian had done and he explained to me why he'd done it... Well. I couldn't exactly complain, could I? He did it for me, really. For the family. To keep us all together. Amy was the one who'd upset the apple cart, so she only had herself to blame. I guess, technically, Felix was also to blame, but you have to look at the bigger picture. Brian was hardly going to get rid of his own son, was he? No. Amy had to be the one to go.

Seb will be upset to find his wife has left him, of course he will, but we'll help him get over it.

It was sheer coincidence that I witnessed Amy's murder. It

was late last night. I was taking a bag of Teddy's used nappies to empty into the outside bin, same as I do most evenings. I watched Brian slit her throat. Watched her sink down behind the huge recycling bin.

Brian was surprised that I was so calm about the whole thing. And that I was prepared to forgive Felix for the affair. I told him that I knew what sort of person Felix was when I married him. That I could forgive a few indiscretions here and there. But that I wouldn't put up with him and Amy doing it right under my nose or shouting to the world about it. No way.

So, here we are in the early hours of the morning, in the middle of a deserted wood. Me and my father-in-law digging a shallow grave for someone who deserves what she got.

After everything I've gone through with my own useless parents, I'm not prepared for Teddy to have to suffer similar years of adultery and neglect. Felix and I need to be here for our son 100 per cent. My little family unit must always come first and I won't tolerate anyone trying to break us apart.

'I think it's deep enough now, what do you think, Nicki, love? Come and have a look?' Brian rests a hand on his shovel and pushes the sweat from his brow.

I walk over to the edge and peer into the muddy hole. 'Yep, that should do it,' I reply, thankful that Brian is prepared to do what it takes to keep this family together.

Personally, I have absolutely zero qualms about burying Amy Fletcher. She put herself in the ground the minute she decided to mess with my marriage. And if anyone else ever tries to steal my husband, I'll happily do the same again.

A LETTER FROM SHALINI

Dear reader,

Thank you for choosing to read *The Daughter-in-Law*. I do hope you enjoyed it.

If you'd like to keep up to date with my latest releases, just sign up here and I'll let you know when I have a new novel coming out.

www.bookouture.com/shalini-boland

I love getting feedback on my books, so if you have a few moments, I'd be really grateful if you'd be kind enough to post a review online or tell your friends about it. A good review absolutely makes my day!

When I'm not writing, reading, walking or spending time with my family, you can reach me via my Facebook page, through Twitter, Goodreads or my website.

Thanks so much,

Shalini Boland x

KEEP IN TOUCH WITH SHALINI

www.shaliniboland.co.uk

facebook.com/ShaliniBolandAuthor

twitter.com/ShaliniBoland

goodreads.com/shaliniboland

ACKNOWLEDGEMENTS

It's always an absolute joy to work with my supremely talented publisher, Natasha Harding. Thank you for everything. For the way you know exactly how to present those structural edits so I don't have a meltdown. For the yummy lunches and catch-up Zoom chats. For the excited messages and calls when one of my books is having a moment. And for generally being an all-round wonderful human being.

Endless thanks to the dedicated team at Bookouture: Jenny Geras, Ruth Tross, Peta Nightingale, Richard King, Sarah Hardy, Kim Nash, Noelle Holten, Mark Alder, Alex Crow, Natalie Butlin, Jess Readett, Alexandra Holmes, Emily Boyce, Saidah Graham, Lizzie Brien, Melanie Price, Occy Carr and everyone else who helped launch this book.

Thanks to my excellent copy editor, Fraser Crichton. Thanks also to Maddy Newquist for your fantastic proof-reading skills. Thank you to designer Lisa Horton for yet another incredible cover.

Thank you to the fabulous Katie Villa who has narrated all my Bookouture books, under the brilliant production of Arran Dutton at the Audio Factory and Bookouture's hard-working and talented audio manager Alba Proko. You guys always do an incredible job of bringing my characters to life.

I feel very lucky to have such loyal and thorough beta readers. Thank you, Terry Harden and Julie Carey. You're amazing!

Thanks to all my lovely readers who take the time to read, review or recommend my novels. It means so, so much. Thanks also to all the fabulous book bloggers and reviewers out there who spread the word. You guys are the absolute best!

I also want to say a huge thank you to loyal readers Michelle Nelson and Mariah Maudlin, to whom I gave starring roles in this novel. I hope you both approve of your characters. Hopefully there'll be lots to chat about at your publication party!

The life of a writer is very solitary, so I'm sending hugs to my family – Pete, Dan, Billie and Jess – for being such great company whenever I emerge from my writing lair.